D0959958

THE ART
OF BEING
Normal

THE ART OF BEING

Normal

LISA WILLIAMSON

Margaret Ferguson Books

FARRAR STRAUS GIROUX

NEW YORK

Farrar Straus Giroux Books for Young Readers
175 Fifth Avenue, New York 10010

Text copyright © 2016 by Lisa Williamson
All rights reserved
Printed in the United States of America
Designed by Elizabeth H. Clark
First edition, 2016
An earlier version of *The Art of Being Normal* was first published in Great Britain by
David Fickling Books, 2015, in a somewhat different form.
1   3   5   7   9   10   8   6   4   2

fiercereads.com

Library of Congress Cataloging-in-Publication Data

Names: Williamson, Lisa, 1980– author.
Title: The art of being normal / Lisa Williamson.
Description: First edition. | New York : Farrar Straus Giroux (BYR), 2016. |
  "Margaret Ferguson Books." | Summary: David Piper, always an outsider, forms
  an unlikely friendship with Leo Denton who, from the first day at his new school
  wants only to be invisible, but when David's deepest secret gets out, that he wants
  to be a girl, things get very messy for both of them.
Identifiers: LCCN 2015022213 | ISBN 9780374302375 (hardback) | ISBN
  9780374302399 (e-book)
Subjects: | CYAC: Transgender people—Fiction. | Friendship—Fiction. |
  Secrets—Fiction. | High schools—Fiction. | Schools—Fiction. | BISAC:
  JUVENILE FICTION / Social Issues / Friendship.
Classification: LCC PZ7.1.W56 Art 2016 | DDC [Fic]—dc23
LC record available at http://lccn.loc.gov/2015022213

Our books may be purchased for promotional, educational, or business use.
Please contact your local bookseller or the Macmillan Corporate and
Premium Sales Department at (800) 221-7945 ext. 5442 or by e-mail at
MacmillanSpecialMarkets@macmillan.com.

For Matt

THE ART
OF BEING
Normal

DAVID

When I was eight years old, my class was told to write about what we wanted to be when we grew up. Then our teacher, Ms. Box, went around the room asking each of us to stand up and share what we had written. Zachary Olsen wanted to play soccer for England. Lexi Taylor wanted to be an actress. Harry Beaumont planned on being prime minister. Simon Allen wanted to be Harry Potter, so badly that the previous term he had scratched a lightning bolt onto his forehead with a pair of scissors.

But I didn't want to be any of these things.

This is what I wrote:

I want to be a girl.

DAVID

FIVE AND A HALF YEARS LATER

My party guests are singing "Happy Birthday." It does not sound good.

My little sister, Livvy, is barely even singing. At eleven, she's already decided family birthday parties are totally embarrassing, leaving Mum and Dad to honk out the rest of the tune, Mum's reedy soprano clashing with Dad's flat bass. It is so bad Phil, the family dog, has retreated to his bed. I don't blame him; the whole party is pretty depressing. Even the blue balloons Dad blew up look pale and sad, especially the ones with *Fourteen Today!* scrawled on them in black marker. I'm not even sure the underwhelming events unfolding before me qualify as a party in the first place.

"Make a wish!" Mum says. She has the cake tipped at an angle so I won't notice it's wonky. It says *Happy Birthday David!* in bloodred icing across the top, the *day* in *Birthday* scrunched up where she must have run out of room. Fourteen blue candles form a circle around the edge of the cake, dripping wax in the buttercream.

"Hurry up!" Livvy says.

But I won't be rushed. I lean forward, tuck my hair behind my ears, and shut my eyes. I block out Livvy's whining and Mum's cajoling and Dad's fiddling with the settings on the camera, and suddenly everything sounds sort of muffled and far away.

I wait a few seconds before opening my eyes and blowing out all the candles in one go. Everyone applauds. Dad pulls on a party popper but it doesn't pop and by the time he's got another one out of the package Mum has started taking the candles off the cake, and the moment has passed.

"What did you wish for? Something stupid, I bet," Livvy says, twirling a piece of golden-brown hair around her middle finger.

"He can't tell you, silly, otherwise it won't come true," Mum says, taking the cake into the kitchen to be sliced.

"Yeah," I say, sticking my tongue out at Livvy. She sticks hers out right back.

"Where are your two friends again?" she asks, putting extra emphasis on the *two*.

"I've told you, Felix is at Math Camp in Florida and Essie is visiting her dad in Leamington Spa."

Leaving me festering alone in Eden Park all summer, I add silently.

"That's too bad," Livvy says with zero sympathy. "Dad, how many people did I have at my birthday party?"

"Forty-five. All on roller skates. Utter carnage," Dad mutters grimly, ejecting the memory card from the camera and putting it into his laptop.

The first photo that pops up on the screen is of me. My eyes are closed midblink and my forehead is shiny.

"Dad," I moan. "Do you have to do that now?"

"Just doing some red-eye removal before I e-mail them over to your grandmother," he says, clicking away at the mouse. "She was so sad she couldn't make it."

This is not true. Granny has bridge on Wednesday evenings and doesn't miss it for anyone, especially her least-favorite grandchild. Livvy is Granny's favorite. But then Livvy is everyone's favorite.

Mum returns to the living room with pieces of cake on plates and sets them down on the table.

"Look at all these leftovers," she says, frowning as she surveys the mountains of picked-at food. "We're going to have enough pigs in a blanket and brownies to last us until Christmas. I just hope I've got enough plastic wrap to cover it all."

Great. A fridge full of food to remind me just how wildly unpopular I am.

After cake and intensive plastic-wrap action, there are presents. From Mum and Dad I get a new backpack for school, the *Gossip Girl* DVD box set, and a check for one hundred pounds. Livvy gives me a box of candy and a shiny red case for my iPhone.

Then we all sit on the sofa and watch a film called *Freaky Friday*. It's about a mother and daughter who eat an enchanted fortune cookie that makes them magically swap bodies for the day. Dear World, if only it were that straightforward. Dad nods off halfway through and starts snoring.

That night I can't sleep. I'm awake for so long my eyes get used to the dark and I can make out the outlines of my framed posters on the walls and the tiny shadow of a mosquito darting back and forth across the ceiling.

I am fourteen and time is running out.

DAVID

It's the last Friday of summer vacation. I have been fourteen years old for exactly nine days.

I'm lying on the sofa with the curtains closed. Dad's at work (he's an accountant) and Mum is with a client (she works from home as a Web site designer). Livvy is at her best friend, Cressy's, house. I'm watching an old episode of *America's Next Top Model* with a package of double chocolate chip cookies balanced on my stomach. Tyra Banks has just told Ashley she is not going to be America's Next Top Model. Ashley is in tears and all the other girls are hugging her even though they spent almost the entire episode going on about how much they hated Ashley and wanted her to leave. America's Next Top Model house is nothing if not brutal.

Ashley's tears are interrupted by the sound of a key turning in the front door. I sit up, carefully placing the cookies on the coffee table beside me.

"David, I'm home," Mum calls.

She's back early from her client meeting.

I frown as I listen to her kick off her shoes and drop her keys in the dish by the door. I quickly grab the crochet blanket at my feet, pulling it up over my body and tucking it under my chin, getting into position just before Mum walks into the living room.

Immediately she pulls a face.

"What?" I ask, wiping cookie crumbs from my mouth.

"You might want to open the curtains, David," she says, hands on hips.

"But then I won't be able to see the screen clearly."

She ignores me and marches over to the window, throwing open the curtains. The late-afternoon sun floods the room, making the air look dusty. I shield my eyes.

"Oh for heaven's sake, David," Mum says. "You're not a vampire."

"I might be," I mutter.

She tuts.

"Look," she says, gesturing toward the window. "It's beautiful out. Are you seriously telling me you prefer lying around in the dark all day rather than being outside?"

"Correct."

She narrows her eyes before perching on the sofa by my feet.

"No wonder you're so pasty," she says, tracing her finger down the side of my bare foot. I kick her hand away.

"Would you rather I lie in the sun all day and get skin cancer?"

"No, David," she says, sighing. "What I'd *rather* is see you doing something with your summer vacation other than staying indoors watching TV for hours on end. If you're not doing that, you're holed up in your room on the computer."

The phone rings. Saved by the bell. As Mum stands up the blanket snags on her wedding ring. I reach to grab it but it's too late, she's already looking down at me, a quizzical expression on her face.

"David, are you wearing my nightie?"

It's the nightie Mum packed to take to the hospital when she had Livvy. I don't think she's worn it since; Mum and Dad usually sleep naked. I know this because I've bumped into them on the landing in the middle of the night enough times to be scarred for life.

"It's so hot out, I thought it might keep me cool," I say quickly. "You know, like those long white dress things Arab men wear."

"Hmmmmm," Mum says.

"You'd better get that," I say, nodding toward the phone.

· · · · ·

I keep the nightie on for dinner, figuring it'll be less suspicious that way.

"You look like such a weirdo," Livvy says, her eyes narrowing with vague disgust.

"Now, Livvy," Mum says.

"But he does!" Livvy protests.

Mum and Dad exchange looks. I concentrate really hard on balancing peas on my fork.

After dinner I go upstairs. I take out the list I made at the beginning of summer vacation and sit cross-legged on my bed with it spread out in front of me.

Things to achieve this summer, by David Piper:
1. Grow my hair long enough to tie back in a ponytail
2. Watch every season of *Project Runway* in chronological order
3. Beat Dad at Wii Tennis
4. Teach my dog, Phil, to dance so we can enter *Britain's Got Talent* next year and win 250,000 pounds
5. Tell Mum and Dad

I had one glorious week of being able to scrape my hair into the tiniest of ponytails. But school rules dictate boys' hair can be no more than collar length, so last week Mum took me to the barber to have it cut. Points two and three were achieved with ease during the first two weeks of the break. I quickly realized four was a lost cause; Phil isn't a natural performer.

Five I've been putting off. I've practiced plenty. I've got a whole speech prepared. I recite it in my head when I'm in the shower, and whisper it into the darkness when I'm lying in bed at night.

I've tried writing it down too. If my parents looked hard enough they'd find endless unfinished drafts stuffed in my desk. Last week though, I actually completed a letter. Not only that, I nearly pushed it beneath Mum and Dad's bedroom door. I was right outside, crouched down by the thin shaft of light, listening to them mill about as they got ready for bed. All it would take was one push and it would be done; my secret would be lying there on the carpet, ready to be discovered. But in that moment, it was like my hand was paralyzed. And in the end I just couldn't do it and went racing back to my room, letter still in hand, my heart pounding like crazy inside my chest.

Mum and Dad like to think they're really cool and open-minded just because they saw a Red Hot Chili Peppers concert once and voted for the Green Party in the last election, but I'm not so sure. When I was younger, I used to overhear them talking about me. They'd speak in hushed voices and tell each other it was all "a phase," that I would "grow out of it," in exactly the same way you might talk about a child who wets the bed.

My friends Essie and Felix know of course. The three of us tell each other everything. That's why this summer has been so hard. Without them to talk to, some days I've felt like I might burst. But Essie and Felix knowing isn't enough. For anything to happen, I have to tell Mum and Dad.

Tomorrow. I'll definitely tell them tomorrow.

I climb off the bed, open my door a crack, and listen. Mum, Dad, and Livvy are downstairs watching TV. The muffled sound of canned laughter drifts up the stairs. Although I'm pretty sure they'll stay put until the end of the program, I lock my door. Satisfied I won't be disturbed, I retrieve the small purple notebook and tape measure I keep locked in the metal box at the bottom of my sock drawer. I position myself in front of the mirror that hangs on the back of my bedroom door, pull the nightie off over my head, and step out of my underpants.

An inspection is due.

As usual, I start by standing against the door frame and measuring my height: 168 centimeters. Again, no change. I allow myself a tiny sigh of relief.

Then I press my palms against my chest. I will it to be soft and spongy but the muscle beneath my skin feels hard like stone. I take the tape measure and wrap it around my hips. No change. I go straight up and down, like a human ruler. I am the opposite of Mum with her fleshy curves—hips and butt and boobs.

I move up closer to the mirror, so close to the glass I have to fight to stop myself from going cross-eyed. I lift my chin and run my fingers over my Adam's apple, then over my chin and cheeks. Some days I swear I can feel stubble pushing up against my skin, sharp and prickly, but for now the surface remains smooth and unbroken. I pout my lips and long for them to be plumper, pinker. I have my dad's lips—thin, with a jagged Cupid's bow. Unfortunately I appear to have inherited pretty much Dad's everything. I skip over my hair (sludge brown and badly behaved, no matter how much gel I use on it), eyes (gray, boring), nose (pointy-ish), and ears (sticky-outy), instead turning my head slowly until I am almost in profile, so I can admire my cheekbones. They are sharp and high and probably the only part of my face I like.

I move downward to my penis, which I hate with a passion. I hate everything about it: its size, its color, the way it has a complete mind of its own. I discover it has grown an entire two millimeters since last week. I check it twice but the tape measure doesn't lie. I frown and write it down.

I inspect my hands and feet last. Sometimes I think I hate them the most, maybe even more than my private parts, because they're always there, on show. They're clumsy and hairy and so pale they're almost translucent. Even worse, they're huge and getting huger. My new school shoes are two whole sizes bigger than last year's pair. When I tried them on in the store I felt like a circus clown.

I take one last look in the mirror, at the stranger staring back at me. I shiver. This week's inspection is over.

LEO

"*Leo!*" *my little sister, Tia, calls.*

I close my eyes and try to block her out.

It's hot. It's been hot for days now. I've got the windows and doors open and I'm still dying. I'm lying on my twin sister, Amber's, bunk trying my hardest to keep cool.

At night I sleep on the bottom bunk because Amber says she gets claustrophobic, but when Amber's not around I like to hang out on the top. If you lie with your head at the end closest to the window, you can't see the other houses or the garbage cans or the crazy old lady from across the way who stands in her front yard and yells for hours on end. All you can see is the sky and the tops of the trees and if you concentrate really hard you can almost convince yourself you're not in Cloverdale anymore.

"Leo!" Tia yells again.

I sigh and sit up. Tia is seven and a complete pain in the neck. Mam let her have a pair of high heels for her last birthday and when she's not watching TV she clomps around the house in them, talking in an American accent.

Tia's dad is Tony. He's in prison, doing time for fencing stolen goods.

My dad is Jimmy. He left when I was a baby. I miss him.

"Leo, I'm hungry!" Tia wails.

"Then eat something!"

"There's nothing to eat!"

"Tough!"

She starts to cry. It's earsplitting. I sigh and heave myself off the bunk.

I find Tia at the bottom of the stairs, fat tears rolling down her face. She's short for her age and paper clip–skinny. As soon as she sees me her tears stop and she breaks into this big dopey smile.

She follows me into the kitchen, which is a complete mess, the sink piled high with dishes. I search the cupboards and fridge. Tia's right, there's nothing to eat and God knows what time Mam's going to be back. She left just before lunch, saying she was off to the bingo hall with Auntie Kerry. There's no money in the tin so I take the cushions off the sofa and check the inside of the washing machine and the pockets of the coats in the front hall closet. We line up the coins on the coffee table. It's not a bad haul—four pounds.

"Stay here and don't answer the door," I tell Tia. She'll only dawdle if I take her with me.

I put my hoodie on and walk fast, my head bowed, sweat trickling down my back and sides.

Outside the store there's a bunch of guys from my old school. Luckily they're distracted, mucking around on their bikes, so I yank my hood up, pulling the drawstring tight so all you can see are my eyes. I buy bread, soda, dishwashing soap, and a chocolate Swiss roll that's past its expiration date.

When I get home I put the *Tangled* DVD on for Tia and give her a glass of soda and a slice of the Swiss roll while I wash the dishes and stick bread in the toaster. When I sit down on the sofa she scampers over to me and plants a wet kiss on my cheek.

"Thanks, Leo," she says. Her mouth is chocolaty.

"Get off," I tell her. But she clings to me like a monkey, and I'm too tired to fight her off.

Later that night, Mam is still out so I put Tia to bed. Amber's staying over at her boyfriend, Carl's, house. Carl is sixteen, a year older than us. Amber met him at the indoor ice skating rink in town last year. She was showing off, trying to skate backward and fell and hit her head on the ice. Carl looked after her and bought her a cherry slush. Amber said it was like a scene from a movie. Amber's sappy like that sometimes. When she's not being sappy, she's as hard as nails.

I lie on the sofa and watch some stupid action movie on TV with lots of guns and explosions. It's almost finished when the security light outside the front door comes on. I sit up and check the time. It's nearly midnight. I can make out shadows behind the swirly glass. Mam is laughing as she tries and fails to get her key in the lock. I hear a second laugh—a guy's. Great. More fumbling. The door finally swings open and they fall into the front hallway, collapsing on the stairs giggling as the front door shuts behind them. Mam lifts her head and notices me watching. She stops giggling and clambers to her feet. She puts an unsteady hand on the door frame and glares.

"What are you doing up?" she asks.

I don't say anything. The guy gets up too, wiping his hands on his jeans. I don't recognize him.

"Hello there,'" he says, holding up his hand in greeting, "I'm Spike."

Spike has inky-black hair and is wearing a battered leather jacket. Mam goes to the kitchen to get him a drink. Spike sits down on the sofa next to me and takes off his shoes, plonking his feet on the coffee table. His socks don't match.

"Who are you then?" he asks, wiggling his toes and putting his hands behind his head.

"None of your business," I reply.

Mam comes back, a can of beer in each hand.

"Don't be so rude," she says, handing one to Spike. "Tell Spike your name."

"Leo," I say, rolling my eyes.

"I saw that!" Mam barks. She takes a slurp of her beer and turns to Spike.

"Right little so-and-so this one is. Dunno where he gets it from. Must be from his father's side."

"Don't talk about my dad like that," I say, standing up.

"I'll talk about him how I like, thank you very much," Mam replies, rummaging in her purse. "He's a good-for-nothing bastard."

"He. Is. Not." I growl, separating each word.

18

"Oh really?" Mam continues, lighting a cigarette and taking a greedy puff on it. "Where is he then? If he's so marvelous, where the hell is he, Leo? Eh?"

I don't have an answer for her.

"Exactly," she says.

I can feel the familiar knot in my stomach forming, my body tensing, my skin getting hot and clammy, my vision fogging. I move over to the window and try to use the techniques my therapist, Jenny, taught me; roll my shoulders, count to ten, close my eyes, picture myself on a deserted beach, et cetera.

When I open my eyes and turn around Mam has moved to join Spike on the sofa, giggling away like I'm not even in the room. She notices me watching and stops what she's doing.

"And what do you think you're looking at?" she asks.

"Nothing," I mutter.

"Then get lost, will ya."

It's not a question.

I slam the living room door so hard the entire house shakes.

LEO

Family legend goes that Mam's waters broke as she was waiting to pick up takeout from the Taj Mahal Curry House on Spring Street. Family legend also goes that she was still clutching the naan when she gave birth to Amber an hour later. I took another half hour. Auntie Kerry says I had to be dragged out with forceps. I must have known that I'd be better off staying where I was.

My first memory is of my dad changing my diaper. Amber reckons you can't remember stuff that far back, but she's wrong. In the memory I'm lying on the living room floor and Dad is singing. It's not a real song, just something made up and silly. He has a nice voice. It's only a short memory, just a few seconds, but it's as real as anything.

After that, the next memory I have is knocking Mam's cup of tea off the coffee table and scalding my chest. I still have the scar. It's the shape of an eagle with half of one wing missing. I was two and a half by then, and Dad was long gone. I wish I could remember more about him but I can't—that one memory is all I've got. I've tried searching for him on the Internet but finding him is easier said than done. Do you know how many James Dentons there are out there? More than you might think, and so far none of them have turned out to be my dad.

I only have one picture of him. I took it from Mam's room when I was a kid. It's a full-length shot of him standing next to a burgundy Ford Fiesta. He must have just finished washing it because it's really shiny and there's a bucket of soapy water at his feet. I wish the photo was at a different angle because then I might be able to read the license plate, but it was taken side-on, with Dad leaning up against the passenger window. He has his arms folded across his chest and is grinning proudly at the camera. He has good teeth—white and straight. I think I must take after him because Mam's got horrible teeth, yellow from a lifetime of cigarettes. He's tall with sandy-brown hair, just like mine. It's too far away to really know whether I've got his eyes or nose or anything else. On the back there's a date written in Mam's scratchy handwriting. Seven months before Amber and I were born.

One New Year's Eve, tipsy on cheap white wine, Auntie Kerry let it slip that Dad was a carpenter. I like the idea of that, of him working with his hands and making beautiful things from scratch. Auntie Kerry also let it slip that she reckons he went down south to live by the sea, but no one seems to know this for sure. Any time I ask questions, people clam up or get angry and the subject is always closed before it even gets started.

I wonder what he'd think if he could see me now—standing

in front of the bathroom mirror wearing an Eden Park School blazer over my T-shirt.

It's the night after Spike came home with Mam, the end of the last day of summer vacation. I heard Spike leave early this morning, whistling as he went down the stairs. Mam spent the day in bed with a "migraine." She must be feeling better now though, because ten minutes ago I saw her leave the house and climb into a battered white Peugeot, Spike behind the wheel. Not that I care. Amber is over at Carl's and Tia is in bed so I have the place to myself.

I stare at my reflection, at the snazzy-looking stranger staring back. It's the first time I've tried on my blazer since the beginning of summer vacation, and it's weird how different it makes me look. There are no blazers at Cloverdale School, just yellow-and-navy sweatshirts that get pilly after one wash. I was given special coupons so I could buy this one and some school pants from a fancy shop in town. When I modeled for Mam she burst out laughing. I straighten the lapels and relax my shoulders. I ordered it a size too big so it's a bit baggy on me. I don't mind though; I prefer it that way. It smells different from my other clothes—expensive and new. It's burgundy with thin navy stripes and a crest on the right breast pocket with the school motto—*Aequitās et inceptum*—stitched underneath. The other day, I went to the library and looked up what it meant on the computer. Apparently it's Latin for "Fairness and Initiative." We'll see.

The Eden Park district is on the opposite side of the city from the Cloverdale district. Mam and I went to the school for a meeting back in the spring. Eden Park itself was exactly how I imagined it, all green and lush with tree-lined streets and little cafés selling organic-this and homemade-that. And even though Eden Park School is a regular public school, just like Cloverdale, the similarities stop there. Not only did the school look different, with its nice buildings and tidy grounds, it felt different too: clean and neat and orderly. About a million miles away from Cloverdale School.

Jenny came with Mam and me to the meeting. Mam spoke in a snooty voice that I know she thinks makes her sound smart. She always uses it when she's around doctors and teachers. We met with Ms. Logan, the guidance counselor, and Mr. Toolan, the head teacher. They asked lots of questions. Then Mam and I waited outside while they talked with Jenny. A few times students walked past and gave us funny looks. They looked rich. I could tell by their neatly ironed uniforms and Hollister backpacks. Mam and I must have stuck out like a sore thumb.

After more talking and questions, I was offered a place for year eleven. Jenny was really excited for me. Supposedly people move just so they can be in the Eden Park school district. Jenny thinks it'll be a "fresh start" and "an opportunity to make some friends." Jenny's obsessed with me making friends. She goes on about my "social isolation" like it's a contagious disease. After all these years she still doesn't get that social isolation is exactly what I'm after.

"Leo?" Tia calls from her bedroom.

I step out into the hallway. Tia's door is ajar as usual, so she can see the landing light.

"Leo?" she says again, louder this time. I sigh and push open her door.

Tia's room is tiny and a complete wreck, clothes and stuffed animals everywhere and crayon scribbles all over the walls. She sits cross-legged under the duvet she inherited from Amber. The cover was once a Flower Fairies print, it's now so faded and worn that some of the fairies are missing faces or limbs, ghostly white smudges in their place.

"What do you want?" I ask wearily.

"Where's Amber?"

"Over at Carl's. She'll be back soon."

"Will you tuck me in?"

I sigh and kneel down next to Tia's bed. She beams and shimmies into a lying-down position. Snot clings to her tiny nostrils. I pull the duvet up under her chin and turn to go.

"That's not the right way," she whines.

I roll my eyes.

"Please, Leo?"

"For Pete's sake, Tia."

I lean over and begin tucking the duvet underneath her, working my way down her spindly little body until she looks like a mummy.

"How's that?" I ask.

"Perfect."

"Can I go now?"

She nods.

"Leo?"

"What?"

24

"I like your jacket."

I look down. I still have the blazer on.

"Oh yeah?"

"Yeah, it's really nice. You look handsome. Like Prince Eric from *The Little Mermaid*."

I shake my head. "Thanks, Tia."

She smiles serenely and shuts her eyes. "You're welcome."

DAVID

"David!" Mum yells up the stairs. "Time to get up!"

I turn onto my stomach and pull a pillow over my head. A few more minutes pass before my bedroom door creaks open.

"Rise and shine," Mum singsongs, creeping across the carpet and peeling back the duvet.

I snatch it from her and pull it over my head.

"Five more minutes," I say, my voice muffled.

"No way. Up. Now. I won't have you making Livvy late on her first day."

Livvy is starting at Eden Park School today.

I heave myself out of bed and glance in the mirror. I look awful—sweaty and pale with dark circles under my eyes and crease marks across my cheeks. I never sleep well the night before the first day back.

By 8 a.m. I'm sitting in the passenger seat of the car. Livvy is still outside posing for photographs while Mum weeps behind the lens. Livvy is very photogenic; everyone says so. Mum and

Dad often joke her real dad's the milkman. No one *ever* makes similar jokes about my parentage.

Livvy cocks her head and smiles angelically. The way the sunlight hits her, I can see the outline of her bra through her blouse. She already wears a 32A. She and Mum went shopping for it over the summer, and when they got home they acted all giggly and secretive.

"Look after her, David!" Mum says when she drops us off outside the school gates.

As we start to walk up the drive, I place a protective hand on Livvy's shoulder. Immediately she grunts, shaking it off.

"Don't walk so close to me!" she hisses.

"But you heard Mum, I'm supposed to look after you," I point out.

"Well, don't. I don't want people to know we're related," she says, quickening her pace. I let her go, watching as she strides confidently toward the lower-school building, her long hair flying out behind her.

"Nice," I mutter to myself, recalling a time when Livvy used to follow me around the house, sweetly begging me to play with her.

I hear two voices calling my name. I grin and spin around. Essie and Felix are heading toward me, waving madly.

Essie is tall (almost a head taller than Felix) with masses of (currently black) hair, pale blue eyes, and stupidly long legs. Beside her Felix is immaculate as usual, his fair hair combed into a neat side part and his face tanned from the Florida sun.

I skip toward them and we collide in a messy group hug.

"When did your little sister get so hot?" Felix asks as we separate.

"Ew, don't be such a pervert, she's only eleven!" I cry. At the same time Essie punches him on the shoulder, sending Felix staggering back a few steps.

"Ow!" he cries, clutching his shoulder.

"Er, hello? Girlfriend? Right here?" Essie says.

Felix and Essie got together at the Christmas ball last year. I left the dance floor to buy some chips and a Coke and by the time I returned, they were chewing each other's faces off to an Enrique Iglesias song. I didn't even know they liked each other that way so it all came as a surprise. Felix and Essie claim it was as much of a shock for them ("I blame Enrique," Essie often says, usually when Felix is annoying her).

"How was Math Camp?" I ask Felix. I can't imagine anything more hideous.

"Awesome," he replies.

"I missed you both so much," I say, as we head toward the upper-school building, instinctively falling into step with each other. "My birthday party was beyond miserable without you."

"Don't talk to me about miserable," Essie says. "I've been in stepmonster hell for the past six weeks. Can you believe she tried to make me take my nose ring out?"

"Oh God, don't get her started," Felix moans. "It's all she talked about last night."

I stop walking.

"You guys hung out last night? Why didn't you call me?"

Essie and Felix exchange looks.

"It was kind of boyfriend-girlfriend hanging out," Essie says. "If you know what I mean."

"Yeah," Felix echoes, turning a bit red and pushing his glasses up his nose. I notice his skin is peeling around his hairline.

"Oh, right," I say. "Never mind."

We keep walking.

Although I'm obviously thrilled my two best friends in the entire world are in love, I still can't help but get slightly freaked out by the idea of them "together." I don't know if they've had sex or anything yet and I haven't asked. Which bothers me. Up to now, we've always told one another everything and all of a sudden one topic, and a pretty major one at that, is unofficially off limits. To me anyway.

· · · · ·

I get to my homeroom early so I can reserve a seat near the front, as close to Mr. Collins as possible, even if that means sitting next to Simon Allen, who always stinks of plasticine. The same kids have homeroom together for all of upper school so I know what to expect and this way I can guarantee people like Harry Beaumont and Tom Kelly won't be sitting anywhere near me. Homeroom only lasts for twenty minutes but it feels like an eternity some days. For about the thousandth time I wish I was in the same homeroom as Essie and Felix. They're just next door but it feels like light years away. At least we have Biology and History together this year so it's not a complete disaster.

Bam! The spitball strikes me hard on the back of my neck. I twist around in my seat. Harry is pretending to tie his shoelaces. Everyone around him is sniggering. I peel the spitball off my skin and flick it onto the floor where it lands with a dull splat. It's fat, moist, and heavy. He's been practicing.

"Hey, Freak Show!" he calls.

I pretend not to hear him. "Freak Show" has been Harry's nickname for me for years. A lot of other kids call me it too, but Harry's the one responsible for its longevity.

"Aw, c'mon, Freak Show," he says coaxingly. "That's not very polite, is it? I'm trying to have a nice conversation with you and you've got your back turned to me."

I sigh and twist around in my seat again. Harry has stood up and is now lounging on Lexi Taylor's desk while she giggles like a hyena. Lexi is Harry's current girlfriend. She thinks she's superhot because apparently modeling bridesmaid dresses in the fashion show at the Eden Park Summer Fair last year somehow makes her Naomi Campbell.

"Was that your little sister I saw you arrive with this morning?" he asks.

"What's it to you?"

"No need to be touchy! I was only asking."

I sigh. "Yes, she's my sister. Why?"

"It's just that she looked, well, almost normal."

Laughter ripples across the classroom. Harry basks in it, a slow grin spreading across his face. I try not to let my irritation show.

"So what I'm trying to work out is this," he says. "Which one of you is adopted?"

Mr. Collins breezes into the classroom, oblivious. "Welcome back, everyone! Harry, sit down, please."

Harry slides off the desk, smirking.

"I reckon the smart money's on you, Freak Show."

DAVID

Lunchtime. I take a Coke from the fridge and put it next to the plate of lukewarm congealed mac and cheese already on my tray.

"Well, I heard he got expelled," a year-eleven girl with frizzy brown hair in front of me is saying.

"Who?" her friend asks.

"The new kid."

"Expelled? What for?" someone else asks.

"I don't know. It must be something bad though. I've heard it's almost impossible to get expelled from Cloverdale School."

I've heard of Cloverdale School. It has a reputation for being really rough and scary, always in the papers for poor student scores.

"I know why he got expelled," one of the boys chimes in proudly. "Apparently he went nuts during wood shop and chopped off the teacher's index finger with a junior hacksaw."

There's a collective gasp. Apart from the frizzy-haired girl who says, "I'm not surprised. You can tell he's a bit crazy, just look at his eyes."

I follow their gaze to a boy sitting alone at a table in the far corner of the cafeteria, glaring at a plate of fries. I'm too far away to tell if his eyes are "crazy" or not.

"How has he ended up here, then?" someone else asks.

"I don't know but I'm not going to go anywhere near him," another boy says. "To have been expelled from Cloverdale he must be a real maniac."

I pay for my food and find Essie and Felix at our usual table in the corner. I pass the popular kids in the center of the room, shrieking and laughing and showing off—the star attractions. Their hangers-on are eating at the surrounding tables, forming a protective barrier, leaving the more out-there groups to populate the outer tables. Over in the opposite corner, the emo kids huddle around an MP3 player, listening intently, bobbing their heads in time to the music. A few tables over, the clever, nerdy kids are debating passionately about the latest Marvel movie.

Essie, Felix, and I don't fit into any particular group. Essie thinks this is a good thing. It was Essie who came up with our name—the Non-Conformists (or the NCs for short), not that anyone ever calls us that.

"Hey, Davido," Essie says as I slide into my seat. "We're discussing which has more nutritional content, today's delicious mac and cheese"—she leans in and sniffs her plate—"or a can of dog food."

"I vote for the dog food," Felix says cheerfully, his mouth full, spraying pumpkin-and-tahini-millet-ball crumbs in all directions. He's allergic to pretty much everything so his mum prepares him a macrobiotic lunch every day.

"I vote for the dog food too," I say, unfolding a paper napkin. "I once tasted some of Phil's kibble and it wasn't all that bad."

"You did what?" Felix says, putting down his carton of carrot juice.

"How have we not heard this story before?" Essie demands.

"Mum caught me eating from our old dog's bowl one morning," I say. "I guess I must have just been really hungry. In my defense I was only about three at the time."

"And this is precisely why we love you, David Piper," Essie says. "Pass the salt, will you?"

I can't quite pinpoint the moment Essie, Felix, and I became best friends. I only know we somehow gravitated toward one another like magnets, and by the end of our first year at primary school, I couldn't imagine the world without the three of us in it together.

As I pass the salt to Essie, my eyes fall on the new boy. He's sitting two tables away, still staring at his food. Up closer, he doesn't *look* crazy. In fact, he's sort of cute with his snub nose, messy light brown hair falling across his forehead, and the most incredible cheekbones.

I lean in.

"Hey, do either of you know anything about the new boy in year eleven?"

"Only that he got expelled from Cloverdale School and is meant to be a violent lunatic," Felix says, his voice carelessly loud.

"Sssshhhh, he might hear you!"

I peer over Felix's shoulder but the boy is still having a staring competition with his fries.

"I feel bad that he's on his own," I say. "Should I ask him to sit with us?"

Felix raises his eyebrows. "Did the words 'violent' and 'lunatic' not raise even the faintest alarm bells?"

"Oh don't be so boring!" Essie says. "Anyone who has an official screw loose is more than welcome at our table. Go for it, Mother Teresa, spread some NC love."

I hesitate, suddenly afraid.

"Why don't you do it?" I say.

"I don't want to scare him off," Essie says. "A lot of men are intimidated by strong women."

Felix and I roll our eyes at each other.

"No, definitely best you go, David," she continues. "You're nice and unthreatening."

"Gee, thanks," I say sarcastically, pushing back my chair and making my way over to the boy's table.

"Hi," I say, hovering at his side.

I notice a red free-school-meals token poking out from under his tray. The boy doesn't respond.

"I'm David Piper," I say, extending my hand. "I'm in year ten. Nice to meet you."

The boy ignores me and takes a swig from his Coke instead, wiping his mouth on the sleeve of his blazer. My hand hovers awkwardly in midair. He finally looks at it before sighing again and shaking it once, firmly.

"Leo Denton," he says gruffly.

He raises his eyes to meet mine, and I have to catch my breath for a moment, because, wow, that year-eleven girl was totally wrong. Leo's eyes aren't crazy at all; they're beautiful, hypnotic, like looking through a kaleidoscope almost—sea green with amber flecks around the pupils.

"Can I help you?" Leo asks.

I realize I'm staring.

"Er—yes—sorry," I stammer, dragging my eyes away from his. "It's just that my friends over there and I . . ."

I point to Essie and Felix. Helpfully, Essie has plastered her top lip to her gums and Felix has flipped his eyelids inside out.

"Er, well, we were wondering if you'd like to eat lunch with us?"

I hold my breath. Leo is looking at me like I've got two heads.

"No thanks," he says finally.

"We're not weird, honestly." I glance back at Essie and Felix. "Well, we are a bit . . ."

"Look, thanks, but no thanks. I'm done anyway."

And with that, Leo stands up, dumps his tray on the cart, picks up his Coke, and heads for the door.

I amble back to our table.

"He wasn't interested," I report.

"What?" Essie cries, outraged.

I shrug and sit down.

"Psychopaths do tend to be loners," Felix muses.

"He didn't seem very psychopathic," I point out.

"They never do," Felix replies loftily.

I crane my neck to look out the window but Leo has already disappeared from view.

"Olsen alert! Olsen alert!" Essie starts to hiss.

"Where?" I say, turning my attention back to the table, instinctively sitting up straight.

"Behind you. Over by Harry's table."

I slowly turn around in my seat. And there he is. Zachary Olsen. Otherwise known as the love of my life.

I have loved Zachary Olsen ever since we shared the same wading pool, aged four. The fact I was once in such close proximity to his semi-naked body is sometimes too much to bear. The fact he clearly has no recollection that our semi-naked bodies ever shared a wading pool is even worse. Zachary is everything I am not—a half-Norwegian love god complete with shaggy blond hair and tanned six-pack. He's captain of the soccer *and* rugby teams. He's crazily popular. He *always* has a girlfriend. He basically stands for everything we Non-Conformists claim is wrong with the world. And yet I am completely in love with him. Unfortunately he doesn't appear to know I'm alive.

Today he has his arm slung around Chloe Hollins's shoulder, indicating she is his current girlfriend (death to Chloe) and is laughing at something Harry has just said. Even Zachary's fraternizing with the enemy does little to dampen my love for him. He could probably torture kittens and rob old ladies at gunpoint and I'd still adore him.

I watch as he and Chloe saunter out of the cafeteria, looking smug and sexy. Essie reaches across and gives my hand a squeeze. Which says it all really. I am a hopeless case. In about a billion different ways.

LEO

My first day at Eden Park School is okay. Even though it follows a similar pattern to Cloverdale—three hour-long classes in the morning, two more after lunch, the timetable rotating each day—it manages to feel totally different. Everyone pays attention in class for one thing, like they actually want to be there, and as a result the time seems to pass more quickly. Even better, apart from some year-ten kid who tries to talk to me at lunch, no one comes near me. Not that I'm invisible exactly. All day kids have been staring at me. At first I can't work out why but then I notice the *way* they're staring at me. They're scared. So I play up to it. I act the hard man and stare right back, and every time they chicken out first. Who cares *why* they're scared. As long as they leave me alone, I don't care what they think.

The bell rings for the end of the day. The hallway is packed but as I walk down it, kids scramble to make way for me, parting like the Red Sea. It would actually be pretty funny if it wasn't so strange. I'm almost at the end of the hallway when this girl appears out of nowhere and bumps into me.

Her eyes spring open in surprise and I can't help wondering what kind of idiot walks around with their eyes closed.

"Jesus, sorry!" she says, laughing, lowering the massive pair of red headphones she's wearing so they're hanging around her neck. "I was totally not looking where I was going. Are you okay?"

She has black curly hair that shoots out in all directions, and light brown eyes almost the exact same color as her skin. Basically, she's gorgeous. I quickly chase the thought out of my head.

"It's just that I was listening to the most incredible song," the girl continues. "I'm obsessed with it. Want to hear?"

She thrusts the headphones at me.

"No thanks," I say, squeezing past her, careful my body doesn't touch hers.

"Hey!" she calls after me.

Reluctantly I turn around and raise my eyes to meet hers. Her lashes are stupidly long. I hate that I notice this.

"You're new, right?"

"Yeah, I'm new," I say.

She breaks into a fresh grin.

"Well, in that case, welcome to Eden Park School, new boy."

. . . . .

I arrive home to discover Spike's Peugeot parked at a funny angle outside our house, as if he's abandoned it at the scene of a crime.

He stayed over again last night. This morning the bathroom sink was full of black stubble.

I push open the front door. Spike is sitting on the sofa with Mam perched on his knee. He's whispering in her ear and she's giggling like a little girl. His hand is on her butt.

I slam the door shut. It makes the two of them jump. Mam glares at me and straightens her miniskirt.

She's always going on about how she's as skinny now as she was when she was fifteen, and insists on wearing the skimpiest of clothes to prove it. It's her eyes that give the game away— dead and tired, like life's sucked all the sparkle right out of them.

"How you doing?" Spike says over her shoulder. He takes in my blazer and lets out a whistle. "Wow, what have you got on? You go to Hogwarts or something?"

I ignore him and wander into the kitchen. I open the cookie jar. It's empty apart from a few crumbs.

"Excuse me, Spike's talking to you," Mam barks after me.

"It's the Eden Park School uniform," I say, replacing the lid.

"Eden Park, eh?" Spike replies. "You must be smart."

I shrug.

"Just because you're wearing a fancy blazer, it doesn't mean you're better than us, so don't go getting ideas above your station," Mam says.

"Like I would dare," I say under my breath.

"What did you say?" she asks sharply.

"Nothing. Can I go now?"

"Please do. I've had enough of your miserable face."

40

. . . . .

I find Amber sitting on her bunk, brushing her white-blond clip-in hair extensions.

"Why aren't you at Carl's?" I ask.

"Fight," she says. "I found a load of texts on his phone from some girl at the ice rink."

"Oh."

Carl and Amber have a huge argument at least once a month.

I sniff. The room smells rank—of chemicals and moldy cookies.

"Jesus, Amber, it stinks in here!"

"Keep your hair on, it's only fake-tan spray," she says.

Amber always says she'd rather die than be "all gross and pale." When I was a kid I used to tan in the summer but my legs haven't seen the sun in forever and these days they're so white they're almost fluorescent.

"Well, it smells nasty," I tell her, wrinkling my nose.

"Sorry," she replies breezily, then asks, "So how was school?"

"All right," I reply, hanging up my blazer and taking off my tie. I drop to the floor and start to do my daily push-ups, banging them out fast.

"Are the kids really rich?" she asks.

"I dunno. Some are I guess."

"Did you make any friends?"

She's relentless. I pause mid-push-up.

"You're as bad as Jenny."

"Well, did you?"

I think of the boy in the cafeteria and the girl who bumped into me in the hallway.

"Nah," I say. "No point."

Amber makes a face but doesn't push it. I flip onto my back and start to do my stomach crunches. I hear the bathroom door opening and closing. A few seconds later Spike starts singing an old Elvis song.

I crawl over to the wall and give it a thump.

"Shut up!" I yell.

"Oh, leave him be," Amber says.

"You're joking, aren't you?"

"He seems harmless enough."

"He's a tool, Amber."

"He's not that bad. Tia likes him."

"Tia likes everyone."

"He's better than the last one at least," Amber points out.

"Not hard." I snort.

Mam's last boyfriend did a runner with our television. But then Mam's boyfriends always do a runner eventually. She'll drive Spike away before too long, just like she did Dad. Not that I'd care if Spike left. Dad is the only one I care about.

LEO

My first class on Tuesday is English, one of my least favorite subjects. I prefer subjects with wrong or right answers, formulas, and rules.

I get there early, choosing a desk next to the window about halfway back. I sit down and begin to unpack my stuff.

"Hey, do you have a pen I can borrow? Mine leaked all over me!"

I look up. It's her. The girl with the headphones, sitting at the desk right in front of me. She's twisted around in her seat so her elbows are resting on my desk, her chin cupped in her hands.

"So, do you?" she asks.

"Do I what?" I ask stupidly.

She rolls her eyes and laughs. "Do. You. Have. A. Pen?" she asks again, separating each word for me.

"Oh yeah, 'course I do, hang on."

I fumble in my pencil case, trying to find the least chewed pen I can.

"Here," I say, handing it over. "Keep it."

"Thanks, new boy! Oh God, how rude am I? I haven't introduced myself properly. I'm Alicia Baker," she says, offering her hand for me to shake. "Excuse the ink."

"I'm Leo," I say, shaking her hand once, then dropping it.

"Oh, I know who you are," she says.

The teacher, Ms. Jennings, claps to get our attention. Alicia smiles at me before turning to face the front of the class.

Shit.

I'm not here to meet girls. Girls let you down. They trick you, manipulate you. Girls can't be trusted. Fact. But at the same time I can't ignore this funny feeling in my stomach; it's a bit like when I used to dive from the highest board at the swimming pool. As Ms. Jennings takes attendance, Alicia sneaks another glance at me over her shoulder. I look away fast, pretending I haven't seen her, and fix my eyes on the clock above Ms. Jennings's head, so hard my vision goes all blurry.

I blink. Ms. Jennings is saying my name.

"Denton? Leo Denton?" she asks, frowning, her eyes searching the room.

"Er, yeah, here, miss," I say, raising my hand. Half the class turn around in their seats to look at me.

"Stay awake please, Mr. Denton," she says through pursed lips, before continuing down the roll.

The rest of the class is taken up with handing out books, filling in forms, listening to Ms. Jennings talk.

The bell finally rings. I start to pack up my things and can feel Alicia watching me. I look up. She's smiling again. She has a dimple in each cheek. Her teeth are crazy white.

"Laters, daydreamer," she says, as she puts her headphones on before linking arms with some blond girl and gliding out of the classroom.

. . . . .

The next time I have English, I try not to look at Alicia as I walk up the aisle to my desk. But then I make the mistake of glancing down at her, and there she is, smiling away, totally oblivious to how it's messing with my head.

Ms. Jennings dims the lights. We're watching a movie version of *Twelfth Night*, the play we're studying this term. At first I try to concentrate on the movie but after a few minutes I find myself staring at the back of Alicia's head. She usually wears her hair down but today it's up and I can see her neck.

Outside it's raining and the classroom is warm. I place my hand against the window. The condensation feels good—cool and wet. When I take my hand away, it leaves a print behind. Next to it I draw a circle with my index finger. Ms. Jennings looks up from her marking. I put my damp hand into my lap and wipe it on my pants.

A second later Alicia twists sideways in her seat and adds eyes and a smiley face to my circle. Before I can stop myself I'm leaning forward, adding big ears and a tuft of hair. And I can just tell, by the way the muscles in her neck contract, that Alicia is smiling.

"Ahem?"

At the front of the classroom, Ms. Jennings is frowning at us, her eyebrows raised. Alicia lets out a tiny giggle. I fight to keep my lips from curling into a smile.

For the rest of the class I force myself to look at the screen and nowhere else.

By the time the bell rings, the smiley face has begun to melt and slide down the window, the eyes droopy, the smile now a frown. As I pack away my things, I can sense Alicia watching me. Distracted, I drop my pen. I bend down to pick it up but Alicia is faster.

"Here," she says, pressing it into my hand.

"Thanks," I reply, jamming the pen into my backpack.

I wait for her to move, but she doesn't.

"Leo?" she says.

"Yeah?" I reply, zipping up my backpack and not meeting her eyes.

"Can I ask you a favor?"

I swallow hard.

"What kind of favor?" I ask slowly.

"It's a tiny one, I promise," she says, biting her lower lip. "It's just that I've entered this singing competition online and the winner gets the chance to meet a team of top record execs, but I need way more votes if I'm going to make it through to the final. So I was wondering whether you'd vote for me? I've been pestering everyone else on Facebook and Twitter, but I couldn't find you."

My skin prickles as I picture Alicia searching for me online.

"I think it's really okay by the way," she adds.

I frown.

"That you're not on Facebook, I mean," she continues. "I wish I wasn't on there a lot of the time. It can mess with your head, you know?"

I don't answer her.

"You, er, sing then?" I ask instead.

"Oh, yeah," she says, looking at her feet, shy suddenly. "I write my own stuff too, and post videos—on YouTube and stuff."

"Oh, right, okay," I murmur.

"So you'll vote for me?"

"What do I have to do?"

"Do you have your phone?"

I shake my head. I don't want Alicia to see my crappy old Nokia.

"Give me your hand."

Before I can say or do anything, she's grabbing my hand and placing it in hers. Her skin is soft and her nails are short and neat and painted with clear polish. I let my hand go limp and hope she doesn't notice my bitten-down nails. She scrawls on the back of my hand with a pen, the nib dragging at my skin. When she's done, she pauses and looks up.

"Freckly hands," she says.

"Eh?"

"I've always wanted freckles," she continues. "My gran reckons they're kisses from the sun. Cute, huh?"

I shrug.

Alicia taps the back of my hand with the pen.

47

"Well, that's the Web site. I'm listed as Alicia B."

"Alicia B," I repeat.

"To vote for me, you just have to click on my name and watch my video. I'm about halfway down, I think."

"Okay."

"Amazeballs. Thank you, Leo, I really appreciate this."

It's only then she lets go of my hand and heads for the door.

. . . . .

After school, instead of going straight home, I go to the computer lab. Apart from one other kid and the teacher on duty, it's empty.

I take a set of headphones from the stack at the front and sit down at one of the monitors in the back row. I type the Web address printed on my hand. I scroll down until I find Alicia B and click on her name.

Alicia's face flashes up on the screen. She's sitting on the end of a bed cross-legged, a guitar on her lap and her face frozen in a smile. I press Play.

"Hi! I'm Alicia B," she says directly to the camera. "This is a song I wrote called 'Deep Down with Love.' I really hope you like it and, if you do, that you'll vote for me! Thanks!"

She begins to sing. And she's amazing. I watch the video a couple more times, even though I'm only allowed to vote once. I'm about to leave when I remember her talking about posting stuff on YouTube, so I type in *Alicia B* and up come more videos.

Some are of her singing songs by people like Adele or Leona Lewis. But it's her own music I like the best, songs with really sad lyrics about love going wrong. At the end of each one she always waits a few beats before breaking into a big smile to remind you it's all pretend.

Because I'm pretty sure Alicia Baker is the sort of girl who breaks hearts, not the other way around.

· · · · ·

When I get home, Spike is in the kitchen reading the newspaper and eating toast. Does he ever go to work? According to Mam he's a delivery driver for some bakery downtown.

"What are you doing here?" I ask, taking off my blazer and tie and draping them over the back of a chair.

"Hello to you too," he says cheerfully.

"Where's Mam?"

"She's got a shift at the Laundromat, then she's going to catch a movie with your auntie Kerry. Girls' night, you know."

"That still doesn't explain why you're here," I say.

"I offered to pick Tia up from school and make you kids some dinner."

"Right."

I open the bread box, it's empty. I glance at Spike's plate. There must be five slices of toast there.

"Here, have some of this," Spike says quickly, noticing my frown. "It'll keep you going."

"No thanks."

"Don't be silly. I can't eat this anyway. What's mine is yours, kiddo."

I go into the living room, sit down, and turn on the TV. It's one of those programs about people searching for houses abroad. I can feel Spike watching me. I look over my shoulder. He's leaning against the door frame, balancing the plate of toast on his hand.

"Spain's a lovely place," he says, nodding toward the screen. "Ever been, Leo?"

"No," I mutter.

"It's fantastic," he says. "Although I always say you can't beat Thailand. Now that's one beautiful country. The nicest people too. God, the times I had in Thailand, kiddo," he says, letting out a low whistle. "People are always telling me I should write a book about my travels, you know.'

"Then why don't you?" I say.

The way he's talking it's like he's had these grand adventures.

He sighs. "Don't have the time, kiddo."

The other day he left his wallet on the coffee table and I had a quick look through it. His driver's license says his name is Kevin. So much for *Spike*. His address is somewhere in Manchester. Apart from that there was a bit of cash, some receipts, and a folded-up strip of photos of him and Mam taken in one of those passport-photo booths. In the first shot they were grinning at the camera, in the second they were doing bunny ears behind each other's heads, in the third and fourth, they were kissing. Gross.

Spike comes to sit next to me.

"Go on," he says. "Have some."

The toast drips with butter. It smells so good. In spite of myself I take a slice, but only 'cause I'm starving. I rip it in half and stuff the smaller piece into my mouth, swallowing it down whole. It scrapes the back of my throat.

Spike takes a bite and munches for a few seconds, his lips smacking.

"Actually, Leo, I'm glad your mam's not home. I think we got off on the wrong foot. This might be a good chance for us to have a chat, you know, man to man."

I wonder what Mam's told him about me.

"Thanks but no thanks," I say, swallowing the other piece of toast in one go and standing up.

"Leo, wait, will ya?"

I turn. Spike is looking at me. With his floppy hair and droopy eyes, he reminds me of the spaniel Auntie Kerry had for a bit, until it peed in her underwear drawer and she took it to the rescue center.

"I really like your mam. You know that don't you, kiddo?" he says.

The idea of anyone being into my disaster zone of a mother seems pretty unlikely to me.

"She's a special lady, Leo, and I know it's very early days, but if things work out, and I hope they do, I'm going to do right by you and your sisters. I'm not like the others, I'm not going to disappear the minute things get a bit rough."

"Whatever," I say, looking out the window. "I'm fifteen. In a year or so, I'll be out of here anyway."

"I know. I'm just saying, it must be hard for you guys, not having a dad on the scene."

I spin around. "Keep my dad out of this. You don't know anything about him."

"Now hang on a minute, kiddo, I might know more than you think," Spike says.

"You don't know anything," I spit, heading for the door.

"Leo," Spike calls. "Come back, Leo!"

I grab my hoodie and slam the front door behind me.

As I stomp across the yard I hear one of the upstairs windows open and Tia's thin little voice calling my name. I ignore her and keep walking.

I head for the old Cloverdale pool.

It's still light out when I arrive so I lie on my back on the bottom of the empty pool with my hoodie propped under my head as a pillow. Above me, the fading sunlight shines through the glass roof and warms my face. Already I feel a bit calmer. I spread my fingers out. The surface of the pool beneath me feels cool and sort of damp, and the whole place stinks of chlorine, which is odd because there hasn't been any water in here for a couple of years now. I like breathing it in, taking big gulps and letting it fill up my lungs and nostrils.

When the city council announced they were going to close down the Cloverdale swimming pool a few years ago, everyone made a big fuss and signed a petition, but it didn't do any good; they went ahead and closed it anyway. They're building a new recreation center about a mile away, with a gym and a café and Zumba classes. It won't be the same though.

I used to swim here when I was a kid. On sunny days, you'd get blinded doing the backstroke. I liked it best when it was raining. I used to love how it got really dark and the rain would thunder on the roof and you could imagine you were swimming down the Amazon in the middle of a tropical storm.

Gav used to bring me and Amber here on Saturday mornings while Mam stayed in bed and slept off her hangover. Gav was Mam's boyfriend at the time. He taught us to swim in the shallow end—backstroke and front crawl. Amber didn't like getting her hair wet and would cough and splutter every time she got water in her mouth. But I loved it. Gav used to say I was a real water baby.

I liked Gav. He was one of the better ones. Of course he was too soft and let Mam walk all over him, until one day he must have finally had enough because he left the house in the morning and never came back.

Anyway, when we had swimming at primary school a couple of years later, I was the best in the class. I'd whip through the water, fast and strong, everyone else way behind me. A scout for the county youth team spotted me and I started going to extra classes after school and competing in races and winning medals and trophies. But then one day I stopped. Just like that. And I haven't been in the water since. I was ten. I miss it. I miss the way it made me feel—calm and in control. I miss the muffled sounds of voices when my head was underwater. Sometimes I think life would be about a thousand times easier if I could do everything underwater, with no one bothering me, everyone's words distorted and faraway, and me just under the surface, fast and untouchable.

As I lie here, Spike's words keep echoing in my head: "I might know more than you think." Part of me wishes I'd stayed and asked him what he meant. But then Spike would only have Mam's story and who knows what crap she's been telling him.

No, the only person who can really tell me the truth is long gone.

DAVID

At lunchtime on Monday, the cafeteria is packed, everyone willing to put up with the stench of boiled cabbage and burned parsnips in exchange for warmth. The weather turned over the weekend. According to the newspaper it's set to be the coldest September on record since the 1940s.

Essie, Felix, and I look over at Leo who is wolfing down a slice of pizza.

"I wonder where he goes?" I ponder, watching as he finishes, deposits his empty tray, and heads for the door.

"To howl at the moon?" Essie suggests.

"Ha-ha."

"Why do you care anyway?" she asks.

"I was just speculating," I say, poking at my food with my fork.

"Did I tell you he's in my math class?" Felix asks.

"Are you serious?" I say.

I can't help but be surprised that Leo is in the special advanced class. Immediately I feel ashamed for judging him so quickly. I mentally add "good at math" to the irritatingly sparse list of facts I know about him, the list all the more irritating because I haven't quite worked out why I'm so interested in the first place.

"What's he like in it?" I ask.

"No wielding of weapons so far," Felix says. "In fact, he hardly says a word. He can obviously do the work though."

"I can't believe you didn't tell me sooner," I say.

"What is it with you and this kid?" Essie asks. "You're obsessed with him."

"No I'm not. I find him interesting, that's all. Don't you?"

"Moderately," Essie says with a yawn.

"You're just annoyed he didn't jump at the chance to eat lunch with us that time," I say.

"No, I'm not, although based on that alone, the boy clearly has no taste." She narrows her eyes at me. "You don't have a crush on him, do you?"

"Just because I find someone interesting does not mean I have a crush on them."

"It's okay if you do. I'm just surprised. I didn't think bad boys were your type. Poor Zachary," she says, "ousted by the new boy."

"I do not have a crush on Leo Denton," I say, probably a bit too loudly because the girls sitting at the next table peer over their shoulders at us with rare interest.

"I don't," I repeat, in a low voice.

"Okay, okay," Essie says, holding up her hands in mock surrender. "I believe you."

"Thank you," I say.

"Although thousands wouldn't," she adds, smiling wickedly.

I don't see Leo again until after school. As Mum drives Livvy and me home, I spot him slumped against the bus stop, his hands shoved in his pockets, eyes staring out into space. It's so weird, because the feeling I get when I look at him is totally different from how I feel when I see Zachary around school. I don't have butterflies or feel like I'm about to vomit. I'm still capable of speech. I don't turn the color of a tomato. And yet I definitely feel something. I just haven't worked out what the *thing* is yet, and it's driving me mad.

. . . . .

Every evening before dinner, Dad sits down in his favorite armchair and reads the newspaper while drinking a cup of milky tea. Tonight I position myself on the sofa opposite him and pretend to study my French vocabulary for Madame Fournier's test tomorrow morning. I'm pretending because what I'm really doing is watching Dad's face for clues while he reads—a telltale raise of the eyebrows, a furrow of the brow, perhaps a smile, some hint of disapproval or otherwise. Because on page twenty-three of the newspaper there is an article about a teenage girl in America who has just been elected homecoming queen at her school. I'm not sure what a homecoming queen does, apart from wear a crown and sash, ride in a parade, and wave at people. But that's not the bit of the story I'm interested in. Because the girl in the article, in her glittery evening gown and high heels, was born a boy.

As he reads, Dad's face remains frustratingly unchanged.

I peek over the top of my vocab list as he takes yet another noisy slurp of tea, and leisurely turns the page.

"Anything interesting?" I ask casually.

"Not really," Dad replies.

After half an hour he's finished. He sets the newspaper down on the arm of the chair and heads off to the kitchen to rinse his mug and help Mum prepare dinner. As soon as he is out of the room, I swipe the newspaper and run upstairs, two at a time, closing my bedroom door behind me.

My bedroom is my sanctuary. Last year, for my thirteenth birthday, Mum and Dad let me paint it any color I liked. The shade I really wanted was a gorgeous hot pink, but I was too afraid to ask for it. I ended up going for a deep red instead, which, according to Essie, is very "womblike." Dad refers to my bedroom as "the cave," in a deep gravelly voice he thinks is hilarious. My walls are decorated with framed prints, mostly black-and-white shots of New York City, or vintage film posters, and photo collages of Essie, Felix, and me through the years.

I turn on the Christmas lights that loop their way around the room, and clamber onto my bed, spreading the newspaper out in front of me. I turn to page twenty-three and sigh. The page is dominated by a photograph of the beaming homecoming queen, black hair cascading down her tanned shoulders. My finger traces the contours of her face and the curves of her body in its sparkling dress. According to the article she is sixteen. She looks older, twenty-one maybe. Could I look like that in two years? I try to imagine myself on the school stage, wearing a glittering ball dress and smiling serenely as I wave down at my cheering classmates, Zachary (crowned homecoming king, naturally) on my arm, gazing at me adoringly. But the image fails to form properly in my head. It feels silly and fake, like a halfhearted game of let's pretend.

Taking a pair of scissors from my desk, I carefully cut out the article, then reach under my bed and pull out my bulging scrapbook.

My scrapbook represents four years of careful curation. At the front, the pages are populated with postcards, candy wrappers, and movie tickets. After a while I started gluing in anything I found interesting or beautiful—a peacock feather collected on a school trip to Newstead Abbey; a Kleenex imprinted with a pink lipstick pout, swiped from Mum's dressing table; pictures of beautiful women snipped out of magazines. My favorites are the old movie stars—Elizabeth Taylor dripping with diamonds, Marilyn Monroe on a beach in a gleaming white swimsuit, Audrey Hepburn wearing long black gloves and pearls. These days, my movie stars mingle with clippings from newspapers and medical journals, statistics and tables, facts and figures.

I open the scrapbook to the most recent page. It smells sweet from the perfume sample I added last week. I shut my eyes and bury my nose in the pages for a moment, inhaling deeply. On the opposite page I carefully stick the article into place, smoothing it down so there are no bubbles or creases.

I glance at my phone. Twenty minutes until dinner. Just enough time for an inspection. I lock my door and turn on some music to make the process more bearable. I pick out Lady Gaga's *Born This Way* album, cranking up the volume to maximum.

I'm finished and have just put on my underpants when the door handle begins to rattle.

"David?" Livvy calls over the music. "Let me in!"

"Hang on!" I yell, pulling on my bathrobe, tying the belt tightly around my waist. I turn off the music and as I unlock the door, I remember my inspection notebook is lying open on my pillow. In a panic I pick it up and chuck it in my backpack before leaping back into the center of the room.

Livvy enters cautiously, wrinkling her nose as she spots me standing ramrod straight, wearing my bathrobe hours before bedtime.

"Didn't you hear us yelling for you to come to dinner?"

"Obviously not."

"Why was your door locked?" she asks.

"I was changing."

"Like any of us are interested in watching you get changed."

I make a face. She returns an uglier one.

"David! Livvy!" Mum calls from downstairs. "Dinner's getting cold."

Livvy stays put, her eyes narrow with suspicion.

"Go on," I say, gently nudging her toward the door. "You heard what Mum said, dinner's getting cold. I'll be down in a sec."

Reluctantly, she lets me usher her out of the room.

DAVID

That night I pass out on my bed surrounded by my French notes. I have feverish dreams where I find myself in the body of Madame Fournier, only I can't speak French, and have to hide in the supply closet.

I oversleep the next morning, waking up when Mum bangs on the door telling me she's leaving in ten minutes. In a stupor I stumble about, pulling on my school uniform, trying to tame my slept-on hair, throwing books and folders into my backpack, before clattering down the stairs and into the car, my eyes still sticky with sleep.

The morning doesn't get much better. First period today is Gym, a subject at which I do not excel. It's the only class I share with Zachary and while it's hardly a chance for me to shine, it's an excellent opportunity to look at his legs. This term we are doing rugby. Ordinarily my tactic is to keep as far away from the ball and other players as possible. But today an overly enthusiastic student teacher is covering the class and forces me into the scrum. The low point is Simon Allen sitting on my head.

In French the test goes spectacularly badly. When I hand in my paper at the end of the class, Madame Fournier is already frowning, as if she can predict my failure.

In Math we are studying Alegbra. Mr. Steele may as well be speaking Elvish for all I understand. Unable to keep up, I spend most of the class doodling. It takes me by surprise when I realize the hunched-over figure I've drawn in the corner of my paper looks more than a bit like Leo Denton.

By lunchtime I am thoroughly exhausted. Harry, Tom, and Lexi are behind me in the cafeteria line, Harry and Tom taking turns flicking my ears, making Lexi squeal with laughter every time.

"Very mature, guys," I say, trying to sound as bored as possible.

"Oh c'mon, lighten up, Freak Show," Harry says. "It's just a bit of fun."

He flicks me again on the right earlobe, hard. I flinch. The three of them crack up.

I fix my eyes on the back of the head of the kid in front of me and concentrate on staying very still, trying to resist the urge to abandon the line altogether. Occasionally, if I ignore him for long enough, Harry gets bored and moves on to a fresh victim.

"Where are your friends? Beauty and the geek? No, wait, hang on, let me rephrase that, this is Essie Staines we're talking about after all. Where are the mutant and the geek?" he crows.

"What did you call my friends?" I ask, annoyance propelling me around to face him.

"The mutant and the geek," Harry replies innocently. "Got a problem with that, Freak Show?"

I bite down hard on my lip.

"So where are they? Off mutating somewhere?"

"They're at band practice," I say.

"Oooooh, band practice," Harry says in a lisping high voice.

I turn away from him. Up ahead the lunch ladies are ladling out food in what seems like slow motion.

"God, this line is killing me," Lexi says, sighing. "Entertain me, Harry?"

"Isn't being in my company entertainment enough?" Harry asks. Lexi giggles.

"Hey, how about a quick round of kiss, marry, throw off a cliff?" Tom suggests.

"Fine," Lexi says. "Anything to break this tedium."

"I've got an amazing one for Lex," Tom says.

"Go on then, Tommy-boy," Harry says. "Do your worst."

"Okay," Tom says. "So here are your choices, Lexi. Mr. Wilton—"

"Gross!" Lexi squeals. Mr. Wilton teaches History and is at least seventy.

"Mr. Stacey . . ." Tom continues.

Lexi squeals again. Mr. Stacey teaches English and is a complete pervert. There's a rumor he tried to get Caitlin Myers drunk on the year-twelve trip to Toulouse last term.

"And finally, year ten's very own . . ." I hear Tom perform a drumroll on his thighs. ". . . David Piper."

"Genius!" Harry exclaims, high-fiving Tom. "Pure genius!"

I try to concentrate on the menu, debating beef stew versus vegetarian lasagna.

"So c'mon then, Lex, the man has spoken, what's the verdict?" Harry says.

"Easy," Lexi replies. "I'd kiss Mr. Stacey, because at least you'd know he'd be into it, I'd marry Mr. Wilton because he might die soon and I'd get all his money in the will, and I'd throw Freak Show off the cliff."

"Aw, poor Freak Show!" Harry says.

"Like I care," I say under my breath, reaching for a bottle of water.

"What did you say?" Harry asks.

I rest my tray on the counter, take a deep breath, and turn all the way around to face him.

"Do you honestly think I care whether Bubble Brain here wants to throw me off a cliff or not?"

Tom sniggers.

"What did you call me?" Lexi asks, her face suddenly bright red.

"Bubble Brain," I say, sounding a thousand times more confident than I feel. There's a line with Harry and I have a feeling I'm teetering dangerously on the edge of it.

"Harry, are you going to let him speak to me like that?" Lexi demands.

Harry walks around me in a slow circle. My heartbeat speeds

up. He stops behind me, his body pressed against mine, his chin resting on my shoulder. I can feel his breath warm on my cheek. It smells of cigarettes masked with mints.

"Apologize to my girlfriend," he growls in my ear.

I consider my options. I could, of course, do what Harry has asked, and apologize to Lexi. This would probably be the most sensible option in the long run. However, it would also haunt me for days. I'd wake up in the middle of the night thinking of the kick-ass things I *could* have said. Alternatively, I could channel my inner Essie and reel off a long list of Lexi's other "attributes" in addition to being a bubble brain. This would be the most satisfying option but is potentially very dangerous. What I don't consider is what I actually end up doing, possibly the most dangerous option of all.

"I'm waiting, Freak Show," Harry whispers, his breath tickling the back of my ear.

I elbow him in the stomach. He's not expecting it and doubles over in pain.

Lexi rushes forward and puts her arms around Harry. He shakes her off and charges at me. The force of his push sends me flying into the kids behind me. My backpack drops from my shoulder and falls to the floor. I bend down to pick it up, but Tom gets there first, scooping his foot underneath it and kicking it to Harry who proceeds to kick it around in a circle.

"Beaumont, don't be such a child," a year-eleven girl says.

For a second I think Harry is going to listen to her because he stops and picks up the backpack and starts to move toward me. I hold out my hands to take it from him, but at the last second a huge grin spreads across his face and he chucks it over my head to Tom instead. As it's sailing through the air, I remember.

My inspection notebook is in there.

Panic floods my chest.

"Give it back," I say to Tom.

"Give it back," he mimics in a high-pitched squeak.

"You could at least ask nicely," Harry says.

"Give it back, please!" I say, urgency creeping into my voice.

"Now that's much better," Harry says. "But you know what, Freak Show? We're not done yet."

He chucks the backpack to Lexi this time, who shrieks with delight before throwing it to Tom.

"Look, just give it back!"

I'm yelling now. But they keep throwing and I'm piggy in the middle, jumping helplessly. Tom throws the backpack to Harry. It arches high over my head. I reach for it, my fingers just grazing the shoulder straps before it lands in Harry's arms. Instead of throwing it back to Tom, he holds it to his chest, rocking it like a newborn baby, a fresh grin on his face.

"You know what I think? That the lady doth protest too much," he says, slowly undoing the zipper.

No, no, no.

"Harry," I say in a low whisper. "I'm begging you, just give it back."

"You're begging me, are you?" he says. "How very, very interesting."

Not taking his eyes off mine, he turns the bag upside down.

My pencil case falls out and springs open, pens and pencils scattering in all directions. Half a bottle of water comes tumbling after it, a packet of chewing gum, my keys, books, and folders, papers floating innocently to the ground like oversize confetti. And finally, my purple notebook. I drop to my knees to pick it up but Harry is one step ahead of me, snatching it in one swift movement.

"Now what do we have here?" he announces to the growing audience. "Does Freak Show keep a diary? Dear Diary, why am I such a weirdo loser?" he recites in a high voice.

More and more kids are gathering to watch. I look around desperately for a teacher or lunch lady but I can't see anyone over the heads of the small crowd that circles us.

Including Zachary Olsen's.

Suddenly I feel very dizzy.

"Give it a rest, Harry," someone says, possibly the year-eleven girl again. But Harry's having too much fun to even consider quitting now. He opens the notebook at random. His eyes dart down the page, widening with excitement, like he can't quite believe his luck.

"Harry, please," I say, glancing sideways at Zachary who is frowning slightly. But it's useless; nothing's going to stop Harry now.

"Guys, guys, listen to this!" he cries. 'Height, 165 centimeters; hips, 66 centimeters; Adam's apple, small but visible." He looks up at me, shaking his head. "What the hell is this, Freak Show?"

I lunge toward him, trying to make a grab for the notebook but Tom gets hold of my arms, pinning them behind my back.

"Get off me!" I yell, twisting against him.

"Pubic hair, coarser, more wiry!" Harry continues to crow. "Oh my God, listen to this! Penis length, six and a half centimeters!"

There's an explosion of laughter. I'm screaming now, thinking maybe if I make enough noise I can drown Harry out. At one point I think I hear someone telling him to stop, but over the din I can't be sure.

"Shutupshutupshutup!" I chant, my eyes squeezed shut. Perhaps if I don't open them I can pretend this is a horrible dream, that Zachary Olsen isn't standing there listening to Harry recite the fluctuating size of my penis. I feel water building under my eyelids, threatening to spill. But I can't cry in front of them. *I won't.*

The punch shuts us up.

It sounds unreal, like a sound effect from an action film. I open my eyes. Harry is on the floor, blood gushing from his nose, his eyes wide with shock. At first I think maybe I've had some kind of out-of-body experience and I'm the one responsible. But then I realize Tom's arms are still around me. I follow Harry's sight line. Standing over him is Leo, the kid from Cloverdale School, staring at his fist like it doesn't belong to him.

LEO

I'm in the head teacher's office. Mr. Toolan is looking at my file and frowning.

My left leg is jiggling up and down. Most of the time I can disguise how I feel, but when I'm nervous my left leg manages to override my brain every time.

Mr. Toolan puts my file down on his desk and sighs. "I'm not going to sugarcoat this, Leo. This is not a good start."

I flex my hands. My knuckles on one hand are red and tingly from the punch.

"I hoped *never* to see you in this office and yet less than two weeks into your first term, here you are. And for hitting another student no less," Mr. Toolan continues.

I look down at my shoes. I'm still wearing last year's pair. They're scuffed at the toes and the laces are starting to fray.

There's a knock at the door. It's Ms. Logan, the guidance counselor.

"I came as soon as I heard," she says, slipping into the seat beside me.

"Are you going to kick me out?" I ask. They're the first words I've spoken since I arrived.

Mr. Toolan and Ms. Logan exchange looks.

"How about you start by telling us what happened," Mr. Toolan says.

I clear my throat and lean forward in my chair.

"This kid was getting picked on, really getting laid into. And no one was standing up for him, not enough to do anything anyway, they all just let it happen."

"So at this point, why didn't you alert a teacher? Why did you take it upon yourself to sort it out with your fists?" Mr. Toolan asks.

I close my eyes. But it's still a blur. All I can see are flashing images: David who came over to talk to me in the cafeteria that first day, looking hurt and humiliated, on the verge of tears; then the other kid, the one I punched, looking smug and proud. The next thing I remember is me standing over him as he lay on the floor, blood pouring from his nose, and a couple of teachers grabbing my arms and marching me out of the cafeteria. Everything in between is hazy.

"Well?" Mr. Toolan says.

I open my eyes.

"I don't know, sir. I just . . . lost it, I suppose."

"Well, 'losing it,' as you put it, is simply not acceptable behavior."

I look at my feet again.

Mr. Toolan takes off his glasses and rubs his eyes. He has red marks on either side of his nose. I glance at Ms. Logan, trying to work out exactly how much trouble I'm in, but she refuses to look at me.

Mr. Toolan puts his glasses back on and props his elbows on the desk, his chin resting on his clasped hands.

"Do you know why I accepted you as a pupil here, Leo?"

"No, sir," I say.

"It was not just your clear aptitude in mathematics that secured you a place here. I saw something special, someone worth taking a chance on. I saw a young person who wanted to put his past behind him, work hard, and keep his head down."

"And I do! Look, sir, you weren't there, you didn't see what really happened. He was asking for it!"

Mr. Toolan holds up his hand to silence me.

I grip the wooden arms of the chair.

"Leo, I don't think you're comprehending the seriousness of the situation. You're fortunate Harry's nose wasn't broken."

He's the fortunate one, I want to say. I take a deep breath before speaking.

"Look, sir, I get that I shouldn't have hit him. And if I could turn back time, I wouldn't have. But you didn't hear what he was saying to that kid, he was destroying him and it just wasn't right!"

"I don't care, Leo," Mr. Toolan interrupts. "The bottom line is, Eden Park students do not physically attack their peers, end of story. Do you understand me?"

"But, sir—"

"Do you understand me, Leo?" Mr. Toolan repeats.

71

"Yes, sir."

The room is suddenly very quiet apart from the ticking of an unseen clock.

"So are you going to expel me?"

Mr. Toolan sighs. "No, I am not going to expel you, Leo. You will be in detention for the next month, starting tomorrow, and on probation for the remainder of your time here. If you take even a step out of line, I will have no choice but to take more permanent action. Does that sound fair?"

All I can do is nod.

"I'll have to call home too, of course, and inform your mother. Physical violence toward a fellow student is very serious and considering the circumstances, she needs to be kept in the loop."

Like she'll care.

"I'll also be speaking to Ms. Harding."

He's talking about Jenny. Great. I have an appointment with her on Friday. I can already picture her face—sad and disappointed.

"That's everything, Leo," he says. "You're dismissed."

He bows his head and begins to scribble in my file.

I nod and stand up. My left leg is still trembling.

Outside Mr. Toolan's office, Harry is sitting with his head resting against the wall and a massive wad of tissue held to his nose. Some blond girl is practically straddling him as she coos in his ear and strokes his hair.

"Maniac," she spits over her shoulder as I pass.

I give her the finger. Her eyes bulge but she doesn't say anything else.

On the other side of the glass, in the secretary's office, David is writing his statement. When he notices me, he breaks into a smile and waves.

Thank you! he mouths.

I frown and look away, pushing open the door to the empty playground. Afternoon classes have already started. The fresh air hits my face—cold and sharp.

I haven't been expelled. But I've got to be extra careful now. Any more slipups and I'm out. Whatever way I see it, Eden Park is going to look good on my college applications. If I get thrown out now, people will want to know why I've left two schools in the space of eight months, and that's the last thing I need. Good grades from Eden Park are my ticket out of Cloverdale. They'll guarantee me a place at a decent college for years twelve and thirteen, and a decent university after that. All I need to do is keep my head down, keep in control. But at the same time the unfairness of it all burns in my chest.

I go back inside and head to my next class.

DAVID

When I come out of Mr. Toolan's office, Felix and Essie are waiting. They jump up from their chairs and fling their arms around me like I'm a soldier returning from battle.

"Oh my God, are you okay?" Essie cries, holding me at arm's length, inspecting me for injuries.

"I'm fine," I say. "What are you guys doing here? Shouldn't you be in Art by now?"

"Art, schmart," Essie replies.

"What the hell happened, dude?" Felix asks over her.

We sit down. I start with the ear flicking and end with Leo getting carted off to Mr. Toolan's office, a mixture of anger and bewilderment on his face.

"But why was your inspection notebook in your bag in the first place?" Felix asks. "I thought you kept it locked away?"

"It wasn't on purpose," I say grimly, "believe me."

"I still can't believe that Cloverdale kid punched Harry

Beaumont!" Essie interrupts, shaking her head in wonder. "Was it amazing? I bet it was amazing!"

"I don't know. I had my eyes closed," I admit. "It sounded pretty amazing though. It was really loud. And Harry's nose was bleeding a ton afterward."

"Awesome," Felix says, his eyes dancing. Harry broke Felix's glasses back in year eight and Felix has been patiently waiting for Harry to get his comeuppance ever since.

"You should totally invite him to have lunch with us," Essie says.

"Who? Harry?" I ask.

"No, you idiot!" she cries. "What's-his-name! The junior-hacksaw-wielding maniac!"

"You mean Leo?" I reply.

"Of course I mean Leo!" Essie exclaims. "I want to shake his hand for doing what we've all wanted to do for years!"

"Fine, I'll ask when I see him in detention. I don't know if he'll say yes though."

"Hang on a second, detention? How come *you* got detention?" Felix demands. "*You* were the victim!"

"For elbowing Harry in the stomach," I say, rolling my eyes. "A week. At least Mr. Toolan let me off with a warning. He says if anything like that happens again, he'll have to call home. Harry got a week too. Leo got an entire month. For a single punch. That's pretty harsh, don't you think?"

Essie shrugs, swinging her legs. "You know what Mr. Toolan's like, always going on about how we're 'young ladies and gentlemen,'" she says, imitating his deep voice.

"Essie's right," Felix adds. "He has a really low tolerance for physical violence."

"Psychological torture on the other hand . . ." Essie says. "God, things are messed up in this place sometimes. If the teachers had any sense, they would have socked Harry in the face themselves years ago. Ugh, he's such an animal."

We sit in silence for a few moments.

"It is strange though, when you think about it," Felix says.

"What is?" Essie asks.

"That the school would accept Leo as a pupil in the first place. They make out spots here are like gold dust and yet Mr. Toolan, who prides himself on running such a 'peaceful' school, goes and lets in some kid with a history of violence. That's weird, right?"

"I suppose," I say.

"And what's weirder still is this," Felix continues. "Do either of you know what a junior hacksaw actually looks like?"

Essie and I shake our heads. Felix takes out his phone and after a few seconds of tapping, passes it over to us. We peer at the picture on the screen.

"*That's* a junior hacksaw?" I say. The saw on the screen is small and flimsy, nothing like the massive weapon I'd envisioned Leo swinging about the hallways of Cloverdale School.

"It looks like it could barely saw a KitKat in half, never mind a finger," Essie scoffs.

"Exactly, my friends," Felix says, folding his arms, sitting back in his chair, and looking rather proud of himself. "Exactly."

LEO

At the end of the day, I'm heading out of school when I hear someone calling my name. I turn around to see Alicia running toward me. My heartbeat quickens as she approaches.

"Hey Leo," she says breathlessly.

"Hey."

"You walk really fast, did you know that?"

I shrug.

She's wearing different earrings today, tiny silver ladybugs in place of her usual gold hearts.

Not knowing what else to do, I turn around and keep walking. Alicia falls into step with me.

"I heard about you," she says.

I glance at her and try to read her face. I get the feeling Alicia Baker might not be the sort of girl who is turned on by violence.

"Oh yeah?" I say, trying to sound nonchalant.

"Yeah, defending that year-ten kid."

"Oh that. Stupid of me. Dunno what I was thinking."

"It wasn't stupid at all. I think it was sweet of you."

"Yeah?"

She nods.

"Mr. Toolan didn't think so," I say. "Detention for a month, starting tomorrow."

"Harsh."

"Tell me about it."

I don't mention the probation.

We reach the gates. I expect Alicia to leave me and head home but instead she follows me over to the bus stop, sitting down next to me on the curb.

"I mean it," she continues, tucking her skirt around her legs. "It was really sweet of you to do what you did. Not enough people stand up for the underdog around here. That Harry Beaumont kid is such an idiot too. It was about time someone gave him a taste of his own medicine."

There's a pause.

"Leo, can I ask you something?" she says.

"Er, yeah, okay," I say.

"Why did you really change schools? There's a stupid rumor going around, about you chopping off a teacher's finger, or something crazy like that, but I don't believe it for one second."

I've overheard snatches of the same rumor. I have no idea where it came from but figured there was no harm in letting it fly; anything to reinforce my image as the tough guy from the wrong side of the tracks.

"Why don't you believe it?" I ask carefully.

"Because. You're not like that."

"What makes you so sure?"

"Oh, I don't know, let's just say I'm a very perceptive person," she says, smiling.

I don't smile back, searching the street. Where the hell is the bus?

"So come on, what really happened?" she asks.

I glance over Alicia's shoulder. Other kids are giving us curious looks. I try to ignore them.

"You can tell me. I won't blab it around, I promise, cross my heart," Alicia says, running her finger across her chest.

But Alicia doesn't know what she's signing up for. The truth is bigger than she could ever imagine.

"Okay," I say. "But you really can't tell anyone."

"Your secret is safe with me," Alicia replies solemnly, moving in closer so her thigh is almost touching mine. God, she smells good. My mind is whirring: What should I say?

"The thing is," I begin, my voice lowered, "I got in with a bad group at my old school. And I could see how stuff was going to go for me if I stayed. And, well, I didn't want that for myself, so I got a transfer."

"You can do that?"

"Under special circumstances, yeah."

"Wow, that's a pretty grown-up decision to make."

I shrug, as if it's no big deal.

"Why don't you tell people that then?" she asks. "Why do you let them go around making stories up about you getting expelled?"

I shrug again. "None of their business. I figure they can think what they like. The most important thing is that I know the truth, you know?"

I look down at my fingers. I can feel Alicia's gaze on me. Quickly, I take the opportunity to change the subject.

"I voted for you by the way," I say. "In that singing competition."

"You did?" Alicia asks.

"Of course. You were great."

"You really think so?"

"Definitely. Best on there by miles."

"Aw, thanks, Leo," she says.

And it feels sort of good to have made her feel good.

"You know who you remind me of?" I continue. "This singer my gran used to like when she was alive. Shit, I've forgotten her name now, Ella something—"

Alicia grips my arm.

"Oh my God, not Ella Fitzgerald?" she says.

"Yeah, that's it."

"Ella Fitzgerald is my inspiration!" Alicia says, her eyes shining. "You honestly think I sound like her, Leo?"

"I said so, didn't I?"

She beams.

"Leo?"

"Yeah."

"Can I ask you something else?"

"Er, okay," I say.

"How come you don't participate in Gym? It's the only other class we have together and you're always on the bench."

I am totally aware Gym is the only other class I share with Alicia and how good she looks in her tiny pleated gym skirt and tight polo shirt.

"Knee problems from a soccer injury a few years back," I lie smoothly, in the swing of things now.

"That must be hard, not being able to play anymore," she says, her arms clasped around her knees.

"It's not great, but what can you do? It's not like I was good enough to play professionally or anything," I say with a modest shrug.

The bus is coming up the hill. I stand but Alicia stays where she is, watching me, her head to the side.

"What?" I ask, feeling self-conscious as her eyes roam over my face. "What are you looking at?"

She smiles.

"You're interesting, Leo Denton, do you know that?"

Alicia is looking at me as if I have all these layers, and the whole time our eyes are locked together. As I reluctantly board the bus, I forget all about Harry Beaumont and Mr. Toolan and being on probation and my million other problems. Even the voice in my head, the one warning me to make a run for it and that girls are no good, is fading by the second. Because everything is canceled out by my heart going wild in my chest, like it's going to burst out of me and dance right across the street.

DAVID

The next day, Harry's nose has swollen to almost twice its normal size and has turned a deep purple. Even better is the fact that, so far anyway, the revelations in my notebook appear to have been overshadowed by the news that someone finally punched Harry Beaumont. The fact that this someone is the alleged maniac from Cloverdale School is just the cherry on top. Not that the contents of my notebook have been entirely forgotten. As I walk between classes I notice that some kids are making weird shapes with their hands. It takes me a few seconds to work out they're indicating roughly six and a half centimeters between their thumbs and index fingers. And even though I'm not exactly thrilled by this, I'm mainly just grateful no one has worked out why I was writing all this stuff down in the first place.

To cover up my detention I tell Mum and Livvy I'm helping out with the costumes for the school musical for a week and will get the bus home. Livvy frowns but doesn't say anything, and

I'm thankful news of yesterday's events does not appear to have reached the lower-school building yet.

. . . . .

After school I head to detention. I haven't had one since I was in year eight, when Essie, Felix, and I tied ourselves together for Children in Need and caused a mass pileup at the bottom of the stairs in the art wing. This is my first solo offense and I can't help but feel a tiny bit badass as I sign in with ancient Mr. Wilton.

Two girls are sitting in opposite corners of the classroom with matching tearstained faces. I slide into a seat in the front row and take out my math homework and pencil case. Harry walks in, his nose looking even more purple than it did this morning. He glares at me before making his way to the back of the room. A few seconds later Leo enters. His eyes sort of float over me as he walks past and chooses a seat by the window. He slumps down so low in his seat, his chin is almost level with the desk.

"Welcome, everyone," Mr. Wilton growls. "Your one-hour detention begins now."

He sets a stopwatch, sits down behind his desk, and promptly falls asleep.

I try to do my homework but I can't concentrate. Harry is listening to music through his headphones and must have it turned up to the maximum because I can clearly hear the lyrics and tinny bass line. To my left Leo has a copy of *Twelfth Night* propped open. I don't think he's reading it though. I can tell by the way his eyes are staring at the same spot on the page, like they're about to burn right through the book. He must notice me watching because he looks over sharply. Quickly I pretend to scowl at a math problem. I try not to look again.

The rest of the hour creeps by, the hands of the clock dragging their way around the face. Finally Mr. Wilton's stopwatch starts beeping. I begin to pack up my things. As he passes, Harry knocks my math book off the desk.

"Later, Freak Show," he calls over his shoulder.

I sigh and drop to my knees.

"Why does he call you that?"

It takes me a moment to register that Leo is speaking to me.

"Sorry?" I say, blinking up at him.

"Freak Show. Why does he call you that?"

I consider my answer. Leo punched Harry in the face for me, which surely indicates he's on my side at least to some degree. I'm assuming he also heard Harry spout the contents of my notebook before punching him, which bodes well. But at the same time, I can't help but feel cautious.

"It's kind of historical," I say, straightening up.

Leo frowns. "How do you mean?"

"Harry's been calling me that since we were, like, eight years old," I reply, shoving the book into my backpack.

"But why?"

"I don't know. Because I'm different?"

"Isn't everyone?"

"Not at Eden Park School."

I pull on my coat and we begin to walk down the deserted hallway.

"So you just let him?" Leo continues.

"It's not a case of letting him," I say. "Let's just say it's complicated."

Leo raises an eyebrow but doesn't say anything else.

"Harry Beaumont is kind of the unofficial king of year ten," I say.

"But why? He's a dickhead."

"He's on the soccer team and runs track for the county. Oh, and he's on the Ball Committee, which automatically grants him godlike status around here."

"Ball Committee?"

"You didn't have balls at Cloverdale?"

Leo lets out a single laugh. "No."

"We have two, one before Christmas and one at the end of spring term. And Harry is in charge this year. He's promising a snow machine at the Christmas one. Whoop-de-doo."

"And people actually care about this stuff?"

"They really do."

Leo shakes his head.

"At least I'm not alone when it comes to dealing with Harry's abuse," I add brightly. "He has it in for pretty much anyone who doesn't fit the mold. Yesterday was just my turn, that's all. Thanks by the way. Much appreciated."

"Don't mention it," Leo murmurs, pushing open the main doors.

We step outside. It's begun to rain. I fish in my backpack for my umbrella.

"Are you taking the bus?" I ask.

Leo nods.

"Me too."

I open up my umbrella.

"Want to come under?" I ask.

"No thanks."

We begin to walk down the drive toward the bus stop.

"You shouldn't let him," Leo says after a moment.

"Pardon?"

"Harry. You shouldn't let him call you that."

"It's only another two years. Then, if my parents let me, I'm going to complete years twelve and thirteen at a college in the city rather than stay on here."

"Me too," Leo says.

"Really? Cool. Maybe we'll end up at the same place."

Leo shrugs.

"As long as Harry isn't there, I don't care where I end up."

"So until then you're just going to put up with it?"

"I know it sounds pathetic but it's honestly easier to try and ignore Harry. You never know, he might get bored eventually. Hey, it would be different if I knew I had a personal bodyguard on hand to beat him up every time he gives me grief, but I have a feeling yesterday was probably a one-off—"

"Yeah," Leo says quickly. "I'm on probation so probably best I keep my head down."

"You're on probation? Just for what happened yesterday?"

"Yeah," Leo says. "Er, new policy I think. Zero tolerance or something."

"Oh, right. God, I'm sorry."

Leo shrugs. "Not really your fault, is it?"

He doesn't say it with a whole lot of conviction though.

The rain is falling faster now, hammering down on my umbrella. I try again to coax Leo under but he pretends not to hear me. His eyes look even greener in the eerie gray light.

We reach the street as the number fourteen bus comes juddering up the hill.

"That's me," Leo says, taking his bus pass out of his pocket.

"What's Cloverdale School like?" I blurt.

He gives me a sharp look.

"Why do you want to know?"

"It's just you hear all this stuff about it so I was curious . . ."

Leo sighs. "You really want to know what Cloverdale is like?"

I nod eagerly.

"It's a shit-hole," he says. "Pure and simple. See ya."

I watch as he breaks into a jog toward the bus stop, his blazer flying out behind him like a cape.

LEO

As I make my way to the back of the bus, I replay the conversation with David in my head. It's so messed up. This Harry guy gets away with picking on all these kids, and here I am with four weeks' detention, and probation, my entire future at Eden Park School at risk, just because I actually stood up to him. I feel angry even thinking about it. Like I want to find out where Harry lives and punch him again, only harder this time. A familiar feeling bubbles in my chest like hot lava. I remember describing it to Jenny once. She wrote something down in my file with a frown on her face.

"Volcanoes are unpredictable, Leo, uncontrollable," she said. "They erupt. We need to work at keeping the one inside you dormant, or at the very least, from causing as little mass destruction as possible."

I'm so agitated I get off the bus three stops early so I can cool off by walking the rest of the way home.

I'm heading across the bridge when a car drives past and I do a double take. It's a beat-up burgundy Ford Fiesta. Before I have the chance to think, I'm bolting after it, running so hard I feel like my legs and chest might explode. I finally catch up with it at a traffic light and peer inside, my chest heaving up and down. The driver is an Indian lady wearing a bright pink sari. There are a couple of kids in the back. The lady doesn't notice me but one of the kids presses his face up against the window, squishing his nose against the glass and crossing his eyes at me. I stare back until the light changes and they speed away.

It was stupid of me to even think it could be Dad behind the wheel. He's long gone from here, I know it. I can feel it in my bones.

Sometimes, if I can't sleep at night or I'm bored on the bus or in classes, I imagine this parallel universe where Dad is still around. In it he takes me to soccer games, helps me with my homework, and calls me "son," like he's really proud of me. He makes Mam nicer too: younger, prettier, happier. Parallel-universe Mam always remembers to buy toilet paper, cooks roast dinners on Sunday, and laughs a lot. With Dad around, our house isn't a pigsty. It's spick-and-span and if things get broken, they get mended or replaced. I try not to think about it too much though; there's no point when it's all a stupid fantasy anyway.

When I get home Spike and Tia are sitting on the sofa watching cartoons with the curtains closed. The sink is full of dirty plates and mugs and there's a new kidney-shaped stain on the carpet.

More and more of Spike's belongings have appeared around the house: an old waffle iron in the kitchen, a set of weights in

89

the living room, a book of "inspirational" quotes, tattered and dog-eared, propped on the back of the toilet in the bathroom. It's like his stuff is mutating on a daily basis.

"Leo!" Tia squeals the second she spots me, jumping up and running over to me, chucking her skinny arms around my waist.

"What's up, kiddo!" Spike says.

I roll my eyes and wish he would call me by my actual name for once.

Tia presses her cheek against my belly, her feet balanced on mine.

"Dance with me?" she begs.

"No. C'mon, get off, T," I say. Reluctantly she lets go of me, her lower lip sticking out in a sulk.

"Where's Mam?" I ask Spike.

"Upstairs. Getting ready for bingo with Auntie Kerry later," he replies.

"Surprise, surprise," I say, going into the kitchen and opening the cupboards. As usual they're bare apart from an ancient can of tuna fish and half a box of stale crackers. I can't remember the last time Mam did a supermarket shop.

"Big jackpot going. You never know, tonight might be her lucky night," Spike says, rubbing his hands together. "Imagine that, eh? Your mam a millionairess?"

"Like Kim Kardashian?" Tia asks.

"Exactly like Kim Kardashian," Spike says.

I shake my head. Who are they kidding? I open the fridge. Something in there stinks and I slam it shut.

"I was thinking, would you kids like fish-and-chips tonight?" Spike asks. "My treat."

Tia lets out this big gasp. "Really?"

"Yeah, why not. Leo?"

Part of me wants to say no, just to rain on his smug parade. But already I have the smell of fish-and-chips in my nostrils and I'm practically drooling.

"Whatever," I say.

"Fish 'n' chips, fish 'n' chips," Tia chants, jumping up and down on the sofa.

"What about Amber? She'll want some too, I bet?" Spike says.

"She's here?" I ask.

He jerks his head upward.

I trudge up the stairs, bumping into Mam on the landing. She has a pink towel wrapped around her body and another on her head, turban-style. Both are stained from the bleach she uses to dye her roots every few weeks.

"You're late," she says, adjusting the towel under her armpits. Her arms are scrawny and birdlike.

"Like you care," I reply.

"Hey, I heard that," she snaps.

"You were meant to," I say, trying to push past her.

She grabs hold of my sleeve and pulls me back so we're facing each other. I'm only an inch or so taller than her but because she's so skinny it feels like much more.

"I've told you once and I'll tell you again," she says, getting in close so I can smell her breath—toothpaste and cigarettes.

"Just because you're going to that fancy school now, it doesn't mean you're any better than the rest of us, all right?"

"What? Wanting to do well is a crime?" I ask.

"There you go," she says. "Mouthing off again. The sooner you finish your exams and get a job to earn your keep, the better."

"What, like you?"

Mam never holds down a job for long. She's been at the Laundromat since May—a bit of a record for her.

"Speaking of that school of yours," she says. "The head teacher left a voice mail message and when I called him back he didn't sound too happy."

I look at my feet.

"Not so mouthy now, are you?" she says.

I go to push past her but she blocks my way.

"What does that mean anyway?" she asks, pointing at the embroidered crest on my blazer.

"Like you actually want to know."

"What? I'm not allowed to ask my own kid a question now?"

"It's the school motto," I say reluctantly. "Latin for 'fairness and initiative.'"

She lets out a short laugh.

"Fairness? Well, that's where they've got it wrong. Because life isn't fair, Leo, and the sooner people are taught that, the better off they'll be."

She folds her arms, like she's proud of herself. I could argue with her, try to explain that's not what the motto means, but I can't be bothered. Because even though she got that bit wrong, she's right about one thing—life *isn't* fair.

"Are we done?" I ask.

She just shakes her head and sweeps past me into her bedroom. A few seconds later the roar of the hair dryer starts up.

I open my bedroom door to find Amber sitting on her bunk, painting her toenails bright pink.

"Spike's going to get fish-and-chips. You want anything?" I ask.

"Just a couple of hot dogs for me, thanks. No buns." Amber says.

"That's it? No chips?"

"No thanks, I'm cutting out the carbs."

Amber's always on some sort of crazy diet.

"You're nuts," I say. "If you get any skinnier there'll be nothing left of you."

"Whatever, I'm huge," she says, pinching a nonexistent roll of fat on her stomach. "By Hollywood standards I'm practically obese. Why're you so late?"

"Detention."

She sits up straight. "You're joking?"

"Nope."

"What happened?"

I tell her all the bits I remember, finishing with Mr. Toolan's warning—one more step out of line and I'm out.

"Jenny's going to go ape-shit," Amber says.

"I know."

"What are you going to do?" Amber asks.

"Nothing much I can do except try and keep out of trouble from now on."

"So this kid you stood up for, who is he?"

"No one."

"That's too bad. I thought you were going to say you'd finally got yourself a friend."

"Why is everyone so obsessed with me making friends?"

"Because. It's normal," Amber says.

I look up at her. "Normal? And since when have I been normal, Amber?"

Because "normal" kids don't have six files' worth of notes. "Normal" kids don't see therapists. "Normal" kids don't have mothers like mine, who tell you life isn't fair with messed-up glee, like the unfairness of life is pretty much the only thing they know for sure. I've spent my whole life being told I'm the complete opposite of "normal."

Normal. I start to say it over and over again, pacing up and down, agitation gushing through my arms and legs, making me want to lash out and go wild. Amber leans over and grabs my shoulder.

"All right, bad word. I'm sorry. Calm down, Leo."

I shake her off, but stop pacing.

"Here, come up," she says, moving across to make room.

I climb up the ladder to join Amber on her bunk. We sit cross-legged, our knees touching, the top of my head brushing the ceiling. I'm trembling.

"I don't get why you're so against the concept of opening up to someone," Amber says softly. "Having some kind of meaningful relationship with someone who isn't your sister or your therapist."

94

I almost open my mouth to tell her about Alicia, just to shut her up, but at the last second I stop myself.

"I don't want you to let what happened in February dictate the rest of your life."

I stiffen. Amber never mentions February. It's an unspoken rule between us. My eyes fall shut and all of a sudden I'm back in the woods, the cold on my body, tears pouring down my face. I open my eyes. My breathing is fast and raggedy.

"Sorry," Amber says. "I didn't mean to upset you. Come here."

She puts her arms around me. I let her. My breathing begins to return to normal.

"I just want you to be happy, little bro. Move on and all that," she whispers into my hair.

"I know," I say. "Just let me do things my way, okay?"

She sighs. "Okay."

By the time we make it downstairs, Mam is getting ready to leave, a slash of red lipstick across her mouth, lighter in hand.

"Be lucky!" Spike yells after her.

She totters down the path with one arm raised, her fingers crossed.

We eat our fish-and-chips on our laps in the living room while watching old episodes of *Total Wipeout* on TV. Spike and Tia laugh like crazy the whole time. Amber steals half my chips. She doesn't mention February again.

DAVID

In Thursday's detention, the two girls are gone so it's just Harry, Leo, and me. Harry is already there when I arrive, sprawled in his chair at the back of the room, listening to his lame music again. The swelling has gone down a bit but his nose has turned a pleasingly disgusting shade of yellow. I can't help but smirk to myself as I sit down. I'm taking out my homework when Leo comes in. I mouth, *Hi*. He hesitates a moment before mouthing, *Hi* back, frowning the whole time.

Mr. Wilton sets his stopwatch and promptly falls asleep, his snores loud and immediate.

Unable to concentrate on my homework, I rip a piece of paper out of the back of my notebook and begin to sketch Mr. Wilton, snoozing away in his chair. I exaggerate his bushy eyebrows and round belly. I draw a thought bubble above his head and in it, a busty girl in a bikini, pouting with her hands on her hips. I fold the page into quarters and aim it at Leo's desk. It lands a few centimeters from his right hand. He picks it up and smooths it out on the desk. For a second I'm certain I detect a change in his face, not quite a smile, but something in that direction. But just as quick, his expression is blank again and he's refolding the piece of paper and pushing it to the very edge of his desk.

Finally the stopwatch goes off. Mr. Wilton groggily dismisses us, although Harry is already out the door before he's finished speaking, his footsteps thundering down the hallway. Leo starts to hand me back the picture.

"Keep it," I say.

"You don't want it?"

"I drew it for you."

Leo frowns.

"What I mean," I say quickly, "is that it's just a sketch, nothing special. Keep it. Or throw it in the garbage. Whatever."

Leo gives me a weird look but tucks the picture inside his copy of *Twelfth Night* anyway.

"It's good, you know," Leo says as we walk down the hallway.

"Sorry?"

"The picture you drew. It's good."

I smile shyly. "Thank you."

"Do you take art classes?" he asks.

"No. Textiles."

"What? Sewing?"

"Yes, although I can barely thread a needle, much to Ms. Fratton's dismay. I'm more into the design side of things, fashion and stuff. What about you? Are you into art?"

"Nah. I'm shit at that sort of thing. Can't draw to save my life."

"What are you good at?" I ask.

"Math," Leo says without hesitation. "Numbers."

"I'm awful at math," I say. "It's my worst subject by far. Anything with right or wrong answers I'm generally terrible at. Funny how everyone's brain is wired so differently, isn't it?"

"Hmmm," Leo mutters, looking at the ground.

We're halfway down the drive when I spot Mum's car parked just outside the school gates.

I swear under my breath. What is she doing here? I told her I would take the bus home.

"What?" Leo asks.

"Nothing."

I consider pretending I've forgotten something and turning around but Mum has already noticed me.

"Yoo-hoo! David!" she calls, getting out of the car and waving.

"Is that your mum?" Leo asks, nodding toward her.

"Unfortunately," I reply.

From the backseat of the car, Phil notices me and starts barking, bouncing up and down on the seat.

"You've got a dog," Leo says, his eyes lighting up in a way I've never seen before.

"Oh yeah. That's Phil."

"Phil? What, as in short for Philip?"

"I know, lame, right? Blame my dad. He has a thing about giving all our pets human names. Our goldfish are called Julie and Dawn, and our last dog was called Graham."

"But that's cool," Leo says. "Way better than calling a dog something dumb like Fluffy or Lucky."

"I suppose. It's a bit embarrassing though, when you take him off his leash in the park and yell 'Phil' and about half the men there turn around."

"What breed is he?" Leo asks.

"We don't know. We got him from a rescue center about four years ago. We think there might be some Jack Russell in him, maybe some spaniel. We're not really sure though. He's a total mutt."

"He's cool looking."

We reach the car.

"Hi, darling," Mum says, pushing her sunglasses up on her head. "Thought you might appreciate a ride home after such a long day."

I can sense Leo looking at me.

"Hi there," she says, extending her hand to Leo. "I don't think we've met before. I'm Jo, David's mum."

"Leo," Leo replies, shaking her hand.

"Nice to meet you, Leo. Are you working on the musical too?" Mum asks.

"Musical?" Leo says with a frown.

"Yeah, er, Leo's working backstage, building scenery," I say quickly, widening my eyes at him. "Aren't you, Leo?"

"Yeah, backstage," Leo echoes, thankfully taking my cue.

"What show are they doing this year?" she says, directing her question to Leo. He shoots me a panicked look over her shoulder. I try to mouth the words *Oh! What a Lovely War* at him but it's too late; Leo is already telling Mum we're doing *Grease*.

"I love *Grease*!" Mum says. "God, I had such a crush on John

Travolta when I was younger. I thought he was a real fox. David, you must remind me when it's on, so I can get some tickets."

"Okay," I say, hoping Mum will have forgotten by the time December rolls around.

Phil is going crazy now, running around in circles on the backseat. I open the door. He bounds out onto the sidewalk, jumping up first at me, then at Leo.

"Phil," Mum says sharply. "Get down!"

"No, it's okay," Leo says. "I love dogs."

"Hello, boy!" he says, kneeling so his face is level with Phil's, rubbing his ears. Knowing he's onto a good thing, Phil rolls onto his back so Leo can scratch his belly.

"You've got a friend for life now, Leo," Mum says.

Leo just grins, not taking his eyes off Phil for a second. He looks totally different with a smile on his face—softer and less intense.

"Can we give you a ride home?" Mum asks after a moment.

Leo gives Phil a final belly rub and straightens up.

"Thanks, but I live kind of far away."

"Whereabouts?" Mum asks.

"Er, Cloverdale," Leo says.

"That's not so far," Mum says. "Come on, jump in."

"Nah, honestly, it's fine," he says, backing away. "My bus is due any minute."

"It's really no bother, Leo. I've got to get some things from the supermarket anyway so it's only a small detour. Go on, save yourself the bus fare."

"Yeah, come on," I add.

Phil licks Leo's hand.

"Okay," Leo says. "Thanks."

Leo insists on sitting in the back with Phil.

"Are you sure?" Mum asks as she starts the car. "It's awfully dog-hairy back there."

"I like it," Leo says, as he massages a blissed-out Phil's ears.

"Do you have a dog of your own?" Mum asks.

Leo shakes his head.

"Do you want one?" I ask. "Phil doesn't eat that much."

"David!" Mum scolds.

"Only joking."

"Do you have any other pets, Leo?" Mum asks.

"Some hamsters once."

"What were their names? Can't be as bad as our pets'," I say.

"Cheryl, my sister named that one," Leo says. "After Cheryl Cole, and, er, Jimmy."

"Who did you name Jimmy after?" I ask.

"My dad," Leo says quietly.

"Wasn't that confusing though? Bet your dad and Jimmy the hamster didn't know whether they were coming or going."

"My dad doesn't live with us."

"Oh. Sorry."

Leo doesn't say anything.

"What happened? To the hamsters, I mean," I add quickly.

"Cheryl died. Jimmy escaped."

"Oh. That sucks."

"Shall I put on some music?" Mum says with artificial bright-ness, fiddling with the knobs on the radio. It blares out loudly for a moment and makes Phil jump, sending him cowering under Leo's arm.

"Actually, David," Mum says, "I might have the *Grease* sound track knocking about somewhere. Have a look in the glove compartment. I'm in the mood for it now."

A few seconds later the car is filled with John Travolta and Olivia Newton-John belting out "Summer Nights," Mum singing along tunelessly. I look in the rearview mirror. Leo is staring out the window, his forehead knotted into a frown, his left hand resting gently on Phil's head.

Twenty minutes later we pass a dilapidated sign: WELCOME TO THE CLOVERDALE ESTATE. I sit up straight. Mum flicks the door locks on. I wince and hope Leo didn't notice.

"You'll have to guide me from here, Leo," Mum says, turning down the music.

He leans forward between the front seats and gives her directions.

The estate is like a never-ending maze, the same formation of narrow brown-brick houses, over and over again. Finally, we turn onto Leo's street—Sycamore Gardens according to the graffitied sign.

"This is me," Leo says.

"Which house?" Mum asks.

"Er, that one, number seven. But here is fine," Leo says.

"Okey dokey."

Number seven is the scruffiest-looking house on the street, with peeling paint on the trim and door and a junglelike front garden, the grass almost knee high.

"Thanks for the ride," Leo says.

"You're very welcome," Mum replies.

Leo gives Phil a final belly rub before thanking Mum again and climbing out of the car. He slams the door shut and walks away, his back immediately hunching over.

"Wait a sec," I tell Mum, unlocking the door and jumping out of the car.

"Leo!" I call. "I just wanted to say thanks," I say, catching up with him. "You know, for not letting on to my mum about me being in detention."

"Oh, that. That's okay."

"It's just that if she knew I had detention she'd want to know why and stuff so . . ." I let my voice trail off.

"Yeah, I get it," Leo says, folding his arms. But of course he doesn't get it, not really.

Behind him, the curtains at number seven open for a moment, a face appearing at the glass, before falling shut again.

"Your mum's waiting," Leo says, nodding toward the car. I glance behind me. Mum taps her watch.

"Well, see you tomorrow," I say.

"Yeah."

He turns and makes his way up the path.

"Let's just make sure he gets in all right," Mum says as I climb back in the car.

We sit and watch as Leo disappears through the scratched front door of number seven, to a life full of mystery.

LEO

When I enter the living room, Tia is lying on the sofa watching *Frozen* for at least the hundredth time, a dreamy expression on her face. Through the doorway, I can see Amber in the kitchen kneeling in front of the washing machine.

"Everything all right?" I say, wandering in.

"Not really. Mam left a tissue in her pocket again. Everything's covered in white fluff."

"Where is she?" I ask.

"Down at the pub with Spike."

"Right. What's in the oven?"

"Pizza."

"What kind?"

"Pepperoni. Not sure there's enough for all three of us though. We might have to make some toast as well."

"Thought you were off the carbs?"

"Beggars can't be choosers," Amber says, sighing as she shoves everything in the washing machine again.

"You're home early from detention," she says, adding soap.

"Got a ride."

"Yeah, I saw. Who is he?"

"Who?"

"Who do you think? The kid you were talking to outside."

She closes the washing machine door and turns it on.

"Just a friend."

"Thought you didn't do friends," she says with a smirk.

"I don't. He's no one. Just a kid from detention. His mum dropped me off."

I should have said no to the ride, followed my instincts and got the bus. I saw David's mum lock the car doors when we drove into Cloverdale. And the way David looked at the estate, gawping like he was a kid on an amusement park ride. Not that I blame them. I bet they live in a really nice house, with three bathrooms and a huge kitchen with one of those big shiny fridges you see in American sitcoms, and a huge garden with a neat lawn and flower beds and matching patio furniture.

I pour myself a glass of water and flop down on the sofa next to Tia. She's murmuring along with the lines from the film. She could recite the script in her sleep, easy. I take a sip of water. It tastes funny. Metallic. I should have run the tap for longer.

I try to relax and think of something nice. Alicia pops into my brain. I attempt to shove her away, replace her, but nothing works. I give in, letting thoughts of her take over. She gave me half her stick of chewing gum today, and when I was walking to History, she called me over and made me listen to a song on her headphones. Because we were sharing, our cheeks were almost touching and Alicia kept glancing at me every few seconds to check my reaction, like it was important to her that I liked the song too. I told her I did.

I picture her sitting in her bedroom, her guitar on her lap, curls falling in her face, singing a song just for me.

I close my eyes. I feel better already.

. . . . .

The following morning before school I have an appointment with Jenny at the Sunrise Center. The Sunrise Center is kind of a misleading name. The building is made from gray concrete and the walls inside are painted this really cold mint-green color that makes you feel chilly even on a boiling-hot day. They put posters and paintings up on the walls but there's still no getting away from the fact that it's a depressing place for kids with "problems." Mam used to come to my appointments with me, talking in her snooty voice and sucking up to Jenny, acting like I wasn't even there. As soon as I was old enough to take the bus here on my own, she stopped coming, which suits me just fine.

I've been seeing Jenny ever since the doctor first referred me, back when I was seven, so she knows me pretty well by now, or at least she thinks she does. It's annoying though because I hardly know anything about her apart from the fact she probably has a cat 'cause there's always cat hair all over her tights. Sometimes I try to ask her personal questions but she always manages to avoid answering them and then turns them around and asks me *why* I'm asking and before I know it, I'm answering yet another question. On the whole though, Jenny is all right. When I was younger I used to get mad a lot and storm out of the room or shout at her. Once I threw her potted plant out the window. It smashed on the hood of someone's car and set the alarm off. Jenny was cool and businesslike about it, which somehow was way worse than if she'd just screamed at me.

I wait in the reception area of the Adolescent Department. There are two other kids also waiting, a boy and a girl. The boy plays on his phone. The girl reads a magazine. None of us speak. It's an unofficial rule.

Jenny pops her head around the door.

"Leo?"

She's wearing her blank friendly face but she's not fooling me. There's no hiding the tightness in her lips and the disappointment in her eyes. I follow her to her office.

It's small and narrow with the same mint-green walls. There are four chairs arranged around a small square coffee table with a box of tissues set upon it. You always know you're in for a good time when there's a box of Kleenex on permanent standby—and this is no ordinary box, it's a *jumbo* box.

Jenny closes the door and we sit down.

"So how's it going, Leo?" she asks, taking a gulp of tea.

"Is that a new sweater?" I ask.

Jenny looks down. "No, not particularly."

"It suits you."

"Thanks. So what's been happening? How's school?"

"Where'd you get it from?"

She puts down her mug of tea and looks at me.

"Leo, we're here to talk about you, not my fashion choices. I had a call from Mr. Toolan on Tuesday," she adds.

Here we go. "Oh, yeah?"

"Afraid so, Leo. He said you hit a fellow pupil. Do you want to tell me about it?"

"He deserved it."

"Oh, Leo," Jenny says, sighing. "We've worked on this. You can't go lashing out at people like that, whether they deserve it or not."

"But he was bullying another kid."

"I know," Jenny says gently. "And I appreciate you were trying to help, but surely you can see you went about this the wrong way."

"Maybe," I say, pulling at my tie and curling it around my index finger.

"I'm disappointed, Leo. Eden Park is such a great school. I'd hate to see you waste this opportunity."

There's a long pause.

"Leo, the bottom line is you can't go around punching people, no matter how much they annoy or anger you. No excuses."

I shrug and look out the window. The sky is filled with dull white clouds.

Jenny sighs. "How is everything else going?" she asks, changing tack. "How are you getting on with the other students?"

I shrug again. "Okay."

I can't help but think about Alicia. Not that I'm going to tell Jenny about her. She'd only make a big deal out of it and ask me a billion questions I don't want to answer.

"Have you found anyone there you feel you can trust? Who you can talk to when things get confusing or difficult?"

"Nope," I reply, drumming my fingers on the wooden arms of my chair.

Jenny shifts position in her chair.

"I know you find it hard to trust your peers, and I understand your caution, Leo, I do, but you can't live your entire life in this hard shell, no matter how much you think you want to. I don't want you to miss out on possible friendships, healthy, fulfilling ones, because of what happened back in February. I'm concerned about your social isolation."

Social isolation. Again. She's obsessed with it.

"I do fine by myself," I say firmly.

Jenny lowers my file on to her lap.

"Friends isn't a dirty word, Leo."

I look her in the eye. "It is to me."

"I just want to see you participating in a positive way, Leo."

"Participating?" I ask, screwing up my face. "Participating in what?"

Jenny sighs again. "In life, Leo. I want you to start participating in life."

. . . . .

That afternoon, I'm the first to arrive in detention. All day I've been annoyed with Jenny and her lecture about social isolation. A few minutes later Harry comes in, heading straight for the back of the classroom. Then David, giving me a quick wave as he sits

109

down. I nod. Today we're joined by two boys. As I try to get through the rest of *Twelfth Night*, I can feel one of them looking at me, staring at me, like I'm a waxwork at Madame Tussauds. I turn my head sharply and fix him with a glare. His eyes widen with fright before he looks away.

I still can't concentrate. Out of the corner of my eye I see David bent over his work, his left hand propping up his forehead. Every few seconds he lets out a sigh. I watch as he rips a page out of his notebook and tosses it aside. I lean in. I recognize the cover of the math textbook he's working from. It's one I completed a couple of years ago.

In front of me, Mr. Wilton is snoring. I glance over my shoulder. Harry has his eyes closed and the two boys are sulking. I stand up and cross the aisle, sliding into the seat next to David. He looks up in surprise. I peer at the piece of paper he ripped out. It's a mess of scribbles and cross-outs.

"You're making this way more complicated than it needs to be," I say.

"I am?" David whispers.

"Big-time. Once you've got the formula straight, simultaneous equations are really simple to solve."

"For geniuses like you and my friend Felix maybe," he says miserably.

"Nah, I'm serious. Let me show you."

I pick up David's pen. I begin to write, David leaning in to watch.

"See, once you've done that, it's clear what the total value of x is. Then all you need to do is divide that by—what?"

David peers at the paper.

"I don't know."

"Yes, you do. Take your time. The answer's there, you just need to find it."

He continues to stare at the page, his face getting redder and redder.

In front of us, Mr. Wilton stirs. We lower our voices.

"Five?" David whispers back doubtfully.

"Exactly."

"Really?"

"Yep."

"But that's really simple."

"Told you. Want to try another?"

. . . . .

On Monday I'm in detention doing my English homework when a folded-up piece of paper comes sailing through the air and lands on my desk. I glance over at David. He's looking straight ahead although his lips are twitching as if resisting a smile. I open it. It's another drawing. This time it's of a dog that looks like Phil. Next to the dog is a speech bubble containing the words *Bow wow, bow bow, woof, woof, BARK!* and an asterisk guiding me to a footnote in the bottom corner: *Doggy translation: I aced my math homework!!! Mr. Steele almost fainted. Thanks a trillion. David.*

I look up. David is smiling hopefully. And even though the note is pretty cheesy, I can't help smiling back.

LEO

It's Tuesday. Ms. Jennings announces that we are going to be working in pairs to discuss the symbolism in *Twelfth Night*. Because this kid Matt is out sick with mono, there's an odd number of students so she puts me in a three with Alicia and Ruby, the girl who sits next to Alicia. Ruby's a bit annoying but okay.

I keep my cool, nodding casually as Alicia and Ruby turn their desks around so they're facing me. Alicia's knee touches mine for a second.

"God, I've got such a hangover," Ruby announces, flopping her head on her desk.

Alicia rolls her eyes. "You've always got a hangover. It's, like, Tuesday, Rubes. Who gets that messed up on a school night?"

Ruby gives Alicia the finger from under her veil of bleached-blond hair. "Leave me alone. I am in a very delicate state right now," she says, her voice muffled.

Alicia shakes her head and grins at me.

"You don't drink then?" I ask.

"Not during the week. Coming to school with a hangover is not my idea of fun."

I wonder where Alicia drinks on the weekend, what she drinks, and whether she's got a boyfriend who buys the drinks for her. I watch out of the corner of my eye as she opens her copy of the book, smoothing out the pages with the palm of her hand.

"I know it's not cool, but I really love this play," Alicia says.

"Oh yeah? What do you love about it?" I ask.

Alicia scrunches up her face to think.

"The humor I guess. And the love story, the way everything is a big muddle but it all comes together right at the last minute. And the way you sort of know that's going to happen the whole way through but when it happens you're still really happy about it. If that makes sense?"

I nod encouragingly.

"But most of all," she continues, leaning forward in her chair, excited, her eyes sparkling (and her excitement is catching because I'm leaning forward too even though I couldn't care less about the play, apart from the fact that Alicia likes it so much), "I love that it has a really kick-ass heroine. I mean Viola is just so brave and feisty. And when you consider this was written like a gazillion years ago, it's even more amazing."

"Even if her part would have been played by a man at the time?" I ask, remembering what Ms. Jennings told us the other day about the all-male casts back when Shakespeare was alive.

"I guess. I mean, the fact a character like her got written all those years ago is big enough. How confusing would that be though? A guy playing a girl pretending to be a guy?" Alicia laughs.

"I hadn't thought about it like that," I say.

There's a pause and I can feel Alicia's eyes still on me, the air between us sort of thick and hazy.

"Have you heard about Becky's party a week from Saturday?" she asks slowly, tracing her finger up and down the page.

"I heard a rumor," I say.

This is an understatement. Becky Somerville is in my homeroom and has such a big mouth you'd have to be living on Mars not to have heard her go on about this party.

"So do you think you might go?" Alicia asks, twirling one of her curls around her finger.

I clear my throat. "I dunno. Parties aren't really my thing."

"What do you mean, parties aren't your thing?" Alicia squeaks. "That's like saying food isn't your thing, or breathing isn't your thing. I mean, who doesn't like parties?"

I look down, cursing myself for saying something so weird. Alicia's right—normal people *do* like parties.

"I'm just not great in crowds," I say. I regret my words straightaway, because I know I'm making it worse, blowing it big-time with my weirdness.

"That's too bad," Alicia says.

"Anyway, I'm not invited," I add. "I don't think Becky is my biggest fan."

Becky treats me like most of my other classmates do, like I'm an exotic animal escaped from the zoo that may or may not be dangerous. Everyone apart from Alicia. Alicia doesn't act like she's scared of me one bit.

"Becky just hasn't taken the time to get to know you yet, that's all," Alicia says. "Because if she did, she'd think differently, I'm sure of it."

I stare at my hands. There's a long pause.

"I was the new kid once."

"Yeah?" I say, raising my head.

"Yep. Back in year eight. My parents moved up here from London halfway through the year."

"And how was it?"

"Hideous."

"Really?"

I can't imagine Alicia's life being anything but golden.

"Uh-huh. In case you haven't noticed, Eden Park isn't the most diverse of schools. You can count the number of black kids here on two hands. I felt like I was walking around with a flashing light on my head half the time. Plus, everyone had friends already. I was a year and a half too late. And there were all these cliques, and rules about who could sit where in the cafeteria, and looking around I just couldn't work out where I was supposed to fit in. For the first few weeks I ate my lunch in the bathroom and cried myself to sleep every night," she says, laughing.

"So what changed?" I ask.

"Well, I forced myself to eat in the cafeteria for a start. Then I joined the drama club and choir, smiled at everyone . . . and eventually I discovered there were lots of nice people, I just had to put myself out there in order to find them. Having my braces removed probably helped too. It's kind of hard to exude confidence when you have a mouthful of metal. And I mean mouthful. My braces were epic."

She laughs again.

"Plus, your rep around school is kind of badass," she adds. "I think I was known simply as the black mute girl for most of my first term."

She tucks a loose curl behind her ear and grins. I like what it does to her eyes.

Alicia clears her throat, then says, "Look, Becky says I can bring someone to her party."

Heat creeps up my neck.

"Oh yeah? Who are you taking?"

She takes a deep breath before looking me straight in the eyes.

"Well, no one at the moment."

"Oh," I say, swallowing hard.

Ruby (who I'd forgotten was even there) lifts her head off the desk and rolls her bloodshot eyes.

"For God's sake, you two are making me die. Leo, Alicia is trying to ask you out, you utter dickhead. Just say you'll go with her to Becky's party, please? Before I bang your stupid heads together."

She plonks her head back down on the desk.

I look at Alicia who is hiding behind her hands. When she lowers them, her cheeks are flushed.

I open my mouth to say something but nothing comes out.

What Ruby is proposing is serious. I mean, it's practically a date. But there's something stopping me from talking myself out of it, something way louder and stronger than the usual voice inside my head.

"So what do you think?" Alicia asks, biting her lower lip. "Do you want to?"

"Er, yeah, okay then," I find myself saying, my steady voice fighting my racing heartbeat and sweaty palms.

"Cool," she says.

There's a pause before she bursts out laughing. And suddenly I'm doing something I haven't done in forever, and it's like I'm having this spooky, out-of-body experience because I'm laughing too.

. . . . .

"Congratulations," I say to David that afternoon, as Mr. Wilton's stopwatch beeps to signal the end of the day's detention. "Five detentions. You're done now, right?"

"I guess so," David says. "It hasn't been all that bad though, not really."

"Nah."

"Maybe I should break the rules more often," he adds with a grin. "Look, I'm sorry you've got another three weeks."

"Don't worry about it."

David clears his throat. "Leo, I was wondering whether you'd consider tutoring me in math. You know, for real."

"Can't you ask someone else?" I ask, frowning.

"My friend Felix maybe, only he's not very good at explaining things. He sort of forgets that not everyone is a genius like him."

"I don't know. I'm not sure I'll be good at it either."

"Oh yes, you would," David says. "You were great the other day. For the first time in forever math actually made some kind of sense."

"Whatever," I say, rolling my eyes.

"I'm serious."

"I don't know if I have the time."

"I'll pay you."

"Don't be stupid."

"I mean it. Please?" David adds. "It would really, really help me out."

I hesitate. The truth is, I kind of enjoyed helping David the other day. I liked watching things click into place for him, him being all proud at being able to solve stuff by himself.

"Just a couple of times a week," he adds. "And if it doesn't work out we can stop anytime. No pressure."

I sigh. "Okay, fine."

He lets out a whoop and for a second I'm scared he's going to hug me.

"Thank you, thank you, thank you!" he chants. "I'll be a model student, I promise."

I shake my head. "You're pretty mental, you know that?"

David just beams back at me. I continue to shake my head, turning away to pack up my stuff.

"Oh, another thing," David says, "which I've been meaning to ask you since last week actually."

"What?"

"Are you free tomorrow at lunchtime?"

"Why?" I ask over my shoulder.

"Do you want to have lunch with me, Essie, and Felix?"

"Why?" I repeat, turning back to face him.

"Because. We want to get to know you better."

"I kind of do lunch alone," I say.

"Oh, please? It'll be fun."

And I don't know whether it's because of Alicia and the party or what, but I find myself saying yes.

. . . . .

The following day it's raining outside and the cafeteria is crowded and stuffy. As I weave my way through the tables and chairs, I pass Harry.

"Psycho!" his girlfriend says.

If only she knew. I ignore her and keep moving.

"You came," David says happily as I set down my tray.

"I said I would, didn't I?" I sit down on the seat beside him. Across from me, David's two friends, whose names he's told me but I've forgotten, are watching me with wide eyes.

The girl has a mass of messy black hair. Her fingernails, stubby and bitten, are painted with chipped black nail polish. She dwarfs the boy beside her, who I recognize from Advanced Math. He's small and slight, and maybe the neatest-looking kid I've ever seen. Seriously, he looks like he might iron his underpants.

Suddenly the girl leaps into motion.

"I'm Essie," she says, leaning across the table to shake my hand. Her voice is husky and theatrical.

"Felix," the boy adds.

"Leo," I say.

"Oh, we know who you are," Essie says. "You're the most famous boy in the school right now."

I raise a single eyebrow and open my can of Coke. It fizzes over the top and I have to slurp down the foam quickly to stop it from spilling all over the table.

"So why did you really get expelled from Cloverdale?" Essie says as I set my can back down.

"Ess!" David hisses.

"What? That's what we all want to know, isn't it?" Essie says.

"But you don't just come out with it!"

Essie pouts and rolls her eyes.

"Let me apologize for my girlfriend, Leo," Felix says. "She has a tendency to get a little, how can I put it? Overexcited."

"You make me sound like an untrained puppy," Essie grumbles.

"If the shoe fits, darling," Felix says, patting her on the hand.

"You two go out?" I say, not even bothering to hide my surprise.

"Yes. Why, do we not look like a couple?" Essie demands.

"I don't know," I say, squeezing ketchup onto the edge of my plate. "What makes anyone look like a couple?"

I think of me and Alicia, how we might look walking down the hallway together, my arm slung around her shoulder, hers around my waist. The thought alone churns up a load of butter-flies in my stomach.

"They reckon women go for men who remind them of their dads," Essie says. "How messed up is that? Luckily Felix is *nothing* like my father."

"It's just the whole Oedipus complex thing in reverse," Felix says, nibbling on what looks like a piece of cardboard. "According to Freud, men want to kill their dads and sleep with their mums."

"Gross," I say, stabbing a fry into my ketchup.

"Unless you've got a hot mum," Felix adds.

"Felix!" Essie and David cry in unison. Essie rips up her roll and starts hurling pieces at Felix's head, David quickly joining in.

"Gluten intolerant! Abuse, abuse!" Felix cries, shielding his head.

They're nuts. Officially. All three of them.

"You still haven't told us why you got expelled," Essie says, having run out of bits of roll to throw.

"What makes you think I was expelled?" I ask carefully.

"There! Told you so!" Felix cries triumphantly, slapping his hand down on the table. "I told you that rumor was garbage!"

"But if you didn't get expelled, why did you leave Cloverdale School?" David asks.

The three of them lean in toward me.

I tell them the same story I told Alicia. When I'm done they slump back in their seats, disappointed.

"How very dull," Essie says. "I much prefer the junior-hacksaw thing."

121

"Sorry," I reply with a shrug.

Just then Essie starts hissing, "Olsen alert!" She jerks her head to the left.

David immediately goes bright red.

"What's an Olsen?" I ask.

"You mean who," Felix says. "Zachary Olsen. Over there."

David goes redder still. I follow his gaze to a tall blond boy standing in the line. I look back at David.

"You like him?" I ask.

"Try head-over-heels in love with him," Essie supplies in a noisy whisper.

"Ess!" David cries, his face practically purple by now.

"Hey, it doesn't bother me," I say. "I mean, I already worked out you were gay if that's what you're worried about."

David peers at me. His face has begun to calm down a bit.

"And you're okay with that?"

"What? You think I'm some kind of homophobe? Because any boy from Cloverdale has got to be a Neanderthal, right?"

"Of course not," David says, flustered. "You just never know . . ."

I sigh. "Look, I don't care who you're into. It's none of my business if you like boys."

"Does that mean you're straight then, Leo?" Essie asks.

Felix rolls his eyes toward the ceiling.

I look her in the eyes, which are a very pale blue, and lined with crusty black eyeliner.

"As a matter of fact, it does," I say. "You ask a lot of questions, you know that?"

"'Curiosity is one of the permanent and certain characteristics of a vigorous intellect,' Leo," she recites.

"Samuel Johnson," I reply, not missing a beat.

Essie blinks at me. "Sorry?"

"The quote. It's by Samuel Johnson, right?"

"You know Samuel Johnson?" Essie asks, her mouth practically hanging open.

"Of course," I say.

This is sort of true. It's one of the quotes from Spike's book that lives in the bathroom. In spite of myself I've started reading it while sitting on the toilet.

"'Don't judge a book by its cover,' eh?" I say.

Essie opens her mouth, then shuts it again.

"English idiom, exact origin unknown," I add, popping a fry into my mouth. I can't help glancing at David. He's grinning like a lunatic.

DAVID

The following Tuesday I'm alone in the cafeteria line when I hear someone say Leo's name. I glance behind me. It's a group of year-eleven girls, their heads bent together in a gossipy huddle. I angle my body sideways so I have a better chance of hearing them, and pretend to study the chalkboard menu on the wall above their heads.

"I'm telling you, Alicia Baker is taking Leo Denton to Becky's party on Saturday," one of the girls, a tall redhead, says. "Ruby Webber told me."

"Lucky Alicia, he's so cute," one of the other girls, a petite blonde, says wistfully.

"Yeah," another girl agrees. "I love the strong, silent type. Bad boys are *always* sexy."

They burst into giggles.

"But isn't he meant to be insane or psychotic or something?" the redhead points out. "Clare Bowman saw him going into the Sunrise Center last week."

The Sunrise Center is on the outskirts of the city, for teenagers with mental health issues. A girl in my year who self-harmed in the school bathroom used to have appointments there. But why does Leo, I wonder. My mind is racing.

"Plus he's kind of short, don't you think?" the redhead continues.

"With eyes like that, who cares," the blonde replies.

It was only a few weeks ago they thought that exact same pair of eyes was "crazy."

. . . . .

All afternoon I can't help thinking about Becky's party. Not that I'd get invited to a year-eleven party in a million years. I don't even get invited to year-ten parties.

When I get home I slump down on the sofa with my laptop and before I can stop myself, my fingers are typing Leo's name into Facebook. I can't find him. He's not on Twitter or Instagram either. I Google his name but the closest I find is a ton of stuff about some Cloverdale girl named Megan Denton who won a load of swimming trophies years ago.

"What are you looking up?"

I jump. Livvy is leaning over the back of the sofa, her long hair brushing my arm.

I slap the lid of my laptop shut.

"Nothing," I snap. "What do you want anyway, sneaking up on me like that?"

"Mum needs help bringing in some groceries," she says.

I remain still, my hands flat against the top of the laptop.

"Go ahead. Tell her I'll be there in a few seconds."

"Weirdo," she replies.

. . . . .

The following day, I meet Leo in the library at lunch for our very first tutoring session. Leo is professional, putting me straight to work. I want to ask him about Becky's party but can't find a suitably casual way of dropping it into a conversation about factoring quadratic equations. In fact I want to ask him lots of things.

As he leans across to pick up my pen to explain something, I can see a cluster of fine light brown freckles across his nose I've never noticed before.

"Hey guys, can I interrupt?"

It's Rachel from my textiles class, one of Harry Beaumont's crew. She's holding a clipboard lined with tinsel and wearing a Santa hat and a plastered-on smile.

"Can I interest you in Christmas Ball tickets?" she asks.

"No, thank you," Leo and I say in unison.

"Are you sure?" Rachel asks. "It's going to be the social event of the year. We'll be transforming the gym into a winter wonderland. Harry Beaumont is even renting a machine that pumps out Styrofoam snow. I promise you, you do not want to miss it."

"I'm okay at the moment, thanks," I say.

"Me too," Leo adds.

Rachel's smile quickly morphs into a pout.

"Suit yourselves," she says snootily, adjusting her Santa hat before stalking away.

"What's the big deal about this ball?" Leo asks. "There are posters for it everywhere and it's not even happening for another three months."

"Christmas Ball fever hits earlier and earlier every year," I say.

"Do you ever go?"

"Ess, Felix, and I always say we're not going to but then at the last minute we end up caving in and buying tickets."

"And what's it like?"

"Oh, you know, hideous. Harry struts around like he's cured the world of famine or something. There's always a huge bowl of disgusting nonalcoholic punch. And the DJ is super-obnoxious and refuses to play requests, yada yada yada . . ."

"So why do you go if you have such a bad time?"

"Oh I don't know. I guess each year there's this flimsy hope that maybe this one will be different. Stupid, right?"

Leo clears his throat. "C'mon, let's finish this equation. You're really close to solving it."

When we start to pack up our things, Leo's wallet slips from his backpack. I drop to my knees to retrieve it. It has fallen open and in the section where you can insert a photograph, there's a picture of a handsome guy with the same sandy-brown mop of hair as Leo.

"Who's that?" I ask, peering closer.

"It's my dad," Leo says, holding out his hand. Reluctantly I pass him back the wallet.

"You look just like him," I say, standing up.

Leo nods slightly.

"Do you get to see him much?" I ask.

Leo shakes his head, shoving the wallet deep into his back pocket.

"Will you see him at Christmas?"

"I doubt it."

"Really? How come?"

"Look, he left when I was a baby, I haven't seen him since."

Now it makes sense why Leo acted so standoffish when I asked about his dad in the car the other week.

"You must at least know where he is?" I ask.

"Nope."

"But doesn't he have to pay, I don't know, child support or something?"

"God knows," Leo says, putting on his backpack.

"Haven't you tried looking for him? Like, on the Internet? Surely he's on Facebook or something."

"Of course I have," Leo snaps. "Do you think I'm an idiot?"

"Sorry."

Leo sighs. "All I know about him is his name and that's he's a carpenter. I don't even know his date of birth."

"You're kidding."

"Nope."

"Wow."

"Yeah," Leo says, his voice flat.

"Do you miss him?" I ask.

Leo looks thoughtful. "Every day."

As soon as the words leave his lips, he looks as if he regrets them, like he's shared too much on the subject.

"Crazy, right?" he adds with a bitter laugh.

"It doesn't sound crazy at all," I say quickly. "It sounds human."

Leo gets a far-off look in his eyes.

"Why did he leave?" I ask.

"They all leave. Without fail. It's what Mam does best, her party trick."

I want to ask more questions but Leo says, "I've got to get going. I'll see you."

I watch as he jogs out of the library.

As I finish packing up my things, I try to imagine my dad leaving me when I was a baby, but it's impossible. I've seen the endless photograph albums of him in hospital scrubs, beaming away as he holds his firstborn child in his arms, or asleep on the sofa with me, tiny and wrinkled, curled up on his chest. He would never have left me and Mum, ever. So what made Leo's dad leave him?

. . . . .

When I climb out of the car after school, Mum lets out a gasp.

"Your pants are halfway up your ankles, David," she says.

The moment we get inside, I run upstairs, lock my door, and take out my inspection notebook and tape measure. Mum is right. I've grown two centimeters in height in less than two weeks. At first I think it's impossible so I measure myself again. And again. But the tape measure doesn't lie. When I write it down in my notebook my hands are trembling and the numbers come out all wobbly. If I can grow two centimeters in the space of two weeks, how many might I grow in six weeks? Or ten?

. . . . .

On Saturday morning Mum insists on taking me into town to buy a couple of pairs of new pants.

"My baby all grown-up," she says, as we pull into a space in an underground parking lot. "You watch, you'll end up taller than your dad!"

Apparently Dad was always one of the shortest kids in the class until, when he was fifteen, he shot up to 188 centimeters pretty much overnight. This is fine if you're a guy. If you're a girl, it's a disaster.

Mum and I head for the store. It's too warm and bustling with shoppers.

In the elevator there's a stroller with twin babies in it. A boy and a girl.

"How old are they?" Mum asks their parents.

"Coming up to eleven months," the mother replies.

"Such a fun age!" Mum says. "They're gorgeous."

"They're a handful!" the father chimes in, and everyone laughs as if he's made an absolutely hilarious joke. The girl baby is asleep. She is all in pink. The boy is awake, a soggy rice cake in one hand, a toy car in the other. He wears denim overalls with a tractor embroidered on the bib. He eyes me wearily. I bet his parents already assume he's going to be a typical boy, that his favorite color will be blue or black or red, that he'll play soccer and like cars and trucks, that one day he'll marry a woman and have babies. And even if he's not typical, even if he likes ballet or baking cakes or kissing boys instead of girls, they'll still imagine that their little boy will grow up to be a man. Because why wouldn't they? As we leave the elevator, the boy and I eyeball each other until he is wheeled out of sight.

In the school uniform department Mum flips through the racks of pants, every so often holding a pair up against me and muttering to herself.

I wander across to the racks of skirts—pleated, flared, long, short. I trail my fingers over them, feigning disinterest, just in case Mum glances across and notices what I'm doing.

In the fitting room, I try on four pairs of navy pants.

"He's having a growth spurt," I hear Mum confide to the salesperson in a stage whisper as she waits on the other side of the curtain.

As Mum pays for the pants, I stare at my feet.

Afterward we head to the food court for lunch and eat at Yo! Sushi. We sit side by side on stools in front of the conveyor belt. I coach Mum on her chopstick technique. She lets me have two portions of the chocolate mochi for dessert.

"This is fun," she says, filling up her glass with fizzy water from the tap built into the bar we are sitting at. "We should do this more often."

My mouth is full so I just nod.

"We're all so busy these days," she continues. "Dad and I with work, you and Livvy with school. I don't feel like you and I have had a real chat in ages. You know, mother-son time."

She pauses and sets down her glass. I feel her eyes settle on me, studying me. I dab the chocolaty corners of my mouth with a napkin.

"Everything's all right, isn't it, darling?" she asks slowly.

"Of course it is. Why do you ask?" I reply, keeping my eye on some cucumber rolls snaking their way around the conveyor belt.

"You've seemed a bit preoccupied lately."

"It's just that school is really busy," I say lamely.

"You would tell me, wouldn't you, if something wasn't okay, or if there was something you wanted to get off your chest? Because your dad and I would understand, you know."

I swallow. Here it is, my opportunity to come out with it. Six little words: I. Want. To. Be. A. Girl. But they stay stubbornly lodged in my throat, choking me into silence. Because the thing Mum thinks I'm not telling her isn't what she's been preparing herself for. She's expecting me to tell her I am gay. I suspect she's been working up to this moment for years, ever since I requested my first Barbie for Christmas, tore around the house in a pair of fairy wings, wrapped a towel around my head and pretended it was a mane of long hair. She's probably even rehearsed her response, practicing in the mirror the right balance between surprise and acceptance. She's certainly dropped enough hints, initiating passionate pro-same-sex-marriage debates around the dinner table and making constant references to her gay second cousin, Chris who lives with his boyfriend, Aaron. But she and

Dad have got the signals all wrong, just like Leo got it wrong in the cafeteria the other day. Because I'm not gay. I'm just a straight girl stuck in a boy's body. But how do I go about telling them that?

"David?" Mum prompts, her eyes big and questioning, full of hope.

"No, Mum," I say, finally finding my voice. "I'm fine. Honestly."

She looks disappointed for a second but hides it quickly, reaching up and tucking a strand of hair behind my ear.

"Well, I'm glad to hear it," she says, patting me on the hand.

As we're paying the bill, a flash of gold catches my eye. I glance across to Nando's on the opposite side of the food court. Alicia Baker, Ruby Webber, and a few other year-eleven girls are squeezed into a booth surrounded by piles of shopping bags. Alicia has produced a shimmery gold top from one of the bags. She holds it up against her torso as the other girls nod their approval.

"Ready to go?" Mum says brightly.

"Sure," I murmur, dragging my eyes away from Alicia and her friends.

· · · · ·

That night, I am home alone. Livvy is sleeping over at Cressy's. Mum and Dad are going to dinner at the house of one of Dad's colleagues. Essie and Felix are having a date night.

"Nothing fluffy or romantic," Essie assured me over Skype,

as Felix lolled on the bed behind her. "Just boyfriend-girlfriend time, you know."

But I don't know. Not really. I've never had a boyfriend or girlfriend (unless you count going out with Leila Shilton for three days when we were six, which I don't). I've never kissed anyone. I've never even held hands. I've probably exchanged a grand total of ten words with Zachary in the past five years. I'm a complete relationship novice. It doesn't help that tonight is the night of Becky Somerville's party and across town in Cloverdale, Leo is getting ready to take Alicia, and I feel like everyone in the entire world is in a twosome except for me.

Mum clearly feels guilty about leaving me by myself because she orders a large pepperoni pizza for me and sends Dad to the store to buy a tub of my favorite Ben & Jerry's ice cream—Phish Food. I wave them off from the door, waiting for ten minutes before heading upstairs.

In my bedroom I drop to my knees and drag out the large box I keep hidden in the back of my closet. Its contents are the result of years of careful collecting. At the bottom are items that no longer fit but I cannot quite bring myself to throw away— the fairy wings Auntie Jane bought me when I was five (I didn't take them off for a week), the pink nightie I swiped from beneath my second cousin Lara's pillow one Christmas, Essie's hated confirmation dress, white and frilly, donated happily. On top of these lie thrift store finds, smuggled into the house under my coat; then cocktail dresses and polyester trouser suits from the 1980s stolen from the back of Mum's closet; more rejects from Essie.

Tonight I select a dress that Essie gave me. It belonged to her mother when she was going through her hippie stage back in the mid-nineties, before Essie was born. It's long, floaty, tie-dyed, and covered with tiny mirrors. I take off my boy clothes, discarding them in a pile on the floor, before slipping it on over my head. I lift up the skirt to my nose and inhale deeply. It still smells of incense, like gingerbread mixed with stale perfume and sea salt.

Next I put on my wig. I bought it earlier this year with money left over from Christmas, running upstairs with it before Mum and Livvy had the chance to demand what was in the mysterious package tucked under my arm. It's a shiny shoulder-length bob, a slightly darker shade of brown than my real hair. I absolutely love it.

I sit down at my desk and take out my makeup bag. Most of it I've bought with my pocket money, other bits I've stolen from Mum, or inherited from Essie. I empty it all, lining it up neatly on my desk, admiring the array of colors. I've been watching lots of online makeup tutorials lately. I position my laptop beside me and search for my favorite: a girl from Texas named CeeCee. She delivers her tutorials in a hypnotic thick Southern drawl. Together, step-by-step, we apply foundation, concealer, blush, eyeliner, smoky eye shadow. The smoky eyes in particular are harder than they look and it takes four attempts before I get my right eye to match my left. I sit back and take in my whole face— the smooth complexion, the hint of girlish blush, my eyes, thick with mascara and mystery. To finish, I take out my favorite lipstick—Diva Red—and drag it across my lips.

The doorbell rings, making me jump. I go into Mum and Dad's bedroom and peek through the curtains. It's the pizza delivery guy. I'd completely forgotten about him. For a moment I consider answering the door as I am. The thought fills me with excitement and fear. But the fear wins out and I'm quickly wiping my mouth on the side of my hand, smearing it bloodred, and pulling my bathrobe on over my dress. As I'm going downstairs, I rip off my wig and shove it in my pocket. I open the front door a crack, just wide enough to pass over the money and receive the pizza, keeping my head down so the delivery man doesn't clock my made-up face. With the door safely shut, I put my wig back on and remove my bathrobe, draping it over the banister.

I take my pizza into the kitchen, get napkins, and pour myself a glass of Coke. Usually I enjoy catching sight of my reflection in the toaster or kettle, the swish of material around my legs, but tonight, for some reason, I feel flat. I eat my pizza in front of the TV, followed by the ice cream, the entire tub in one go, but it's like faking the enjoyment, eating for the sake of it.

I don't have that many chances to dress up undisturbed at home and when I do it's the normal everyday stuff I like doing best—loading the dishwasher, making toast, watching TV. But not tonight. As I load the dishwasher, I feel a tear roll down my cheek. Horrified, I wipe it away. It leaves a watery black smear on my hand. It's only 9 p.m., hours before my parents are due home, but I trudge upstairs anyway, remove my dress and wig, and scrub my face clean. I take a shower in the dark, change into a clean pair of pajamas, and get into bed. I almost Skype Essie and Felix, but at the last second I remember it's their date night and they're probably rolling around naked right now, their thoughts far away from me.

As I lie there in the darkness, unwanted images of Becky's party keep popping into my head. In my mind it is dark and smoky, full of sweaty bodies sighing and swaying, pressing up against each other in slow motion. There's a dull ache in my belly. I turn onto my side so I'm facing the wall. *What's wrong with you?* I ask myself angrily. Then it hits me. I'm lonely. I'm so lonely it physically hurts. The realization makes me feel even worse. Like I've been tricking myself into putting on a brave face this entire time. I roll onto my front, pull my pillow over my head, and recite my French vocabulary in my head over and over and over, until, finally, I fall asleep.

LEO

"What are you doing, Leo?"

I turn around. Tia is standing in the doorway to the bathroom wearing the Hello Kitty pajamas she's been in all day.

It's Saturday night. Becky's party starts in just over two hours.

"What does it look like? I'm fixing my hair."

"But you never do that."

I ignore her and pick up a tub of Spike's hair stuff. I take a sniff before scooping some out with my finger and running it through my hair.

Tia sits on the edge of the bathtub, her toes not quite reaching the floor.

"Where are you going?"

"A party."

"Can I come?"

"No."

"Why not?"

"Because it's a grown-up party."

"But you're not a grown-up. You're only fifteen."

"Fine, it's a teenage party then, just for teenagers."

"Oh. Will there be a piñata and musical chairs?"

"I don't think so."

"Will there be cake and ice cream?"

"I doubt it."

"How can it be a party without cake and ice cream?"

I ignore her. Spike's hair gunk has made the front of my hair look greasy. I dunk my head under the faucet and try to wash it out.

"Leo?" Tia says, pulling at my sleeve.

"What?" I yell over the running water.

"If it turns out there is cake and ice cream, will you save some and bring it back for me?"

I turn off the faucet and straighten up, water dripping down my forehead, and look at her hopeful little face.

"Sure."

On the way out of the bathroom I bump into Mam on the landing. She's just got in from her shift at the Laundromat and looks red-faced and tired.

"What's got into you?" she says accusingly.

"What do you mean?" I ask.

"Acting all cheerful the past few days," she says, narrowing her eyes, like acting cheerful is a sin.

"Don't know what you mean," I say, breezing past her.

She's right though, I've been in a good mood for days now. Things that usually annoy me—Amber using up the hot water in the morning, Tia leaving her cereal bowl in the sink, Spike's singing, pretty much everything Mam does—all this stuff has washed over me.

As I pull on my hoodie and check my reflection one last time, the familiar voice pops into my head, warning me not to get carried away. I ignore it.

. . . . .

Alicia's house sits off a main road behind a pair of massive gates. It's big and symmetrical, with a huge front door twice the width of ours and lots of windows. As I walk up the driveway it seems to get even bigger, looming over me. I reach to press the doorbell and realize my hand is trembling slightly. I shake it hard. Now is not the time for nerves. Tonight is all about being calm, cool, tough.

A tall black man, who I assume must be Alicia's dad, answers the door. His skin is glossy and smooth and his teeth are gleaming white, like Alicia's. Just like the house, he towers over me.

"Can I help you?" he asks in a deep voice.

I clear my throat but my voice still comes out sounding like it doesn't belong to me. "I'm here to pick up Alicia?"

"I'm sorry, young man, but you must be mistaken, my daughter is forbidden to date boys until she is at least twenty-one. On your way now, please," he says, making to shut the door.

"Oh—sorry," I stammer, confused.

"Dad!" Alicia screeches. I look over his shoulder and there she is, standing on the staircase behind him with her hands on her hips, wearing skinny blue jeans and a gold top.

"Don't listen to a single word he says!" she calls.

Her dad breaks into a wide grin. "Only joshing with you, Leo!" he says, laughing and punching me on the arm. "Come in, come in!"

I'm ushered into the foyer. It's huge. We don't even have a proper foyer at home, just a space at the bottom of the stairs that's forever littered with shoes and unopened mail. But Alicia's foyer is as big as our living room, if not bigger. Alicia's mother appears from the kitchen, wearing a striped apron. She looks like a mum from a TV advertisement, with swishy chestnut hair and perfect skin. She takes hold of my shoulders and kisses me on each cheek, telling me how nice it is to meet me.

I'm struck that both Alicia's parents know my name, meaning Alicia must have spoken about me at least a bit.

"Leo, please excuse my super-embarrassing parents. They mistakenly think they're hilarious," Alicia says as she pulls on her coat, guiding me out the front door.

"Back by midnight, please," her dad says, tapping his watch.

"Yes, Dad," Alicia says, rolling her eyes.

In all the commotion I haven't had a chance to look at her properly. It's only now, standing on the doorstep as she wraps a long pink scarf around her neck that I get the opportunity. She has her hair fastened up with a few curls pulled loose so they frame her face and she's wearing makeup. She looks phenomenal.

"You look really nice," I say.

She smiles, "And so do you, Leo Denton."

My stomach does a flip-flop.

Shit.

There is no question which of the houses on Becky's street is having the party. At number twenty-six, the music is already blaring and I can make out the shadowy forms of partygoers through the curtains. We arrive to find Becky greeting each of her guests with a high-pitched squeal and/or perfumed hug. She's wearing a glittery pink dress that makes her look like a fairy on top of a Christmas tree. When we walk in she shrieks especially loud.

"OMG, I'm so beyond excited you are here, Alicia!" she cries in this bizarre American accent, a bit like the one Tia speaks in when she's watched too much Nickelodeon. Becky's greeting for me is a casual, "Hi, Leo," and a slow look up and down, a hint of a smile on her lips.

"Here, let me take your coats," she says, holding out her arms.

Even though it's sweltering, I keep my hoodie on. Alicia takes off her scarf and coat and gives them to Becky.

"God, I love your top," Becky says. "Let me see the back."

Alicia does a twirl. Her top ties around her neck and reveals her smooth brown back. I don't think she's wearing a bra. I swallow.

"Go on into the kitchen," Becky says, waving us through. "My mum's ordered about twenty pizzas."

Becky's mother is the spitting image of Becky, with the same moon face and drawn-on eyebrows. The kitchen counters are piled high with pizza boxes. I help Alicia find a vegetarian slice before finding some ham and mushroom for myself.

"Now, make sure you get a drink from Becky's dad!" Becky's mum says. "We've got beer, wine, liquor, whatever you want. I'm not one of those strict mums. I was young once, believe it or not!"

Becky appears in the doorway.

"Mum!" she says through gritted teeth. "Aren't you and Dad supposed to be leaving?"

"Calm down, darling, I'm just making sure everyone's fed and watered."

"Well, hurry up!"

Alicia and I grin at each other.

Becky's dad is behind the breakfast bar, playing bartender. Bottles of liquor and mixers line the work surface and cans of beer and bottles of wine coolers sit in a plastic tub full of ice in the sink.

"What can I get you?" he says, ignoring me and looking straight at Alicia. She leans forward to inspect the drinks selection and I swear Becky's dad glances down her top.

"Can I get the strawberry daiquiri, please," Alicia asks brightly, pointing at the wine coolers.

"Can of Foster's," I chime in.

"Coming right up," Becky's dad says, winking at Alicia. He makes a big show of tossing the bottle in the air and catching it, like he's a cocktail waiter or something. He even takes the top off with his teeth and spits it out into the garbage can, pausing like he expects us to applaud him. The whole time he keeps his eyes on Alicia.

"Enjoy, darling," he says, handing the bottle over to her.

Almost as an afterthought, he pushes a can of beer toward me, his gaze still lingering on Alicia.

We make our way out of the kitchen with our drinks, balancing our pizza on flimsy paper plates. The living room is packed with kids. The iPod deck is blasting Kanye West. It's weird seeing everyone from school out of uniform. Some of them openly stare at us, whispering as we pass.

Alicia heads for the TV room where it's a bit quieter. We set our drinks down on a coffee table in the corner, but remain standing up, Alicia swaying in time to the music as we eat our pizza. She smiles at me, this gentler version of her usual megawatt grin. And for a moment it's like we're the only two people at the party. But then we're interrupted by some of Alicia's friends, throwing their arms around her, complimenting her on her top, the way she's done her hair, and they are just the first of a steady stream of visitors.

As Alicia receives her subjects, I sit down in a chair and watch her—the way she laughs at jokes that aren't funny, how she leans in and listens intently as secrets are shared, nodding thoughtfully, saying all the right things. At one point she catches my eye and smiles and mouths, *Sorry.*

Around nine, Becky's parents finally leave, making a big show of saying goodbye.

"We're just across the street if you need us! Back at midnight!" Becky's mum calls as Becky practically shoves her out of the door.

"Becky's so lucky," Alicia says when we're finally alone again.

"My parents wouldn't let me have a party without them being there in a million years. And they definitely wouldn't let me have all this booze."

"Nah, my mam wouldn't either," I say.

"Becky's dad was a bit weird, wasn't he?" Alicia says, screwing up her face.

"Yeah, I didn't like him. He was a creep."

"You reckon? I thought he was a bit odd but I wasn't sure."

"Nah, it wasn't right," I say. "The way he was looking at you. He must know you're only fifteen."

Alicia leans forward, so that her breath tickles my ear.

"Nearly sixteen," she whispers.

I exhale. Alicia breaks into a giggle and punches me on the arm.

"You're a real gentleman, you know that, Leo Denton?"

I'm about to answer her when a Rihanna song comes on and Alicia lets out a scream of excitement and jumps up, grabbing me by the hand. I've drunk two cans of Foster's and as I stand up I feel a bit woozy. Alicia seems fine though, swigging from her third wine cooler as she tugs me toward the music.

"I don't really dance," I'm saying, but Alicia either can't hear or she's choosing to ignore me. We're in the center of the living room now, sweaty bodies surrounding us. Someone has turned the music up and the house feels like it's bulging, ready to burst from the booming bass. Alicia is jumping up and down, more strands of hair falling free, flying around her face.

"C'mon, Leo!" she yells over the music. "Dance with me!"

I look around. Everyone is moving, flinging their arms around, and laughing. I don't even know where to start.

"Just do what I do!" Alicia says, grabbing hold of my hands. And maybe it's the beer, or maybe it's the fact it's with her, but I start to dance. I'm just about getting into it when a new song comes on. It's another R&B number, but slower this time, sexy, and immediately Alicia starts grinding up against me, her butt rubbing my crotch. I back away a few steps and she turns around in surprise, frowning slightly. Quickly I mime, *Do you want a drink?* and she relaxes into a smile and nods, before continuing to dance.

I go to the bathroom first, relieved to find it empty. Next to the toilet there's a full-length mirror. What's that all about, I wonder. What kind of weirdo wants to watch themselves take a dump? Becky's creepy dad, I bet. I wash my hands. My face is very pink. I splash cold water over it, trying to cool off.

When I return to the living room, fresh drinks in hand, Becky has turned the music down and is in the center of the room, wobbling about on her glittery pink heels.

"Game time!" she calls, trying to usher everyone into a circle around her. Alicia is already sitting cross-legged on the floor. She pats the spot next to her, but before I can make a move toward it, Ruby plonks herself in the space. Alicia offers an apologetic shrug. I sit down where I am, between Adam, a boy from my English class, and some girl I recognize from school but whose name I don't know. Out of what seems like nowhere, Becky produces an empty wine bottle and everyone goes, "Ooooohhhhh!"

"This game needs no introduction," Becky says. "It's that retro party classic, spin the bottle, people!"

There's lots of whooping.

"You know the rules, if the bottle points to you it's time to get down and dirty!"

Yet more whooping.

"As the birthday girl, I get to spin first."

Becky drops to her knees, flashing her underpants to the crowd. I take a nervous sip of beer and go to stand up.

"Where do you think you're going, Denton?" Becky barks.

"I was gonna sit this one out," I say.

"Oh no you don't," she says. "Joining in is compulsory, right, Alicia?"

Alicia blushes.

Reluctantly I sit back down. Across the circle Alicia smiles at me. I fake a smile back.

Becky spins. As the bottle turns, people clap and yell. I hold my breath, willing it to spin past me. It rests on a kid from my homeroom named Liam. He scoots on his butt into the center of the circle. Becky grabs hold of his face with both hands and shoves her tongue down his throat. Everyone screams. I try to catch Alicia's eye but she's too busy screaming herself, fingers over her eyes. Becky eventually lets go of Liam. Their mouths are all pink and clown-like from friction and smudged lipstick.

"Not bad," she reports to the circle at large. "Six out of ten maybe."

Liam's face turns as pink as the lipstick smeared on his chin. Becky blows him a kiss before squeezing between Alicia and

Ruby. It's Liam's turn to spin. I fixate on the bottle, praying for it not to stop on Alicia.

Couple after couple assembles in the center of the circle, the girls reporting back on the boys' performances like it's an exam: "A for effort," "Eight out of ten," "Needs practice"; the boys slink back to their places triumphant or humiliated. Every spin, I will the bottle not to land on me or Alicia, holding my breath as it inches past us, and I keep telling myself they'll get bored and the party can go back to normal.

"One last spin!" Becky announces, answering my secret prayer.

I dare to relax a little, convinced luck is on my side. This is why it feels like a strange dream when suddenly people are yelling my name and I look down and the neck of the bottle is pointing right at me, like the barrel of a gun. I blink, look up. Ruby is kneeling in the center of the circle, her head cocked.

"I'm not waiting all night," she says coyly. I nod and in what feels like slow motion I edge into the circle on my knees. Everyone starts to chant, "Leo, Leo!" and it's like I'm in the Colosseum in Rome, only instead of being fed to the lions, I'm being fed to Ruby Webber. She's leaning forward now and I can see down her top. I've never noticed her tits before—how big they are, how round, how if she leans forward much more they might spill out of her top altogether. But none of this matters, because even though Ruby is hot, she isn't Alicia. As I edge closer, someone leans across and ruffles my hair, telling me to go for it.

I glance across and there she is. Gorgeous Alicia. Chewing on her thumbnail. We lock eyes for a second and she smiles this sort of brave smile as if to say it's okay. Around me everyone is roaring. Ruby smiles and closes her eyes. I lean in and kiss her very quickly, just a peck, our lips hardly making contact. Her eyes spring open.

"Is that it?" she asks, annoyed and amused at once.

Everyone boos.

I shrug and glance across at Alicia. She is sitting up straight and biting on her lower lip. Becky strides into the circle and puts her hands on my shoulders.

"I have a feeling lover-boy Leo here is saving himself for a certain someone," she crows. A bunch of the girls dissolve into knowing giggles as Ruby returns to the circle.

Becky claps her hands together, "Right, time to spice things up a bit. A new game!"

She goes into the hall and opens the closet under the stairs with a flourish.

"We'll spin again and the lucky couple gets ten minutes of heaven—in here!" Becky says.

She bounces back into the living room

"Your turn, Leo," she says, handing me the bottle and returning to her seat.

I take a deep breath and spin. It seems to turn for an eternity until finally it begins to slow, coming to a stop pointing directly at Becky. Everyone starts whooping. Becky shouts them down, holding up her hands in surrender.

"Sorry, guys, I'm exempt from this round, birthday-girl rules, which means I get to pass to my left, and lo and behold, who is sitting to my left but Miss Alicia Baker!"

Alicia blushes furiously. Becky pulls her to her feet and practically frog-marches the two of us into the hallway while everyone claps and cheers, chanting our names.

"Get in there!" Adam says, his eyes wide and excited on my behalf. I fake a cocky grin in return.

"Go on then!" Becky barks. We squeeze into the closet, nestling between the household items. It smells damp and musty, of rained-on camping gear and stale sleeping bags.

"Enjoy!" Becky singsongs as she slams the door shut and turns out the light, plunging us into darkness. A moment or two later the music starts up, the bass thudding once more. Alicia and I shift around, trying to get comfortable.

"You okay?" I ask.

"Yeah, fine. You?"

"Yeah."

Silence. Alicia breaks it.

"I'm glad you didn't give Ruby a real kiss."

I swallow. "Me too."

More silence. I hear her take a deep breath.

"In case you haven't worked it out yet, I really like you, Leo Denton."

I feel this rush in my chest.

"And I really like you, Alicia Baker."

I imagine Alicia grinning in the dark, her dimples deepening and I'm suddenly desperate to touch them, to explore every single bit of her. I feel for her hand in the dark and find it and she's wrapping her fingers tightly around mine. And then we're kissing. Just like that, our lips like magnets. And it's amazing. Not only that, it's so easy, like the easiest thing in the world. And probably the nicest. At first it's soft, a bit tentative, like our lips are having a polite conversation, but then it's more urgent, hungry, almost like we're feeding off each other. My arms go around her and hers around me. And I forget about everything. I forget about the fact an ironing board is sticking into my back, I forget about Becky and everyone else at the party just inches away from us. The only thing I can think about is kissing Alicia and my hands on her bare back and how this is the best moment of my life bar none. And she's making all these *mmmmmm* noises and then she's kissing my neck and breathing, "Oh, Leo," and my God, I'm so turned on it's unreal. And then she's putting my hand on her boob and I'm about to explode. It feels so good, and the fact that she's put my hand there, that she wants it there, blows my mind. And then her hands are making their way under my layers, under my hoodie, then my shirt, then my T-shirt, searching out skin.

"You've got like a full-on six-pack!" she whispers, excitement in her breath, her hands warm against my stomach. All those hours of sit-ups have paid off. I try to enjoy her reaction but I can't ignore the familiar anxiety building in my belly. My entire body tenses up and I pull away.

"Leo, are you okay?" Alicia asks.

"Yeah, of course," I lie.

"No you're not. What's wrong?"

"Nothing."

"Do you not like me or something?"

"Of course I do!" I almost yell, because the idea of her not realizing how much I like her is crazy.

"Then why have you stopped?"

"It's not you," I begin.

"What? It's not you, it's me?" Alicia says. "Jesus."

"It's not a line!" I say, taking her hands in mine. "Listen to me, I like you so much I could burst, and I want to do stuff with you. God, I want to do everything with you. But not here, not in Becky Somerville's closet under the stairs. You're too special for that," I say, the words tumbling out of my mouth in a panic.

Silence. I bite down hard on my lip.

"You promise you like me?" Alicia says in a small voice.

"God, Alicia, I like you so much it makes me dizzy."

It's the right answer because Alicia lets out this really cute giggle.

There's a thump on the closet door.

"One more minute!" Becky yells.

I lean in to kiss Alicia. She kisses me back. I can feel my anxiety shrinking away. I'm in control again.

For the rest of the evening, Alicia and I are glued to each other's side. For a bit we dance, but mostly we sit on the sofa, Alicia's legs draped over mine, and talk. Alicia tells me about wanting to be a singer but her parents really wanting her to be a doctor, about how much she adores her little brother, about her old life in London. I tell her about sharing a bedroom with Amber, about the funny stuff Tia comes out with sometimes, about my gran dying when I was twelve and how I still miss her.

And it sort of feels good, to be sharing stuff with her, even if I'm carefully editing the bits I'm prepared to share as I go along.

I walk her home. We kiss on the doorstep as the grandfather clock inside strikes twelve.

"Leo, you know the Christmas Ball?" Alicia says.

"Yeah."

"Look, I know it's ages away, but do you want to go together?"

"Er, yeah," I say. "Why not."

She grins and kisses me. And it's amazing all over again.

"Alicia," a man's voice calls from inside.

"My dad," Alicia says, rolling her eyes and tapping her wrist. "Right on time."

She kisses me once more before darting inside.

For a few seconds I'm frozen to the spot, finally able to digest what has just happened.

Alicia likes me. As in, *really* likes me. My entire body is buzzing. I feel epic, alive, like my nerve endings are on fire. The voice at the back of my head tries to interrupt, to remind me about how huge this is, how dangerous, of all the things that could go wrong. But for tonight I'm going to ignore it, drown it out with thoughts of Alicia. And it works 'cause the whole way home I think of nothing and no one else.

DAVID

It's Sunday night. I'm supposed to be doing my math home-work but I can't concentrate. Instead I'm lying on my bed watching YouTube videos on my laptop. The one I'm watching right now is about a boy who lives in America. He has a gravelly voice and stubble on his chin and you'd never guess in a million years that he used to be a girl until he pulls up his T-shirt and shows you something called a chest binder that looks like a thick white crop top and flattens down his breasts. He's waiting to have chest surgery when he turns eighteen. It's sort of mind-bending to think that beneath the binder he has exactly what I want, and that all the things I hate about my body, he'd swap in a heart-beat.

I hear a sound coming from the bathroom. I press Pause and listen.

It's Livvy, calling out for Mum, quietly at first but quickly growing more and more urgent. I get up and head to the land-ing. I knock gently on the bathroom door.

"Mum?" Livvy says.

"No, it's me, Liv. Are you all right?"

"Get Mum."

"But what's up?"

"Just get Mum!" she practically screams.

I race downstairs and find Mum and Dad on the sofa reading.

"Livvy says she needs you. She's in the bathroom," I say breathlessly.

Mum frowns and stands up. I follow her up the stairs.

She knocks on the bathroom door.

"Livvy, sweetheart?" she calls. "It's Mummy."

Livvy opens the door a crack and Mum squeezes in, leaving me to hover on the landing. After a few seconds I hear Mum let out an excited squeal. The door opens and she reappears, her face pink and pleased.

"Mum, what's going on?" I ask.

"Nothing, David. Get on with your homework," she says, shooing me away.

I continue to hover as Mum dashes into her room, returning a few moments later with a package of pads in her hand.

Then it dawns on me. Livvy, my baby sister, has started her period.

Mum ducks into the bathroom, locking it behind her. I can hear her speaking to Livvy in a low voice. A moment later I hear Livvy let out another giggle. Slowly I back away, torn between wanting to listen in and wanting to run as far away as I can.

I shut my bedroom door and sit down on the edge of my bed, wondering how many more moments like this I am going to have to witness: private, female moments from which older brothers are automatically excluded. I try to focus on all the bad things Essie told me about her periods—the stomach cramps and zits and greasy hair, how she feels permanently furious with Felix, but it does little to help.

Later I go downstairs to discover Livvy lying on the sofa with a hot-water bottle resting on her stomach as Mum strokes her hair. I make an excuse about being tired and leave the room.

That night I can't sleep. I can't stop thinking about how I'll never experience what Livvy's experiencing tonight. It's a biological impossibility so unfair it makes my entire body throb.

· · · · ·

The next morning, instead of the cereal and toast we usually have for breakfast on a school day, Mum makes pancakes topped with strawberries and maple syrup in "Livvy's honor." Livvy sits at the head of the table like a queen, smiling serenely upon her subjects. Glossy-haired and clear-skinned, she shows none of the symptoms so gorily described by Essie. Trust Livvy to show early signs of breezing through puberty.

"My baby, all grown up," Mum beams as she pours Livvy a second glass of ceremonial orange juice.

Dad kisses Livvy on the cheek. "This better not mean you'll be bringing home boyfriends soon!" he says with a grin and a conspiratorial wink in my direction.

Livvy rolls her eyes. "Daaaaaad, don't be so lame."

I can tell though, she's pleased.

"Do you want more pancakes, David?" Mum asks, registering my presence at the table for the first time. And even though I am still hungry and could easily eat at least another two, I say no and excuse myself so as not to let them spot the tears in my eyes.

. . . . .

Essie and Felix notice something isn't right the moment they see me during morning break.

"David, what's wrong?" Essie demands.

Her question opens the floodgates. Quickly she and Felix guide me around the corner to the old abandoned bike sheds where I perch on one of the railings and sob like a baby.

"What on earth has happened?" Essie asks, kneeling down in front of me, while Felix rubs my shoulder.

At first I can't talk because I'm crying too hard but eventually I manage to choke out an account of my awful weekend, culminating in the news of Livvy's period.

"Oh, David," Essie says, standing up and hugging me.

"It just sort of hit me all at once," I say between gasps. "That things aren't going to magically fix themselves. They're only going to get worse, way worse."

"Not necessarily," Felix says. "You don't know what's going to happen."

"Yes I do. I'm a disgusting mutant who is only going to get more disgusting and more mutant-like. Did you know I wear a size-nine shoe now?"

157

"Kate Winslet is a size nine," Felix says quickly.

"But that's a girl's size," I say.

Essie ignores me and asks, "How the hell do you know that, Felix?"

"I don't know, I just do. Paris Hilton's feet are even bigger apparently."

"This is getting creepy now, Felix," Essie says.

Their bickering sort of helps me calm down.

"I just feel so . . . lonely," I say.

"Don't say that. You've got us," Essie says, tugging on my tie. And she's right, I do. But they've also got each other.

. . . . .

At lunchtime I meet Leo in the library. Although talking to Essie and Felix helped, I'm still feeling like a bit of me might be missing or broken. I'm certainly not in the mood for trigonometry. Beside me Leo is waiting patiently for me to complete the next problem. He seems more relaxed. I wonder why.

"How was the party on Saturday?" I ask.

"What party?" Leo asks slowly, keeping his eyes on the paper.

"Becky Somerville's. Didn't you go? I thought the whole of year eleven was there."

"Oh *that* party. It was all right," he says. "Nothing special."

"Oh," I say, doodling a star on my page. "That's funny."

"How so?"

"It's just that I heard it was really cool."

I watch his face carefully, alert for clues, certain he's not giving me the full story.

"David?"

"Yes?"

"The hypotenuse?"

"Sorry?"

"Which side of the triangle is the hypotenuse?" he asks, prodding the page with the end of his pen.

"Er, that one," I say, pointing aimlessly.

"No, that's the adjacent. C'mon, you know this stuff, David."

"Clearly I don't," I say, frustration building in my stomach.

Leo sighs. "Look at it again."

I try to look at the page but I can't concentrate. The more I try to focus the more the page blurs, the words and shapes beginning to dance in front of my eyes. I can't help it, I'm mad at him. I'm mad at him for showing signs of popularity. I was convinced he was one of us, a Non-Conformist, and I hate the possibility he might not be.

"Which one is the hypotenuse?" Leo repeats.

"I don't know," I say, horrified to discover a film of tears forming in front of my eyes.

"Yes you do. You're not trying. Just relax and concentrate."

But I can't. I'm too blinded by aimless frustration to focus my thoughts.

"C'mon, David. This is easy."

"I said I don't know," I say, throwing down my pen. "I don't know, okay?"

I expect Leo to flinch but he stays perfectly still, his face unreadable.

"David," he says wearily, like I'm some toddler throwing a tantrum.

I stand up, grabbing my books and shoving them into my backpack.

"David, stop being an idiot and sit down."

"Why should I? I clearly *am* an idiot. You said as much."

"No I didn't. Look, let's try again. We can start at the beginning."

"I'm not in the mood, okay. Let's just call it a day."

I throw a five-pound note down on the table and stalk out of the library.

Leo doesn't come after me.

LEO

The rest of October passes in a blur. Despite David storming out of our math session, we continue to meet. We clear the air but he seems different—quieter and more preoccupied. Sometimes I feel bad taking his money in return for my help, but it's clear he can afford it. Besides it means I have the cash to treat Alicia right.

My detention finally comes to an end. At the same time, all the drama around me hitting Harry seems to have finally died down. Harry still snarls at me in the hallway, but only when there's a protective crowd around him. Alicia is rehearsing for the school musical most lunchtimes, so when I'm not tutoring David in the library, I eat with him, Essie, and Felix in the cafeteria and let their bizarre chatter wash over me. And for once in my life, things actually seem calm. *I* seem calm. Even Jenny notices, although in typical Jenny fashion, she keeps pressing me to find out why.

. . . . .

The Friday before Halloween, Alicia spends the evening with her family.

I roam around my house, restless and impatient, counting down the minutes until I see her tomorrow.

"Will you stop pacing like that, Leo?" Amber demands. "You're like a caged animal or something." She's sitting on her bunk, plucking her eyebrows. She and Carl have made up and are off to the movies later.

"Sorry," I say, lying down on my bunk. I can't keep still though, and after a moment Amber's head appears upside down, her hair brushing the bunk-bed frame.

"What's your deal, Leo?" she asks. "You've been acting really odd lately."

"I don't have a deal," I lie, swatting at her ponytail.

My phone beeps.

"Who's that?" she asks.

"None of your business," I reply.

Amber narrows her eyes but returns to her bunk.

I turn onto my side so I can get my phone out of my back pocket. It's a text from Alicia: *Missing you xoxo.*

I roll onto my back and break into this goofy grin, thankful Amber can't see me. Because it's the sort of grin that would give me away in seconds. And because she's right, I am behaving differently. I can't help it.

I've told Amber I'm tutoring David on the nights I see Alicia so I don't have to spill the beans. I don't know why, but talking out loud about her to anyone, even Amber or Jenny, feels wrong, like it might jinx things. I want to keep Alicia and me in a precious bubble, safe from the outside world, for now at least. But despite this, I can't ignore a niggling feeling of guilt. Most of the time I can keep it buried, but every so often Alicia will smile at me, or tell me some secret, and the guilt creeps up and slices me in two, so sharply it almost takes my breath away. Still, I can't bring myself to tell her the truth.

. . . . .

The following night, Saturday, we go to the movies to watch a Halloween screening of some horror film from the 1970s. The whole way through, Alicia clutches my hand really hard, her nails digging into my flesh during the especially gruesome parts. It sort of hurts after a while, but I don't care.

After the movie I walk her home, even though it's pouring rain. By the time we reach her front door we're drenched. But it's like neither of us has noticed.

"You know what I was thinking tonight?" she asks. "In between screaming like a five-year-old of course."

Wow, she looks good wet.

"No. What?" I ask.

"How you are totally unlike any boy I've ever dated."

I stiffen. Although I know Alicia's been out with other boys, I don't like to dwell on the fact for more than a few seconds. I have to keep reminding myself that she's with me, but it's hard when I'm pretty sure she could have any boy she wanted.

"I mean that in a good way, Leo Denton," she adds. "A very good way. I love that you're not like everyone else," she says, tugging on the drawstrings of my hoodie to pull me closer.

I continue to frown.

"That's a positive thing," she insists. "I like that you're your own person, that you don't care about being popular or tough or showing off. You're different. I like different. I like it a lot."

She rubs her wet nose against mine in an Eskimo kiss. And I get this feeling of déjà vu. Then I remember, Mam used to kiss me and Amber like that when she tucked us in at night. I completely forgot about that until now.

"Do you want to come in?" Alicia asks, her voice suddenly grown-up sounding. "My family's out."

I pull away from her and make a big show of looking at the time on my phone.

"Jesus, I would love to, you have no idea how much. But it's getting kind of late. My mum will be off her rocker if I don't get home soon."

It's a lie. Mam is out with Spike tonight, due back God knows when. But Alicia doesn't know that. She nods, disappointed.

"You do still like me, don't you?" she asks, half-joking, half-serious.

I groan. "Of course I do. I just want things to be special, you know?"

Alicia pouts a little but nods.

"You're right," she says. "I just really, really like you, Leo."

"Tell me about it," I reply, grinning.

She blushes and giggles. And I know I'm off the hook.

We kiss once more before saying a final good night.

As I walk home, even though I'm still buzzing, the same thought keeps popping up and ruining my mood. How much longer can this go on?

. . . . .

The following Thursday is Guy Fawkes night. I go home after school and change out of my uniform before meeting Alicia at the annual bonfire and fireworks display in the Eden Park recreation ground. I have a feeling the Eden Park Guy Fawkes display will be very different from the unofficial Cloverdale ones where kids run riot across the estate, chucking fireworks at one another, the constant wail of fire engines in the background.

Alicia is waiting at the entrance when I arrive, wearing a red wool hat that makes her look really cute and waving a sparkler. When she sees me she drops the sparkler and comes running over, throwing her arms around my neck. It still takes me back when she does this, the way she's so uninhibited about who sees us, like she's proud to be with me.

As we walk into the park, although I'm pretty sure no one from Cloverdale will be here, I pull my hat down low over my head.

In the center of the park there is a huge bonfire. To the left there's a small carnival and a cluster of food stalls.

"Let's go on the ferris wheel!" Alicia says, dragging me toward the lights.

She pays for our tickets and we clamber up a set of rickety steps into the first available car. A boy not much older than us takes our tickets and pulls a bar down onto our laps. Almost immediately we swing upward. Alicia lets out a squeal and clutches my arm.

"Sorry to be such a big kid," she says, her eyes shining. "But I'm crazy about all this stuff."

Our car jerks higher still and the noise below us begins to fade as we creak steadily upward. I look over the side, at the tops of the heads of the people milling around below us. Beside me Alicia gazes down at them, this look of wonder on her face, and in that second I decide I could look at her for days on end and never get bored.

At the top, our car swaying gently as more riders are let on and off down below, Alicia sighs.

"It's so peaceful up here," she says. "I love it."

"I know what you mean," I reply. "It's like I can actually breathe up here, if that makes sense."

"It makes total sense," Alicia says, taking my bare hand and tucking it under her mittened one.

We keep going around. It's being at the top I like best though, where, for a few seconds, I imagine Alicia and I are the only people on the planet.

"Where's Cloverdale from here?" she asks.

I twist around and try to get my bearings.

"I'm not sure. That way, I guess," I say, pointing off to the right.

"Will you take me there some day?"

"Where? Cloverdale? You don't want to see Cloverdale, believe me."

"But I do," she insists, jiggling my arm. "I want to see where you live, see your bedroom, meet your sisters, your mum."

"Nothing much to see," I say casually. "And Mam, she works a lot, she's hardly ever in—"

"You're not ashamed of me, are you, Leo?"

I make a face. "No way."

"Then what's the problem?"

"There isn't one."

I try to imagine Alicia in our cramped living room, perched on the edge of the sofa, drinking a cup of tea. Suddenly Mam is invading the picture, swaying about with a cigarette dangling between her fingers, a can of beer in the other hand. Then Spike is in on the act, wandering in wearing nothing but his cartoon boxer shorts, burping and farting and scratching. Before I know it, Tia's there too, gazing up at Alicia like she's one of her beloved Disney Princesses and asking a ton of dumb questions. All three of them are like ticking time bombs, liable to ruin everything at any time with no warning. And this is without factoring in Amber.

"They do know about me, don't they?" Alicia asks, leaning away from me.

"Of course they do," I lie. "I haven't stopped talking about you!"

She relaxes into a smile and snuggles back up against me.

"Tell me more about your mum, Leo. You never talk about her."

I frown and try to work out how to best describe my mess of a mother.

"She's difficult," I say eventually.

"Difficult how?"

"She's one of those people whose mood sort of affects the whole house, you know? Like, if she's in a good mood, we can relax, but if she's in a bad one, everyone knows it and feels it."

"Why is she like that, do you think? I mean, there must be a reason for her acting that way?"

I shrug. "I don't know. It's just how she's always been."

"Sounds tough," Alicia says, stroking my hand.

"It's okay. I mean, it could be worse. It's not like she beats or starves us, or anything. She's just not your typical mother, I suppose."

Understatement of the year. My cheeks feel suddenly hot. I always get nervous when I worry that I might have said too much. For a few seconds we sit in silence, the air hazy with smoke from the bonfire.

"Leo?" Alicia says, as our car rocks back and forth.

"Yeah?"

"After the fireworks tonight, do you want to come back to my house?"

I swallow. "Won't your parents be there?"

Alicia grins triumphantly. "Nope. They're at a charity dinner tonight. Won't be back until late. And my brother's staying over at my gran's so we'll have the entire place to ourselves."

She leans in close so her breath tickles my earlobes. "So what do you say?"

Instead of answering, I kiss her. And it's a great kiss, full of longing. But something else too. Fear.

168

After the ferris wheel, we buy hot dogs and pink cotton candy. I hit the targets at the shooting gallery and win Alicia a giant cuddly canary.

As we're making our way toward the bonfire to watch the fireworks, our mouths and fingers sticky from the cotton candy, I hear someone call my name. My first instinct is to freeze up, terrified it's someone from Cloverdale. But then I connect the voice to its owner. David.

"Hey," I say, as David weaves through the crowd toward us, Essie and Felix behind him. In skinny jeans, a fur-lined parka, and a rainbow-striped scarf trailing on the ground, he looks different from when he's in his school uniform—less awkward.

"Hi, Leo. Having a good night?" he asks. He seems nervous despite the fact I saw him at lunch today.

"Yeah, thanks. You?"

"Yeah, good."

He looks from me to Alicia and back again. I clear my throat.

"Er, guys, this is Alicia. Alicia, this is David, Essie, and Felix."

Alicia nods enthusiastically.

"I've seen you around school," she says. "Nice to meet you."

A silence quickly descends, all the more pronounced by the racket surrounding us.

"Well, this is awkward," Essie says loudly, reaching forward and swiping a handful of cotton candy. David elbows her.

Alicia turns to me.

"We should get going if we want to get a good spot at the front," she says.

"Right," I say. "Er, see you guys at school, yeah?"

"Yeah, see you at school," the three of them echo.

Alicia links her arm through mine. As we edge toward the crowd, I glance over my shoulder. Essie and Felix have wandered toward the shooting gallery but David is still looking in our direction, a very slight frown on his face. For a second our eyes meet. He smiles tightly before darting to join them.

At 8 p.m. the fireworks begin. I've never really cared for them, but I guess I just never looked at them in the right way before, because tonight, listening to Alicia gasp and sigh as they splutter and crackle over our heads, I'm a complete fireworks convert.

It's almost enough to distract me from the constant anxiety in my stomach.

LEO

"*You sure they're not going to be back* until late?" I ask as Alicia unlocks her front door.

"I promise you. They go to this dinner every year, and every year they get back at stupid o'clock. Dad's even taken tomorrow off work because of it. Free bar and all that. Seriously, we've got hours."

"Right," I say, following Alicia into the dark foyer, trailing the stuffed canary on the ground behind me.

When we ran into Ruby and Liam and a few other kids from our year, I almost persuaded Alicia we should go with them to Nando's for some food. Not that I particularly wanted to go, but I knew by the time we'd got there and ordered and eaten and argued over the bill, it would probably be too late to go back to Alicia's. But Alicia had made up her mind, whispering something in Ruby's ear before dragging me away from the safety of a crowd.

"You want a drink?" she asks, taking off her coat.

"Er, yeah, please. Water's fine, or Coke if you've got some."

She rolls her eyes. "I meant a real drink."

She takes my hand and leads me into the living room. She flicks on the lights and opens a large glass cabinet containing at least twenty bottles of liquor.

"Vodka okay?" Alicia asks, peering at the label of one of the fuller bottles.

"Sure."

She pours us each a glass. We take a sip in unison. It burns the back of my throat and I have to fight to keep myself from coughing.

"Let's take the bottle up with us," Alicia says, beckoning for me to follow her out of the room and up the stairs.

It's not the first time I've set foot in Alicia's bedroom. But this is the first time I've done so without her parents milling around downstairs and a strict door-open, lights-on policy in operation.

Alicia shuts the door and turns on a lamp, casting a soft pink glow across the room. She turns her back and bends to plug her iPod into its dock. Seconds later the room is filled with soft, jazzy music. My head starts to pulse.

"Ella Fitzgerald," she says, smiling and setting down her empty glass.

I nod.

She holds out her arms. Wordlessly, I move toward them. Our lips meet, mine buzzing with alcohol. This is good. Kissing is distracting, safe. Alicia leads me toward the bed.

"I've still got my shoes on," I say.

"Don't worry about it," Alicia murmurs, falling onto the bed and taking me with her.

"But they're dirty."

"I said, don't worry about it."

I try to concentrate on the kissing again, cupping her face with my hands and focusing on how insanely good her lips feel against mine, how soft her skin is, her fluttery sighs.

"Leo," she whispers between kisses. "Have you got, a, you know?"

"Er, no, I haven't, sorry," I say, my body flooding with relief. "I didn't think . . ."

"That's okay, I've got it covered."

"Great," I lie, the relief exiting my body just as fast as it entered.

We continue to kiss. Alicia's hands snake under my hoodie and T-shirt, my body tensing up the second they do. And suddenly we're back in Becky's closet under the stairs. My breath quickens as Alicia's fingers continue to creep upward. I sit up, panting.

"What's wrong?" she asks.

"Nothing. Just thirsty," I reply.

She pours me a second glass of vodka. As I take a sip, Alicia wriggles out of her top and jeans so she's wearing just her matching bra and panties, pink and satiny, and arranges herself on top of the duvet. I gaze across at her. She looks so sexy and gorgeous. All I want to do is touch her, smell her, be with her. But I know I can't.

I let her pull me down on the bed again. She crawls on top of me so she's straddling me and at first we're just kissing but then she's fiddling with the buttons on my jeans. I push her away and sit up, my heartbeat going wild.

"Is it your first time? Is that it? Because it's mine too. We're in this together," Alicia says, kneeling up on the bed. She looks so beautiful I want to cry.

"It's not that," I say.

"Then what is it? Because every time I touch you, you go totally weird. You claim you're really into me, but every time things get heavy, you push me away."

"I am into you. Shit, Alicia, I think I might even love you."

"And I think I might love you too. So what's the problem?"

The enormity of what she's just said makes my head hurt. I love Alicia. Alicia loves me. I should be walking on air right now. But I'm not. Because I know I'm on the verge of wrecking everything.

"There isn't a problem," I say desperately. "I just can't do this. Not tonight."

"But why?" she pleads. "What's the big secret? We're boyfriend and girlfriend, you should be able to tell me everything."

"Even if it means you'll end up hating me?"

"Don't be stupid," she says. "I couldn't hate you, Leo."

"You don't know that."

"Yes, I do."

I stare at her, beautiful Alicia, her eyes full of fear and hope.

"Just tell me, Leo. I don't want us to have secrets."

My heart feels like it's going about ten thousand miles per hour.

"You don't know what you're letting yourself in for—" I begin.

"For God's sake, Leo, I'm a big girl," she interrupts. "Whatever it is I can handle it. Just tell me."

"Maybe you should get dressed first," I say.

Alicia frowns but climbs off the bed and pulls on a turquoise robe with a Chinese dragon embroidered on the back. She ties the belt around her waist and returns to the bed, sitting cross-legged on the duvet. I hesitate before perching on the edge next to her. She turns so she's facing me side-on.

"What I'm about to say is going to sound really strange," I say, looking straight ahead. "So you've just got to promise me that you'll let me get to the end, okay?"

I dare to look at her. Her face is serious, her eyes unsmiling for once.

"Okay?" I repeat.

She fixes her eyes on mine. "I told you, Leo, whatever it is I can handle it."

I could still make a run for it, but if I do I know I'll lose her for certain. And maybe, just maybe, there's a tiny chance she won't get totally freaked out by what I'm about to say.

I close my eyes. I can hear Alicia breathing next to me and I can tell she's nervous about what might come out of my mouth.

"You know how I've been pulling away from you when we get, you know, intimate," I begin.

Intimate. It seems like such a stupid word. Stiff and formal. It couldn't communicate how I feel when I'm doing stuff with Alicia in a million years. Alicia reaches across and takes my hand in hers. I have to resist the urge to yank it back into my lap. Instead

I try to ignore her thumb gently massaging my palm as I continue to talk.

"Well, there's a reason I've been acting that way. And you've got to believe me when I say it's nothing to do with you, okay?"

Alicia squeezes my hand as if to say, *Go on*, and I know I can't put it off any longer. Suddenly I feel dizzy, like if I opened my eyes, Alicia's bedroom would be spinning at one hundred miles per hour. I take a deep breath.

"Okay, the reason I've been acting so weird is because I'm not who you think I am."

I feel Alicia's grip on my hand slacken ever so slightly.

I need to say it now, quickly, like ripping off a Band-Aid, before I change my mind.

"I wasn't born Leo," I say, my voice growing quieter and quieter, so I'm almost whispering.

Ella has stopped singing. The room is silent.

"I was born a girl."

I keep my eyes closed as Alicia's hand shoots from mine.

DAVID

The day after the fireworks display in Eden Park, Leo doesn't eat lunch in the cafeteria.

"Are he and Alicia Baker going out then?" Essie muses as she picks the carrots out of her chicken potpie with her fork.

"How should I know?" I reply.

"It certainly looked like it last night," she says. "They were all over each other. What a dark horse!"

"Like I said, I don't know," I say irritably.

Essie and Felix exchange looks. I pretend not to notice.

That afternoon, I sit and wait in the library but Leo fails to appear for our arranged math session. When I ask Felix, he reveals Leo missed Advanced Math that morning.

. . . . .

During morning break on Monday, I spot Alicia with Ruby Webber and Becky Somerville outside the bank of vending machines.

"Alicia?"

She doesn't hear me at first. I repeat her name, louder this time.

She turns to face me. Her eyes are bloodshot.

"Yes?" she says, looking through me like I'm a ghost.

"Er, is Leo sick? I haven't seen him since last week. Have you?"

Becky puts a protective arm around Alicia's shoulder.

"No, she hasn't. And she doesn't want to either."

"Becky, don't," Alicia says quietly.

"Why? What's he done?" I ask, looking from Alicia to Becky.

"Only gone and broken my best friend's heart!" Ruby interjects.

"Guys, stop it," Alicia says, looking at her feet.

"What happened?" I ask.

"Like she's going to tell you! Alicia is too upset to even talk to us about it," Ruby says, stroking Alicia's hair. "That's how heartbroken she is."

"But when she is ready to tell us," Becky says, "Leo Denton is going to wish he'd never been born."

Alicia closes her eyes.

"Guys, I said stop," she says softly.

"Not that it's any of your business," Ruby snaps at me. "Now, if you'll excuse us."

She tosses her hair over her shoulder and together she and Becky link arms with Alicia and steer her away from me.

I stare after them. The last time I saw Leo and Alicia together they were at the fireworks, looking totally in love.

This doesn't make any sense.

I would call Leo but I don't have his cell phone number. I suggested exchanging numbers several times but he always resisted, making an excuse or changing the subject.

This is why I find myself boarding the number fourteen bus bound for Cloverdale after school. I text Mum to tell her I'm meeting Leo for extra math tutoring and that I may be late for dinner.

The bus soon leaves behind the tree-lined streets of Eden Park and heads south for unfamiliar territory. We pass Cloverdale School. The building itself resembles a fat office block marooned in the center of a concrete parking lot. Behind the school, I can just make out a tangle of trees, the only greenery in sight. It makes Eden Park School look like a palace in comparison. When we stop a bunch of Cloverdale kids clamber onto the bus, rattling past me, and I can't help but feel glad I chose to sit up front, near the driver.

A few minutes later a robotic voice announces the next stop is Cloverdale Estate—East Side. I press the bell.

Although at least five other people get off the bus at the same stop as me, they quickly scatter, disappearing down alleyways, or into waiting cars, swallowed up by the estate, and within a minute I am alone.

Cloverdale is quiet. I glance over each shoulder before taking out my iPhone and studying the map on the screen.

The recommended route takes me past a row of shops in the center of the estate, some of which are just empty shells with faded signs and whitewashed windows. The last shop is a small supermarket with half its windows boarded up, shards of broken glass sparkling on the sidewalk like glitter. Outside the shop a group of boys wearing the Cloverdale School uniform are shouting and throwing potato chips at each other. I look down to check that my Eden Park blazer is not visible from beneath my coat, and slide my iPhone into my pocket.

It's dusk when I finally enter Sycamore Gardens. I identify Leo's house immediately by its overgrown front yard. I'm relieved to find the living room lights on, and the faint drone of the television just audible as I tread through the trampled grass toward the front door. I look for a doorbell. There isn't one so I knock and wait. A few seconds later the door eases open a crack, constricted by the safety chain, and a small pale face belonging to a little girl peeks up at me through the gap.

"What do you want?" she demands.

"Er, is Leo in?" I ask.

"Nope."

"Tia, who is it?" a female voice calls.

"Don't know, someone for Leo," the kid, who I guess is Tia, calls back.

Another few seconds pass before a second face appears above Tia's, its owner in possession of a very familiar pair of eyes. They appraise me for a moment before the safety chain is released and the door is opened fully, revealing a teenage girl dressed in leopard-print pajamas, with bleached-blond hair piled on top of her head.

"Can I help you?" she asks, folding her arms.

"I'm—looking—for Leo?" I stammer, peering behind her

into the living room. I make out an orange sofa and half of a huge TV set. The girl notices me looking and puts her arm on the door frame to block my view.

"And you are?" she asks.

"Er, David, a friend of Leo's from school."

She raises her eyebrows. "The one he's been spending so much time with?"

"I guess so."

"I'm his sister, Amber."

"Nice to meet you," I say, extending my hand. She stares at me as if to say, *Are you for real?* I drop my hand to my side and pretend to wipe it on my pants.

"Leo's not here," Amber says.

"He's not? Oh. Well, do you know where he is?"

"Down at the pool, I think."

I screw up my face apologetically. "Sorry, where?"

"The pool? The old swimming pool. At the bottom of Renton Road?"

I shake my head.

Amber rolls her eyes again. "You're not from around here, are you?"

"Er, no."

"That was a rhetorical question by the way," she says.

"Oh."

"Tia!" she calls.

By now Tia has scampered back into the living room and is engrossed in a noisy episode of *Horrible Histories*.

"Yeah," Tia calls back.

"I'm going out for about ten minutes. Don't open the door to any strangers."

"Okay!"

Amber grabs a coat from the pile draped over the banister and pulls it on over her pajamas.

"I don't want to be any trouble," I say quickly. "I'm sure I could find it on my phone."

Amber slides her feet into a pair of fluffy pink boots and straightens up.

"No offense, but a kid like you will get eaten alive around here. I'm surprised you made it this far to be honest. Nah, best I take you."

And with that she slams the front door behind us and sets off down Sycamore Gardens, leaving me with no choice but to hurry after her.

Amber walks quickly, her mass of white-blond hair bouncing up and down on her head.

"Leo didn't tell me he had an older sister," I say, as I scurry along beside her.

"Probably because he doesn't," she replies.

"But you said—"

"We're twins."

"You are?" I say in surprise. "Leo never said so."

Amber shrugs.

"That certainly explains it," I continue.

"Explains what?" Amber says sharply.

"Your eyes. They're identical to Leo's."

"Are they?" she murmurs, before taking a sharp right and

leading us down a narrow alleyway. We come out on a main road.

"There it is," she says, pointing across the road toward a large building surrounded by a tall corrugated-iron fence, only its arched roof visible over the top. We cross. Amber leads me around the perimeter of the fence. Every few feet, there are large signs declaring, PRIVATE PROPERTY. TRESPASSERS WILL BE PROSECUTED, pretty much all of them covered with graffiti.

"What is this place again?" I ask.

"The old swimming pool," Amber replies. "Been here since the Victorian times. It closed down a few years ago. There was talk for a while about turning the place into luxury apartments but nothing's happened so far. They've probably finally figured out that anyone with enough money to buy a luxury apartment wouldn't be caught dead living in Cloverdale."

By the time we get around to the back of the building, away from the glow of street lamps, dusk has melted into actual darkness. Amber takes out her phone and shines it over the fence.

"Here we go," she says, loosening one of the fence panels to reveal a small rectangular hole. She motions for me to crawl through it. I hesitate before dropping to my knees. When I reach the other side, I turn, expecting to see Amber crawling after me, but instead she's pulling the fence panel back into place.

"Hey, wait! Aren't you coming?" I ask, panic rising in my voice.

She crouches to peer through the hole and looks at me like I'm crazy.

"I don't think so."

"But where do I go now? Where's Leo?" I ask.

"Inside somewhere," she says, motioning vaguely. "You might need to use your phone to see. It's pretty dark in there."

"Oh, right. Well, er, thanks for bringing me."

"You're welcome," she says.

And just like that, Amber is gone, leaving me alone, crouched in the darkness. I straighten up and wipe my muddy hands on my pants before groping in my pocket for my phone. I adjust the straps on my backpack and begin to walk around the building. I'm shaking and several times I almost trip over the piles of rubble in my path. I look around, noticing the building is built from red brick and decorated with intricate stone carvings. At the front I discover a set of steps sweeping up to an arched entrance held by four pillars. I go up the steps and push at the door, not expecting it to give, but it does and I tumble into the foyer, landing on my hands and knees on a marble floor. As I clamber to my feet, the smell of chlorine hits me. Then the sheer quietness. It's as if all the noise in the world has been sucked out, apart from the sound of my uneven breathing.

I stand up and begin to walk forward. I shine my phone over the reception area. To my right there's an old desk, complete with till and swivel chair. To my left there's a defunct vending machine, empty. In front of me there's a set of turnstiles. I go through them and keep walking. I come to the changing rooms—ladies' on the left, men's on the right. I head into the men's room figuring this will lead me to the pool, and hopefully to Leo. Already I don't have a clue which part of the fence I crawled through and the prospect of spending the night trapped in an abandoned Victorian swimming pool doesn't exactly fill me with delight.

My phone beeps, informing me the battery is low. I decide to conserve the power and slide it back into my pocket, resorting to feeling my way around instead. I let my hands roam over the metal lockers, keys still in locks. Gradually my eyes get used to the dark and I can make out the hooks and benches lining the walls, the showers and urinals. I turn the corner and I'm greeted with a faint glow of light. I make my way toward it.

I step out and realize I'm at the edge of the pool. Above me the clouds have cleared, and the moon glows through the roof, which I can now see is made of glass, casting the entire space with a silvery sheen. Banks of flip-down wooden seats line the length of the pool on each side. At one end there is a three-tiered diving platform, at the other, five windows, tall and narrow. I inch forward and peek down. The pool is empty. Of course it is. And yet I can't help but feel disappointed. I sit on the edge, dangle my legs over the side and marvel at how far down it seems to the bottom with no water distorting the depth. I take out my dying phone and shine it toward the deep end.

"Hey!"

I drop my phone. It makes a loud clatter as it hits the bottom of the pool.

This is it. I'm going to die.

"Hey!" the voice calls again. In my panic I can't identify where it's coming from and it takes several seconds to trace it to a shadowy figure standing on the highest diving board. A moment later a thin beam from a flashlight hits me in the face. I stand up, squinting and shielding my eyes.

"David?" the voice says.

"Leo?"

There's an audible sigh, then a creak of metal as Leo descends the ladder. By the time he reaches the bottom, my heart has just about stopped threatening to burst out of my chest.

Leo strides toward me, one arm straight out in front of him, the flashlight aimed at my head.

"Don't shoot," I joke.

Leo doesn't laugh.

"How did you get here?" he demands, his eyes flashing.

"Your sister brought me," I stammer. "Amber. Hey, how come you didn't tell me you had a twin?"

"She shouldn't have brought you."

"It's not her fault. I asked her where you were."

"Whatever," Leo mutters, lowering the flashlight.

"This place is really cool," I say. "Terrifying but cool. Did you use to swim here? When it was still open, I mean?"

Leo doesn't answer me.

"You shouldn't be here, David," he says.

"But I was worried about you. You haven't been at school since last week."

"I was ill. I am ill."

I study his face in the faint moonlight.

"You don't look ill," I point out.

He ignores me, turning and shining the flashlight over the bottom of the pool.

"You want me to get that?" he asks, nodding at my phone.

"No, I can get it."

He ignores me again and jumps down. He picks up the phone, tossing it to me. I surprise myself by catching it.

"When are you coming back?" I ask as Leo strides to the metal steps, his sneakers squeaking against the tiles. He doesn't answer.

"You can't stop tutoring me now," I continue. "I got a B on a math test the other day. Mr. Steele almost fell off his chair he was so shocked. And it's all because of you."

Leo pauses and sits on the top rung of the steps, his arms hooked around the frame.

"Who says I'm coming back?"

"But you've got to," I say.

Even though Leo has only been at Eden Park School for a couple of months, the thought of him not being around anymore feels wrong.

"According to who?" Leo says.

"I don't know. Me. The authorities."

He snorts.

I sit down next to him, my arms clasping my bent legs.

"What happened, Leo?" I ask. "Why haven't you been at school?"

He just shakes his head.

"Is it something to do with Alicia Baker?"

He turns sharply to face me.

"Why? What has she said?"

"Nothing really. Ruby Webber and Becky Somerville were doing all the talking for her."

"And what did they say?" he demands.

"They didn't say much either," I admit. "Just that Alicia's too heartbroken to tell them what happened."

Leo exhales deeply, frowns, and nods.

"What happened, Leo?" I ask again.

"Nothing," he growls, angling his head away from me.

"It can't be nothing. If it was nothing you wouldn't be hiding here."

"I'm not hiding," he says, jumping back down to the bottom of the pool. I think he lands badly because he swears sharply to himself and limps around in a circle for a moment.

"Are you okay?" I call, clambering down the ladder after him.

"I'm fine," he snaps.

"It can't be nothing," I repeat. "The thing with Alicia, I mean. I saw you together at the fireworks, and you were into each other, and now it's all over?"

"It's none of your business, David."

"But I want to help," I say, glancing upward, the sides of the pool looming high above my head.

"Believe me, you can't," Leo replies.

"Try me," I say, planting myself in front of him. He looks at me for a moment before shaking his head and pushing me gently backward.

"Just go home, David," he says, his voice tired.

"No."

"What?"

I take a deep breath.

"No," I repeat. "Everyone else may have fallen for your

hard-man act, but I haven't. I'm not afraid of you, Leo, not one bit."

Leo squares up to me, his chest all puffed out.

"Oh really?" he says.

"Yes, really," I reply, standing up straight. "And I'm not going anywhere until you talk to me. I'm your friend, Leo."

"You hardly know me, David," he says.

But he's wrong. I do know him. And I want to know him more. I have no idea why. I only know that I'm drawn to him in ways I can't quite explain, and that I can't shift the sneaking suspicion that beneath it all, he gets me, that he's drawn to me too.

"Yes, I do know you," I continue gently. "I know you're kind and sweet and patient."

Leo rolls his eyes.

"But I mean it!" I say. "Please tell me what happened. I'll support you, whatever it is, I promise I will."

Leo lets out a laugh. "That's what she said."

"Who?" I ask. "Alicia?"

"Forget it."

He crouches down, his back to me. He looks small suddenly, just a kid. I crouch down beside him. I want to fix things, make it better, but I don't know how.

"Leo," I find myself saying in a low whisper. "If I tell you something, a secret, something only Essie and Felix know about me, do you promise not to tell anyone?"

"I get what you're doing here," he says. "You tell me some stupid secret and then expect me to tell you all my shit in return, right?"

189

"No. This is something I *want* to tell you. You don't have to tell me anything in return, honestly."

And I mean it. Suddenly I want him to know. I want to open up to him, be vulnerable, with no expectations.

Leo just shrugs.

"So do you promise?" I whisper.

"Look, David, I don't care about your stupid secret, okay?"

"Promise?" I repeat in a loud voice.

"Promise," he says, rolling his eyes, not quite looking at me.

I scoot around so I'm facing him. The surface of the pool feels cold and hard through the thin fabric of my school pants.

"What if I told you I wasn't gay?"

"But you are, you said so yourself. You like that blond kid, what's-his-name, Olsen."

I sigh. I need to come at this from a different angle.

"Let me start again. Remember that time after our first detention together, when you asked me why Harry calls me Freak Show?"

"Yeah," Leo replies, picking at his shoelaces.

"Well, I sort of didn't tell you the whole truth."

He shrugs again.

"What did you want to be when you were a kid?" I ask.

He wrinkles his nose. "I don't know."

"You must have wanted to be something?"

"I said I don't know," he says irritably. "Look, what's this got to do with you being gay or not?"

Despite the cold, my palms are prickling with sweat. I wipe

them on my pants but new beads of sweat appear almost immediately.

"Okay," I begin. "So when I was eight my class was asked to write about what we wanted to be when we grew up."

I close my eyes and just like that, I'm back in Ms. Box's classroom, the smell of leftover school lunches and sweat and grass stains drifting across our bowed heads as we write, my tongue twitching with concentration as my pen speeds across the page, excited by the task I've been given, unaware of what is to come.

I open my eyes. Leo is frowning slightly.

"After we finished writing," I continue slowly, "Ms. Box, she was our teacher that year, asked everyone to stand up and say what they wanted to be in turn. All the other kids wanted to be soccer players and actors and stuff, and I started to get that feeling you sometimes get after an exam, when you come out and at first you're feeling pretty confident but then everyone starts discussing their answers and it suddenly dawns on you that you've totally messed up. Know what I mean?"

Leo nods.

"Well, as Ms. Box went around the room, it was just like that. Because I hadn't written about wanting to be a soccer player or an actor, like everyone else. I hadn't written down anything like that. I just wrote what I really wanted to *be*." I can feel my face turning red. "What I really am."

Leo is looking at me now. Properly. I feel light-headed.

"I wrote I wanted to be a girl," I say, my voice cracking on *girl*. When Leo doesn't say anything, I just keep talking.

I tell him about my scrapbook, my box of dress-up clothes, the endless letters to my parents I've written but never sent. I tell him about all the research I've done on the Internet, the Web sites and forums I've pored over, the YouTube videos I've watched. I even tell him about my weekly inspections and how it feels to look in the mirror and realize my inside and outside don't match up, that they don't even come close.

The entire time he doesn't interrupt. He just stares at me, barely blinking, his expression indecipherable.

"Sometimes," I say, "I look in the mirror and the kid who looks back is like a stranger to me, an alien even. It's like I know the real me is in there somewhere, but for the moment I'm trapped in this freaky body I recognize less and less every day. Does that make any sense at all?"

Leo opens his mouth as if he's about to say something but no sound comes out.

"Of course it doesn't," I say. "How could it?"

"Why are you telling me this?" Leo asks finally.

"I don't know," I admit. "I suppose there was just part of me that wanted to share something important with you. Something really important."

"Right."

A silence hangs between us. Leo is fiddling with the frayed edges of his jeans, and I can only guess that I've totally freaked him out and he's heard enough. I was stupid to think he would react any differently. After all, it's not every day that people turn around and tell you they want to be the opposite sex, least of all some kid you've known a matter of months.

"I suppose you think I'm a freak now," I say, my voice coming out small and sad.

Leo looks up at me sharply. We lock eyes for a moment, Leo's amber flecks flashing in the moonlight.

"I don't think you're a freak, David," he says, his voice slow and careful.

"You don't?"

His eyeballs look shiny, not with tears (I don't think I can even imagine Leo crying), but something close.

"No," he says. "What I mean is, I get it."

I sigh. "That's kind, but you don't get it, Leo, you can't."

He looks at me for a second before swearing under his breath and standing. At first I think he's signaling it's time for us to leave, that the conversation is over, and I make a move to stand up too. But then I realize, instead of walking away, he's taking off his hoodie. Which makes no sense because it's pretty cold in here. I stare up at him, confused. He tosses his hoodie aside. His hair is sticking out in messy tufts. He takes off his sweatshirt, then his shirt, the entire time not saying a word, his face blank but determined, until he's wearing just his white T-shirt. His arms goose pimple immediately. He pauses for a second before lifting up his T-shirt, not over his head, but up to his chin. Instead of skin, his torso is wrapped in what might look to anyone else like a tight white crop top. But not to me. I know exactly what Leo is wearing. And Leo knows I know. And it's like the jigsaw-puzzle pieces that have been floating around in my head for the past couple of months have suddenly slotted together to form a picture.

LEO

"You're a girl?" David whispers, so quietly I can barely hear him.

I let my T-shirt fall back into place. The cold hits me suddenly, sharp and icy. I feel a shiver snake its way up my spine. David jumps to his feet, gathering my clothes and thrusting them into my arms.

"Quick, get them back on or you'll freeze to death," he says, his eyes not quite meeting mine, his forehead scrunched into a frown, like it's hurting his brain to get his head around what he's just seen.

As I pull my clothes back on, I can feel him watching my every move, probably looking for all the clues he missed, those telltale signs that passed him by.

I pull my hoodie on and fold my arms.

"You look like you've seen a ghost," I say.

David nods faintly. Because I suppose, in a way, he has.

"You're a girl," he repeats. This time it's not a question, more a declaration of a fact he now knows to be true.

"Well, technically, but I prefer the term 'natal female,' or 'biological female' if you must," I say.

"But you look like a boy," David says in wonder. "Totally and completely like a boy."

"What can I say, I've had a lot of practice."

There I go again. Being a smart-ass. But David doesn't seem to notice or care. He steps forward, studying my face, walking around me in a slow circle, like I'm a sculpture in an art gallery. I half expect him to reach out and poke me, just to check I'm actually real.

"Are you on hormones and stuff?" he asks.

"Hormone blockers," I say. "They freeze puberty."

"I've read about them on the Internet," David murmurs. "How long have you been on them?"

"Nearly six months now."

"An injection?"

"Yep, every three months."

"Does it hurt?"

I shake my head.

"And how does it feel? Different?"

"I guess."

"Does it mean you don't have periods anymore?"

I stiffen. "Yeah."

"What happens after that?" David continues. "After hormone blockers, I mean."

"Well, next year I'm supposed to move on to testosterone."

"Tes-tos-ter-one," he echoes, sounding out each syllable as if trying on the word for size.

"Two trans kids in one school," I say. "Who'd have thought, huh?"

"I read somewhere that most schools have at least two transgender students," David says. "I always assumed it was a made-up statistic, to trick kids like me into feeling less of a freak. I never in a million years would have guessed the other one would be you."

I smile weakly.

"Do you think there's a transgender version of gaydar?" David continues. "If so, mine is totally off."

I look at my feet. "Yeah, well, no one was supposed to know. It was supposed to be a secret."

I can feel David's eyes still on me, boring into me, like they want to get right inside and burrow under my skin.

"You told Alicia, didn't you?" David says slowly. "That's why she won't talk to you. And why you haven't been coming to school."

"Very perceptive," I say grimly.

Just the mention of Alicia's name makes me feel sick.

"What happened?" David asks.

"What do you think happened?"

David looks at his feet. "Sorry."

"Yeah, well," I mutter, shrugging, thinking maybe if I act like I don't care, I'll stop caring for real.

"Is that why you left Cloverdale School too?" David asks.

I sigh. "Yeah."

"What happened? Were you in disguise there too?"

"Disguise?" I say. "This isn't *Scooby-Doo*, you know."

David blushes. "Sorry, but this vocabulary is kind of new to me. Not to mention the fact I'm still in mild shock from, well . . . this," he says, gesturing at me.

"It's called going stealth," I say. "And no, I wasn't stealth at Cloverdale. Everyone there knew. It was impossible to avoid. I went to primary school with a lot of them and they'd all known me as Megan."

"Megan," David says. "Of course. Jesus, I'm dense."

"What do you mean?" I ask.

"I Googled you and all this stuff came up about a girl called Megan Denton. Hey, weren't you some kind of swimming champion? Is that why you come here?"

"Something like that."

I don't like to talk about my life as Megan. To anyone.

"So when did you start living as Leo?" David asks.

"Just before I went to Cloverdale. I'd just turned eleven."

"And how was it?" David asks. "At school I mean, with everyone knowing?"

I close my eyes for a second, trying to think of a suitable way to sum up life at Cloverdale School, to describe how instead of getting easier every day, things just got harder and harder.

"Hell on earth?" I offer, opening my eyes.

"In what way?"

I shake my head.

"Did something specific happen? To make you leave?" David pushes.

"I don't want to talk about it."

And I don't. If there's one thing I want to dwell on less than Alicia Baker, it's what happened back in February.

"Please?" David asks. "I want to know. I want to understand. Maybe I can help?"

And I don't quite know whether it's because I've said so much already I figure I've got nothing to lose, or because the clouds have moved across the moon, plunging the pool into darkness, or what. But for some reason, I start to speak.

LEO

It was a freezing-cold day in February, one of those gray wintry days when the sun never seems to make it quite high enough into the sky. But I didn't care.

Hannah Brennan had been giving me these looks for weeks. At first it was just a glance in the hallway or a smile across the cafeteria. I'd look behind me to check she wasn't aiming them at anyone else, but quickly I realized they were meant for me. And then they got longer, more seductive. One morning she full-on licked her lips at me. In class she'd been making excuses to talk to me. Asking to borrow paper and stuff, brushing her fingers against mine for a bit too long as I passed over an endless stream of pens and rulers.

I'd never really liked Hannah in particular, no more than any other girl at school. But over the past few weeks I'd begun to notice how nice her butt looked in her tight school skirt, spotted the lacy outline of her bra peeking through her blouse, thought about what it might be like to kiss her. She had a reputation for being a bit wild. There was this rumor about her and one of the student teachers, and another about her and Clare Conroy on the overnight school trip to London . . . Amber reckoned Hannah was a slut. But then that's Amber's standard opinion of anyone she doesn't like. Plus, there was something about Hannah, underneath all the sexiness and bravado: something soft and sweet.

Anyway, I was walking to Chemistry that day when Hannah appeared from nowhere and dragged me into this alcove by the art rooms. She pressed her body against mine, her tits rubbing against my chest, her cheap perfume filling my nostrils.

"Meet me after school," she said breathlessly.

"Where?"

"The woods. Four o'clock."

"But why?"

She smiled this insanely sexy smile.

"Come meet me and I'll show you why."

Then she was gone.

I spent the whole day debating whether or not to go meet her. In Chemistry I was certain I wouldn't. By English, I was certain I would. All day I flip-flopped back and forth. But when the bell rang for the end of the day and I found myself telling Amber I was staying behind to do some extra math work, I knew my mind was made up. I went to the handicapped bathroom near the staff room and checked my reflection. I sucked on two Polo mints at once. It was still only 3:40 p.m. Already the school felt empty. I wandered around the library, not really looking at the books, just killing time. At 3:55 I left and headed across the parking lot, toward the woods.

The woods was kind of an elaborate name for the tangle of bushes and trees at the back of the school. They were officially out of bounds. Not that anyone paid much attention. At lunch and break times they were populated by Alex Bonner and his gang. As I trudged through the undergrowth,

I spotted a used condom. I stepped around it and headed for the small clearing in the center, where I guessed Hannah would be waiting.

I arrived to find it empty. I checked the time. Four o'clock exactly. There was an old wooden crate lying on its side. I turned it up and sat down. Above me the daylight was melting away. It was 4:05. There was a crackle in the undergrowth. I stood. I realized my heart was beating crazy-fast. At first I assumed it was because I was nervous about Hannah, but then I realized it was not nerves, it was fear. Because all of a sudden something didn't feel right. The sound coming toward me was too loud, too heavy to be just one girl.

That's when I started to run.

"She's on the move," someone yelled. It was Robert Marriott, Alex Bonner's right-hand man.

"After her then!" Alex shouted.

I kept running. But I knew I couldn't keep going in a straight line, because if I did I was going to hit the fence surrounding the school. I needed to veer off to the left or right if I had any hope of getting out of there without them catching me. They were gaining on me, their whoops and hollers growing louder every second. From the sound of it, there were eight of them at least, maybe more. The whole crew. I took a sharp left, but I wasn't far enough ahead to do so without them noticing. I was a decent runner, but among the gang was Tyler Williams, who ran track for the county, and he was the one who gained on me, expertly weaving through the trees, negotiating my sudden twists and turns with ease. Suddenly, he was on me and yanked me backward, holding on to me until the taller, stronger boys were able to catch up with him and tackle me to the ground, removing my coat and tossing it aside. Among them was Alex. He took a spool of blue plastic string from his bag and cut off two lengths with a Swiss Army Knife. He passed a length to the boys at my feet and head. Their first two attempts to tie me up failed because I was struggling so much. But then Alex kicked me hard in the stomach. I folded up in pain. The two teams leaped into action, knotting the string tightly around my wrists and ankles as I writhed in the dirt. Alex stood over me.

"If you hadn't turned up today, we'd have left you alone," he said.

He was talking crap. He hadn't left me alone for a single day since I started that stupid school.

"But you pushed your luck," he continued. "You thought you could get your dirty tranny paws on my girlfriend, and for that you're going to have to pay."

"Girl—girlfriend?" I stammered.

"Wait a second, you didn't think Hannah was actually interested in you, did you? Sorry to disappoint, but she's into real men."

Behind him, the other boys sniggered.

"Let's go," he barked.

He strode off, leaving the four biggest boys to hoist me up. I squirmed as much as I could but the string only seemed to get tighter, rubbing painfully against my skin. I was marched back to the clearing and tied against the largest tree, the string digging into my middle.

"I think it's time you remembered what you really are," Alex said. He took the knife from his pocket and exposed the blade. It flashed in the light.

I decided to use the only weapon I had. I screamed. I'd spent so many years purposefully lowering my voice, I didn't even know whether I'd be able to do it and at first the only noise I made was a rattling squeal. But then it switched up and this sound emitted from me I had no idea I was capable of making. The boys backed away in shock.

"Tape her mouth shut!" Alex yelled. Tyler groped in his backpack before dashing over with a roll of duct tape. He ripped off a strip with his teeth and placed it over my mouth. For a second our eyes met. Tyler and I used to play together at preschool. I tried to scream again but the sound was muffled against the tape.

"Now, where was I?" Alex said.

I could see his breath in the air. He walked toward me, his eyes and the knife flashing. Why couldn't he just beat me up, I thought. I'd taken enough beatings to know I could handle them. What was another black eye? But beating me up would have been boring.

He took the knife and sliced through my sweatshirt from the neck downward, then lopped off the sleeves, taking care not to cut through the string holding me in place against the tree. The material fell away, landing at my feet. He did the same with my school shirt, leaving me wearing only my white T-shirt and binder. The cold hit me, so icy it stung.

Alex was cutting through my white T-shirt and I realized I was crying, hot tears running down my face. I closed my eyes. If they were going to do what I thought they were going to do next, I didn't want to see their faces. As I felt the fabric of my T-shirt fall away from my body I heard a collective jeer. Then Alex was sawing through my binder, the knife snagging on the thick material.

"Keep still," he demanded.

I squeezed my eyes shut, my body convulsing, no tears left.

"Alex Bonner!"

The voice of Mrs. Hale, the deputy head, was unmistakable.

The knife bounced off my knee as it dropped to the ground. But still I couldn't open my eyes. I kept them squeezed shut as I was untied, as the tape was carefully removed from my mouth, as Mrs. Hale forced my arms into her coat and radioed for assistance. I finally opened my eyes to be guided *back to school. The last thing I saw was my tattered clothes on the ground and the gleam of Alex's knife on top of them.*

I found out it was the janitor who alerted Mrs. Hale. He saw Alex and his gang heading to the woods and got suspicious. I was later told some of the boys tried to run but were quickly rounded up, along with Hannah.

I was given a uniform to wear from the lost-and-found box. Everything was too big. Mam arrived with Tia in tow to collect me. When Mrs. Hale realized we didn't have a car, she gave us a lift home. Mam didn't say a word, just wore this grim look on her face the whole journey.

I didn't speak for a week.

I never went back to Cloverdale School.

"So what happened? To Alex and everyone?" David whispers, breaking the silence.

I run both hands through my hair. It's the first time I've ever told anyone what happened all in one go like that. Even Jenny only got it in dribs and drabs and never the full story. I feel exhausted but oddly relieved.

"Well?" David prompts.

"They were suspended."

"That's it?"

"What else could they do? Expel ten kids at once?"

"So they made you leave instead?"

"They recommended I transfer elsewhere. For my own safety, they said. I reckon they just couldn't deal with the hassle. I had a tutor come around to my house for the rest of the school year. I'd have been quite happy going on like that but then I got the place at Eden Park and because it's such a good school everyone

204

made a big fuss about me taking it. It was supposed to be a fresh start. What a laugh, eh?" I say, my mouth curling into a fake smile.

"It's not too late. You can still come back," David says, his face hopeful.

"No I can't."

"But you can't leave now."

"Now is exactly when I've got to leave. Before more people find out."

"Alicia might not tell. You might be able to keep it secret after all."

I shake my head.

"You should call her," David says.

"You think I haven't tried already? Her phone's switched off. She doesn't even want to hear my voice, never mind actually talk to me."

There's a long pause.

"Can I ask you something?" David asks. "How did your mum react? When you first told her about wanting to live as a boy?"

"There was never really a moment like that," I say. "It was just always the way I was, from birth practically. She was dismissive at first, when I kept telling her they'd made some big mistake at the hospital. She would tell me to shut up and stuff, but eventually she must have got sick of me begging because when I was seven, she took me to the doctor. And when they took it seriously, and I started seeing my therapist, Jenny, and got referred to a specialist in London, she started taking it seriously too. For a while we were really close, but for the last few years we've just been clashing all the time. We can hardly be in the same room with each other these days without one of us losing it."

"You're lucky though," David says quietly. "To have her just accept you like that, even if you don't get on so well anymore."

I shake my head. "I don't know, lucky isn't the word that springs to mind when I think of Mam."

"And what about your sisters?"

"Amber's always been awesome. And Tia accepted it straight-away, faster than anyone maybe. She just treats me like her big brother now. I don't know if it'll always be that way though. She's not going to be seven forever and kids at her school have already started saying stuff . . ."

Silence. David chews his fingernail and watches me, like he's waiting for me to say something more.

"What are you going to do, Leo?" he asks eventually.

I don't have the words to answer.

DAVID

Leo walks me to the bus stop. The whole time my head is swimming.

Leo is like me. I am like him.

I want to ask him a million questions but don't know where to start. Away from the dark safety of the pool, Leo is silent again. I keep sneaking looks at him out of the corner of my eye, looking for the evidence I've missed, my eyes trailing up and down his body for clues. But he's still the same old Leo—gruff, grumpy, complicated.

By the time we reach the bus stop it's started to drizzle and there's a veil of gray mist in the air.

"Can we finally swap numbers?" I ask.

Leo frowns.

"Unless you want me to come knocking on your door every time you go missing in action," I say.

This does the trick and Leo reluctantly recites his number in a monotone. I immediately call it. Leo's phone lights up in his jeans pocket, his ringtone tinny and harsh.

"And now you have mine," I say. "In case you need me," I add meaningfully.

"Right," he mutters, not looking at me. "You all right to wait on your own?"

"Oh. Yeah, fine."

We stand awkwardly for a second, exposed under the bright lights of the bus stop. He turns to go.

"Wait," I blurt. "Will I see you again?"

The words seem silly the moment they leave my mouth—overly dramatic and sentimental, like lines from a movie or a play.

Leo prods an empty Coke can with his foot. The lights of an approaching bus blink into view. He jerks his head toward it.

"Good timing," he says.

"Yeah," I murmur, fishing around in my bag for bus fare.

"You can wait forever sometimes," Leo adds, his eyes fixed on the road.

I stick my hand out and the bus begins to slow down.

I take a deep breath and say what I want to say quickly.

"It would be a real shame, you know, if you didn't come back to school."

Leo doesn't say a word, aiming his gaze somewhere above my eyebrows.

"I'd really miss you," I add, immediately blushing.

Leo still doesn't reply.

The bus stops and the doors open. I climb on, dropping my

money into the slot. By the time I've settled into my seat, Leo has disappeared from view, swallowed up by Cloverdale Estate.

As the bus rumbles north through the city, the image of Leo lifting his T-shirt to reveal his chest binder plays on Repeat in my head. I am full of excitement and unanswered questions. Then it hits me. Finally, I am not alone. There is someone who understands *exactly* how I feel. The revelation makes me want to shout and sing.

"How was math?" Mum asks when I get home.

"Math was amazing," I reply, chucking myself on the sofa.

"Wow!" she says. "I never thought I'd hear you use the words 'math' and 'amazing' in the same sentence. Leo must be some teacher."

"He is," I say softly. "He's the best."

Mum beams and heats up my dinner in the microwave.

Before I go to bed I text him: *Will I see you at school?*

He doesn't reply. The idea of him not being there anymore makes me feel sick. He has to come back to school now, he just has to.

LEO

When I get home Tia is sitting cross-legged on the floor with Amber on the sofa behind her, her forehead creased with concentration as she tries to force Tia's wispy hair into a French braid. When she sees me, she raises a single eyebrow.

"What was that all about?" she asks.

"None of your beeswax."

"Leo doesn't want to talk. What a surprise," she says to no one in particular.

I ignore her, slumping down on the sofa beside her, exhausted.

She secures the bottom of Tia's braid with a rubber band and taps her on the shoulder.

"All done, T."

Tia beams up at her before crawling over to retrieve the remote control from under the coffee table.

"Where's Mam?" I ask.

"Where else? Down at the pub with Spike. They're celebrating."

"Celebrating? Celebrating what?" I ask.

"Spike moving in."

"Didn't he already do that?"

"Not officially apparently."

I pick up an old copy of *The Sun* from the arm of the sofa and pretend to read it. I can feel Amber watching me.

"Your whole life can't be one big secret, Leo," she says.

"Why not?" I reply, continuing to scan the printed words but taking none of them in.

"Because you're never going to enjoy any of it otherwise. You'll be too busy looking over your shoulder all the time, forever worried people are going to find out. It's no way to live."

"So what do you expect me to do?" I ask, lowering the paper. "Because telling the truth hasn't worked out too well for me so far."

"I don't know, Leo, but you could start by telling me the real reason I've been calling in sick for you since last Friday."

I toss the paper aside and stand up.

"I'm going out."

"But you've only just come in."

"Yeah, well, I'm not in the mood for company."

I leave the room, slamming the door shut behind me.

· · · · ·

Mam is at work on Tuesday so I spend the day on the sofa instead of hiding out at the pool. When Amber drops Tia at home from school I give in and agree to watch DVDs with her.

Anything that means I don't have to think. Because thinking means making decisions. And making decisions suggests you have choices. And right now choices are something I do not have. I made sure of that when I got in too deep with Alicia.

We're about halfway through *The Lion King* when my phone beeps. I leap on it, thinking, hoping it might be Alicia, but it's David.

I spoke to A. Everything's going to be OK. She's not going to tell!

I spoke to A? What is he talking about? Then I realize. A=Alicia.

I text back, my fingers moving fast over the keys.

Wot u mean? Wot u say 2 her?

A few seconds later David's reply comes through.

I asked her if she'd told anyone and she said no. She's not planning to either. Good news!!!

I slam my fists down on the sofa, stirring Tia from her Disney trance and making her jump. How dare David go sticking his nose into my business, talking to Alicia like that. What if someone overheard him?

"You okay, Leo?" Tia asks, her eyes wide and frightened.

"Yeah, T, fine. Sorry I scared you," I say absentmindedly.

My phone beeps again.

Are you still there? Aren't you pleased? She isn't going to tell! It can stay a secret!

He must really think it's that simple. Maybe telling him was a total mistake.

I head into the hallway, shutting the living room door behind me. I sit on the bottom step and dial David's number.

"Hi Leo?" he answers eagerly.

"What the hell did you think you were doing?" I ask. "Talking to Alicia like that?"

"What do you mean?" he asks, his voice small and wounded.

"You had no right to do that, David."

On the other side of the door I can hear Tia singing along to "Hakuna Matata," doing the different voices. I put my hand over my free ear and turn toward the wall in an attempt to block it out.

"But it's okay, she isn't going to tell anyone. She promised," David says. "I thought you'd be pleased."

I let out a low groan. "Just tell me what she said."

"When I asked her, she said she hadn't told anyone and had no plans to."

"That's it?"

"We didn't have much time. I practically had to stalk her to get her alone in the first place. Ruby and Becky barely leave her side."

I breathe out. So Alicia isn't going to talk. But I don't feel relief, not even close.

"Leo?" David says. "You still there?"

"Yeah."

"I thought you'd be glad."

"It's because she's ashamed," I say, my voice flat. "That's the only reason she's going to keep it secret."

"You don't know that—" David begins.

I cut him off. "Yes I do," I say firmly.

There's a pause. I can hear Phil barking in the background.

"I'm sorry I went behind your back," David says quietly.

"Look, I'm sorry I snapped at you," I say with a sigh. "I just don't like people sticking their noses in my business."

"I was just trying to help."

"I know, I know. I just . . ."

I don't know what to think. The only thing I'm certain of is that Alicia hates me. The fact she isn't planning to tell doesn't change that.

"Are you going to come back to school then?" David asks, his voice full of hope.

"Huh?"

"School? You've got to come back."

I rake my hands through my hair and try to visualize walking up the school driveway, eating lunch in the cafeteria. Sitting behind Alicia in English, seeing her in Gym. The first two I can just about handle. The third and fourth . . .

"You have your mock exams soon, don't you?" David adds. "And college applications to fill out? You can't miss all that, Leo, you know you can't."

I wish I hadn't told him my plans. I hate him for being right. Doing well on my exams is my ticket out of Cloverdale. If I do well, I can go on to the big anonymous college in the city, then go to university somewhere far, far away—Scotland or Cornwall or maybe even abroad, start again, fresh. But none of that is possible without my exams under my belt. And for that I have to go back to Eden Park School.

I have to face Alicia.

I let out a sigh. David leaps on it.

"Does that mean I'll see you at school tomorrow?" he asks.

"I don't know. Maybe. Look, I have to go."

I hang up, rest the back of my head against the wall, and close my eyes.

In the living room, Tia is still singing.

DAVID

The following morning I wait for Leo at the bus stop next to school. Opposite me, two buses are parked outside the gates, their engines gently humming, the drivers standing on the sidewalk, chatting and smoking cigarettes. There must be a trip somewhere today.

I check the time on my cell. The first bell rings and I watch as the playground gradually empties. I can just make out Essie and Felix, Essie's newly dyed red hair practically glowing.

I peer down the road looking for Leo's bus, enjoying the sunshine on my face and the brilliant blue sky above me. The morning feels fresh, full of optimism, and I can't help but feel hopeful on Leo's behalf that things are going to be okay.

Finally the bus rumbles into view. I can't see Leo among the passengers getting off and for a moment I'm afraid he's not coming back to school today after all, but then I spot him sloping down the stairs, the last person to get off. He looks tired. His hair is matted, like he's just tumbled out of bed, and he has dark circles that almost resemble bruises, purple and painful-looking, beneath his eyes. When he sees me he frowns.

"What are you doing here?" he asks, shifting his backpack from one shoulder to the other.

"I thought you might appreciate some moral support," I say brightly.

"I'm fine on my own, thanks," he says, squinting in the sun, using his hand as a shield.

"I know you are," I say. "I just wanted to see you, and say hey."

"Well, hey," he replies, rolling his eyes.

In the distance the second bell is ringing.

He sighs. "Come on then."

We cross the road and go through the gates, making our way across the deserted playground.

He pushes open the main door and there's an awkward moment when I realize he's holding it open for me.

"You coming in or what?" he asks as I hesitate.

"Of course," I say, ducking under his arm.

Leo takes an immediate left, toward the year-eleven homerooms.

"If you need me today, for anything, just text me," I say after him.

He shakes his head slightly and keeps walking.

I stop off to use the bathroom and by the time I arrive at my homeroom, everyone else is leaving. Harry pushes past me, crushing me against the door frame. When Mr. Collins sees me he frowns and makes a big show of making a black late mark next to my name in the register. I mouth my apology and head straight to Biology.

Essie and Felix are already there, sitting side by side at our usual work station, their heads bowed together.

"Hey," I say, dragging up a stool.

"David, we've been looking for you!" Essie says, sitting up straight. "Where were you this morning?"

"Stuff to do," I say, pulling my backpack into my lap and taking out my pencil case.

"Does that mean you haven't heard?" Felix asks.

"Heard what?"

The two of them exchange wide-eyed looks.

"About Leo," Essie says.

"What are you talking about?" I ask.

"Wait, you seriously don't know?" Felix says.

I glance around me. The entire class is animated, their loud chatter punctuated with occasional gasps or squeals of laughter. I turn back to Essie and Felix.

"What exactly is going on?"

"Look," Felix says, clearing his throat. "It appears Leo Denton isn't quite who he says he is."

"What do you mean?" I ask, putting my hand on the bench to steady myself.

"Becky Somerville tracked down a kid from Cloverdale School on Facebook," Essie says. "A cousin of her cousin or something, and they told Becky exactly why Leo left."

I swallow. I don't need Essie to say anything else.

"There he is!" Lexi Taylor shouts, pointing out the window. Half of the class sprints over to join her.

"Don't you mean, there *she* is?" Tom quips to a chorus of cruel laughter.

I join their scrum, pushing my way to the front. Beside me, my classmates' noses are practically pressed against the glass, their faces glowing with excitement and scandal.

Below us, oblivious to his gaping audience, Leo is making his way toward the two buses I spotted earlier.

Dr. Spiers enters the room, barking at us to come away from the window and sit down. Reluctantly, we return to our stools.

I sit down, trembling. I pull out my phone. Maybe if I'm quick enough I can warn Leo. I'm halfway through composing my text when Dr. Spiers's hand slams down on the desk, inches from my hand.

"Give it here."

"But, sir, it's an emergency."

"No texting in class. No excuses. Now hand it over."

"Please, sir," I begin to beg.

"Give me the phone, Mr. Piper," Dr. Spiers says in a bored voice, his arm outstretched. "Before I lose my temper."

With my pinkie finger, I manage to press Send on the incomplete text before placing the phone in Dr. Spiers's open palm. I watch as he locks it in his desk drawer.

"You can collect it after school," he says.

I know it is useless to even try to argue with him.

As Dr. Spiers starts the class, I close my eyes and find myself doing something I haven't done since I was a little kid and really wanted a Barbie Dream House for my birthday.

I pray.

I pray for Leo.

LEO

I arrive at homeroom to find the classroom empty except for Mrs. Craig, who instructs me to join my classmates outside. As I make my way back across the playground I remember taking home a letter about the trip, weeks ago, back in October. It's to some gallery in town—a "treat" before we have to knuckle down to study for our exams.

Ahead of me, I can see a line of kids waiting to board a pair of buses. I slow down. It looks like my whole year. Great. I look for Alicia. I can't help it; my eyes seek her out before my brain can stop them. The moment I see her it's like my heart has jumped into my mouth. She's standing with Ruby, her lips pursed and her arms folded across her chest, her mass of black curls held off her face with a silver headband.

I hang back, not wanting her to spot me, and wait to see which bus she boards before choosing the other one.

I'm the last to get on, Mr. Toolan ticking my name off a list as I climb up the steps.

"Welcome back, Leo," he says. "All better now?"

"Yes, thanks, sir," I say, not looking at him.

I hesitate, searching for a seat alone.

"Come along, Leo, we haven't got all day," Mr. Toolan says. "There are plenty of places to sit."

Reluctantly I choose a seat near the front, next to a girl from my French class. Serena, I think her name is. She's quiet in class, only speaking when asked to by Madame Fournier, so I'm pretty confident she won't try to talk to me. As I sit down, her eyes bulge at me before she looks away again. Unable to fit my backpack under the seat in front, I stand up and shove it in the overhead rack. As I tuck in the straps I can feel Serena's eyes on me again, only she's too quick and turns her head to look out of the window before I can catch her in the act. I glance toward the front of the bus. Mr. Toolan is talking to the driver. I sit back down to discover Serena has twisted her body away from mine, one leg crossed over the other, so her back is practically facing me. What is her problem?

The other bus pulls out first, passing us on the left. I scan the windows for Alicia, but the glass is tinted and all I can make out are murky shadows.

My phone vibrates in my pocket. I take it out. It's a text from David, checking up on me I expect.

Leo, whatever you do, don't get on the bus. I think

I stare at it. The message just stops there. He thinks what? Maybe he worked out the trip would mean seeing Alicia and he wanted to warn me. Too late.

As our bus eases its way through the traffic, I try to switch off. I just need to focus on getting through today. I'll worry about tomorrow when it comes. One step at a time. Once we arrive at the gallery, hopefully I'll be able to slip off, keep out of everyone's way until it's time to go home again. I begin to feel a bit better.

Then I hear it.

Megan.

My eyes snap open and I listen carefully. I tell myself I must have imagined it, but I'm not convinced. I glance at Serena. She's wearing a sugary-pink version of the headphones Alicia wears. She's listening to poppy stuff, the sort of thing Tia likes to sing along to. I wish I had an iPod and headphones of my own to drown it out.

I shut my eyes again but this time I can't ignore the sick feeling in my stomach.

· · · · ·

We arrive at the gallery about half an hour later. It looks like a giant sugar cube: square and white and modern. As we're herded off the buses, I come face-to-face with Alicia. She's been crying, I'm certain. Her eyes are red, her face blotchy. She meets my eyes for a second. They flash with panic, then look away again. I want to go over and hold her, make it okay, only I know I can't.

We're being divided into four groups. My heart sinks when I realize I'm in the same one as Alicia. I consider joining one of the other groups but Ms. Jennings has her eye on me.

We're led into the first gallery by our tour guide, an animated

Chinese guy with an American accent. The room is long and white and brightly lit. The paintings on the wall are massive and just the kind of art I hate: the sort that looks like a toddler has done it. I try to listen to what the guide is telling us, anything to distract me from the fact that a tearstained Alicia is standing only a few feet away from me.

"Freak."

The delivery drips with venom and even though I don't know for certain, I'm pretty sure it's directed at me. I try to remain calm and fight the urge to turn around, to find out who the voice belongs to and make them pay for it.

In front of me, the tour guide waves his hands around as he talks about the inspiration behind the painting before us. I don't care, it just looks like a load of red and blue paint chucked on a canvas to me. I try to subtly ease my way to the front of the group, away from the voice. All the time panic is rising inside me. Because all this can only mean one thing—Alicia told and my secret is out.

She said she wouldn't tell. She promised. She lied.

"Tranny."

This time I know who the voice belongs to. Miss Loudmouth herself, Becky Somerville. I whirl around to face her. She smiles smugly.

"What did you call me?" I demand, squaring up against her.

"Tranny," she replies innocently. "I'm so pleased you answered to it."

She smiles sweetly as she notices my clenched fists.

"You're not going to hit a girl are you? Wait, silly me, I'm forgetting it's a fair match. Just go ahead. We'll see how long you last at Eden Park."

I take a deep breath and release my fists. God, I hate her.

Alicia reaches out and pulls Becky back. Becky turns and scowls at her.

"What? She deserves it, after what she did to you," Becky says, putting extra emphasis on *she*. "She's nothing but a dirty lying pervert."

The kids surrounding her make noises in agreement. Their faces are blurring. I feel light-headed.

"So Alicia?" a kid named Charlie says. "I never had you down as a lesbian."

"Oh fuck off," Alicia says.

I've never heard Alicia swear before. It's one of the things I like most about her, that she doesn't feel the need to show off like that, not that she's showing off now; anything but, her face pale with shame.

"She's not a lesbian, you moron," Ruby says angrily. "It's not her fault. Leo, or should I say Megan, totally tricked her."

"Shush!" Ms. Jennings says, glaring at us.

Ruby pauses before lowering her voice.

"Alicia is the victim here."

"Shut up, Ruby," Alicia says.

"But it's true!"

"I said shut up!"

The whole exchange seems to happen in stereo, and I'm

225

certain the walls are starting to spin. I want to scream and shout at them, go crazy and lash out, but I can't. Because my brain is consumed by one single thought.

Alicia isn't who I thought she was. She's not special. She's just like all the rest, just like Hannah.

I need to get away. Now.

The tour guide moves on to the next painting. The moment Ms. Jennings's head is turned, I duck behind another school group before turning and walking straight out of the gallery, as fast as I can.

LEO

It's nearly two when I get back to Cloverdale. It took three buses to get home from the gallery. I didn't have enough money for the third bus so I had to sneak on through the rear doors.

The whole way home my brain is a jumble of thoughts: images of Alicia colliding with flashbacks to the woods, the gallery. It's never going to change. As long as there is a chance of being found out, I'll never be safe, I'll always be waiting. I need to get out of here, and fast.

Spike's car is missing from outside the house; he must be at work for once. As I get closer I can hear the faint roar of the vacuum cleaner.

Mam is home.

I consider turning back but I'm starving and I know that Mam and Spike finally went to the supermarket the other day so the fridge has food in it for the first time in weeks. Plus I know Mam has a shift at the Laundromat at three. If I'm quick, once she's gone I can be out of the house without running into Amber or Tia.

An unwanted picture of Tia realizing I'm gone floats into my head, her lower lip wobbling, her eyelashes wet with the beginnings of tears. I shove it out.

As I put my key in the lock, I hear the vacuum shut off. I close the door behind me and take off my blazer, flinging it over the banister. It lands with the embroidered crest facing up. "Fairness and Initiative"? Give me a break.

I enter the living room. Mam is standing with her hands on her hips, her body angled to the door like she's been waiting for me. The TV, some American reality show, is on Mute.

"And what do you think you're doing here at this time of day?" she demands, pointing at the clock.

She's wearing an old pair of jeans and a faded T-shirt of Spike's, and she has a tea towel wrapped around her head bandanna-style. I prefer her like this, when she's natural. She looks younger and prettier, not that she'd believe you if you told her.

"Well?" she says, following me through to the kitchen.

I open the bread box and take out two slices of bread.

"Half day," I say, grabbing a knife.

"Liar," she replies, not missing a beat.

Slowly I turn to face her.

"You're a liar, Leo," she continues. "Barefaced. I got off the phone with your school a little while ago. According to them you'd done a runner."

"So? What do you care anyway?" I say.

"I can't handle that drama again. No way."

I drop the knife with a clatter and turn around again.

"What drama? All you did was come to one meeting and sign a couple of forms. Jenny sorted the rest out."

"Oh sorry, I forgot, let's bow down to Saint Jenny!" Mam says, raising her hands in the air. "With her fancy university degrees in how to be patronizing. She talks to me like I'm about five years old half the time."

"And why do you reckon that is?"

Mam comes up close so her face is only inches from mine and I can make out the pores on her nose and cheeks.

"You think you're so clever, don't you?" she hisses. "That you know exactly what goes on behind the scenes of everyone's life."

I turn my back on her and march over to the fridge. I take out mayo, ham, and tomatoes, slamming them down on the counter.

"Because you don't, Leo," she continues. "You don't know the half of it."

"I'll tell you what I do know," I say, spooning a thick layer of mayo onto each slice of bread, my hands trembling. "I know that at age fifteen, my life, past, present, and future, was, is, and always will be a pile of shit."

I slap down the ham and start to saw at the tomatoes but the knife I'm using is too dull and I end up with a load of mush. I scrape it onto my sandwich anyway, not caring what it looks like, even what it tastes like anymore.

"That's not my fault, Leo!" Mam shouts. "I know you like to

think everything is, and maybe some bits are, but you cannot blame me for every single bad thing that's ever happened to you!"

There's a beat before I burst into tears.

I think they shock me more than they do Mam. I'm not a crier, even as a kid I hardly ever cried. I'd get angry, scream, throw stuff, but I wouldn't cry. And these days I'm Leo Denton, master of the poker face. But right now I'm powerless to stop the tears from flowing and all I can do is stand there as they rock my body.

"What do you want me to do, Leo?" Mam asks desperately. "What the hell do you expect me to do?"

I can't catch my breath to reply.

"I told you this was going to be hard, Leo. Right at the beginning when you told me how you felt about wanting to be a boy, I warned you, I prepared you the best I could. And I've stood by you, Leo, I have, but there's only so much I can do. I can't turn back time and I can't magic things better. Believe me, if I could I would have done it years ago."

I nod and continue to gasp for air.

"Jesus, if you don't even tell me what's going on, how can I possibly help you?" she asks, pacing back and forth.

I want to tell her but no words form.

She looks up at the clock and swears under her breath.

"Shit, I've got to go."

She rips the tea towel off her head and chucks it on the table, and pulls on the polyester tunic she wears for work over her jeans and T-shirt.

I'm still crying. All I want her to do is stop and hug me, make it okay, just like she used to once upon a time. But she's applying lipstick, refusing to look at me.

"Look, you've just got to pull yourself together, Leo," she says, grabbing her handbag and keys. "And clean this place up while you're at it."

A few seconds later the front door slams shut and I'm alone.

I throw my sandwich at the wall. It hits the tiles with a splat, the cheap white bread sticking for a moment before the whole mess slides down the wall and into the sink.

My tears replaced with anger, I turn and charge up the stairs. I go into my room first, flinging clothes into an old sports bag. I do up the zipper and haul it downstairs. I return to the kitchen and check the tin. It's got less than a fiver in it but I pocket it anyway. I need more though, much more. I head back upstairs to Mam's room. The curtains are still closed and the bed is unmade. The room smells of sleep and stale perfume. I pull open her drawers. They're a mess, a jumble of underwear and tights, but I'm certain Mam must keep a bit of cash somewhere in here. I just need enough to get a train or bus that will put a decent distance between me and Cloverdale. I'll worry about what to do next when I get there. I kneel down and investigate the very bottom drawer. It's full of odds and ends: receipts, batteries, scraps of wrapping paper, old birthday cards. But no cash. I yank at the drawer in frustration. It comes all the way out and I drop it in surprise, trapping my finger beneath it. Cursing, I pick it up and try to slide it back in. It's heavy though and I have trouble lining it up with the runners.

It's then I notice the glint of gold.

I place the drawer on the bed and lie down on my belly. I reach into the gap where the drawer fitted and quickly realize the drawers are not as deep as the frame. My left hand gropes about until it strikes something metal. I pull it out. It's a rectangular box, red with gold trim. It's got dents on each side, as if it's been dropped or thrown on more than a few occasions. I place it on my lap and lift the lid.

The box contains mostly photographs. Quite a few of them are the ones I begged Mam to take down off the walls when I transitioned from Megan to Leo: Amber and me as babies wearing matching pink onesies; the two of us as bridesmaids in peach satin dresses, Amber beaming while I scowled, hating every second; the four of us—me, Amber, Mam, and baby Tia, sitting on the sofa, Tia screaming her head off, the rest of us laughing. Looking at them now, it's like I'm looking at the ghost of some girl I used to know. I put the photos aside.

There are the bracelets we wore as babies in the hospital, tiny things, not much bigger than the circumference of my thumb; our baby-size handprints—red paint on white paper; locks of our hair taped to a piece of cardboard. Beneath these things are several bits of paper. I unfold the first. It's Tia's birth certificate, listing Tony the twit as her dad. Poor Tia.

I realize I've never actually seen my birth certificate before, I've never needed to. Quickly, I unfold the next piece of paper. It's mine.

I wince as I read my birth name, Megan Louise Denton, and see my sex listed as female, there in black-and-white. My eyes float down the page. Then they stop. Something is not right.

My father is listed as Jonathan Denton. Jonathan? But my dad's name is Jimmy. Jimmy Denton.

Then it dawns on me.

I've always assumed Jimmy was short for James. Never Jonathan.

I've been looking for the wrong man.

DAVID

The school day ends just as the year-eleven kids are returning. I look for Leo but can't make him out from the steady stream of students pouring off the buses.

I head to the science lab to retrieve my phone from Dr. Spiers. Before handing it over he insists on lecturing me on the general evils of cell phones. When he finally winds down I have to fight the urge to snatch it from his hands. The moment I'm out in the hallway I check for text messages from Leo. Nothing. I call his number but it goes straight through to voice mail. Unsure what to say, I hang up.

"Sorry I'm late," I say to Mum, as I get into the car.

"No problem," Mum replies, starting the engine.

As we drive past the bus stop, I look for Leo but the shelter is empty.

Livvy twists around in her seat.

"Oh my God, did you hear about that boy in year eleven?" she asks.

"What boy?" I say carefully.

"You know! The one who got kicked out of Cloverdale!"

"Cloverdale? Isn't that your friend, David?" Mum asks, eyeing me through the rearview mirror. "Leo?"

Livvy stares at me, disgusted. "You're friends with Leo Denton?"

"I didn't know he got *kicked out* of Cloverdale," Mum says, frowning.

"He didn't," I say, anger rising in my chest on Leo's behalf. "It wasn't his fault. They made him leave for his own safety."

"And ever since he's been at Eden Park he's been pretending to be a boy, but he's actually a girl named Megan!" Livvy finishes, triumphant.

Mum raises her eyebrows. "Is this true, David?"

Half of me wants to defend Leo and present his side of the story, but the other half knows I'm in dangerous territory if I do. I let that half win.

"How am I supposed to know?" I snap. "We're not even real friends. He just helps me with math, that's all. It's probably a load of made-up garbage."

I angle my body so I'm looking out the window, but I can feel Mum's eyes on me. I'm thankful when she doesn't say anything more on the subject and turns up the radio instead.

. . . . .

It's just after dinner. I'm lying on my bed stalking Zachary's Facebook page on my laptop when my cell buzzes. I lunge for

235

it, desperate for it to be Leo. I let out a sigh of relief when I see his name blinking on the screen. His text is short.

Meet me @ the pool. 8 p.m.

Itching for more details, I ring him back but it goes straight through to voice mail again, so I text him: *Okay.*

I tell Mum I'm going over to Essie's, promising to be back by nine-thirty. She frowns but agrees I can go, providing I text her when I arrive, and when I'm leaving to come back. Before I go I nab the flashlight we keep for emergencies from under the sink, slipping it into my backpack.

As I sit on the bus, I try to think of what Leo could possibly want. And while I hope he's okay, I can't help but feel flattered that I'm the one he's called on in his hour of need.

A distant church bell is striking eight as I squeeze through the hole in the fence outside the pool. I flick on the flashlight, comforted by its fat beam, and start to pick my way across the rubble.

I discover Leo sitting on the lowest of the three diving boards, his legs dangling off the edge.

"Hi!" I call, heading toward him.

Leo raises his hand in silent greeting. I climb up the steps and crawl along the diving board on my hands and knees, the flashlight wedged beneath my chin. Leo turns and smirks as he watches my cautious progress.

"You all right there?" he asks, the amusement in his voice clear.

I ignore him as I shift position so I'm sitting on the edge of the board beside him, our shoulders touching.

I switch off the flashlight and place it behind me. I dare to shimmy forward, curling my fingers so they're gripping the underside of the board and trying not to fixate on the distance between me and the rock-solid surface of the empty pool below.

Leo fidgets beside me, a bundle of nervous energy.

"Thanks for coming," he says.

"Anytime," I murmur, watching his knees jiggle up and down in the moonlight. This is not the Leo I am used to. The Leo I know is steady and solid.

"So what's up?" I ask, confused.

Leo turns to face me. His eyes won't stay still in their sockets.

"I found him," he says.

"Found who?" I ask.

"My dad. Jimmy."

I let out an excited gasp.

"That's great! But how? Did he get in contact?"

"Not quite."

"Then how?"

"What's the name Jimmy short for?" Leo asks.

"James," I reply automatically.

"Yeah, but it's also short for Jonathan, did you know that? All these years I've been Googling the wrong man."

"You're joking!"

"Nope. I found my birth certificate and there it was in black-and-white. I went straight to the library, typed his name into Google, and there he was, fourth entry down. Jonathan Denton & Co. Carpenters, in Tripton-on-Sea."

"And you're sure it's the right one?"

"His picture is on the Web site. It's him all right."

I take my iPhone from my pocket and type *Jonathan Denton carpenter* into Google. Seconds later I'm staring at a picture of Leo's dad. He's sporting a red sweatshirt with *Jonathan Denton & Co.* emblazoned across the front and wearing the same crinkled smile from the photo Leo showed me that day in the library. Leo leans in to look.

"Yep, that's him," he says, his voice glittering with pride. "That's my dad."

"Where's Tripton-on-Sea?" I ask. "I've never heard of it."

"Kent. Some seaside place. Which means my auntie Kerry was actually right, he did go to the coast after leaving Cloverdale."

"So now what?" I ask.

"What do you think? I'm going to go find him."

"You can't just turn up on his doorstep."

"Why not?" Leo asks, clearly annoyed that I've dared question his distinct lack of a plan.

"Well, maybe you should call him first? Warn him?"

"Warn him? Thanks a lot."

"I didn't mean it like that."

Leo shakes his head firmly. "Nah, this has to be done face-to-face. It could be any old crackpot on the phone, but if he sees me in the flesh, he'll know for sure I'm his. You said yourself how much we look alike."

"I guess," I murmur, unconvinced.

"Don't you see?" Leo says, shifting his position so he's facing me side-on, making the entire diving board wobble. "It was almost like it was meant to be. I'm on the verge of running away to God knows where, and then I find my birth certificate and discover exactly where my dad is. I mean, I'm not usually into this kind of thing, fate and crap like that, but it has to mean something, right?"

"Wait, you were planning to run away? Without telling me?"

"You seriously expect me to stick around after what happened at school? In case you missed it, everyone knows, David. It's like Cloverdale all over again."

"But you can't go, not now."

"Are you not listening to me? I'm not setting foot in Eden Park School ever again."

"It wasn't Alicia who told," I say.

Leo flinches at the mention of her name.

"What?"

"It was Becky. She was the one who blabbed. Her cousin's cousin goes to Cloverdale or something."

Leo is silent.

"So maybe you don't have to go away after all," I add.

He rakes his hands through his hair.

"It doesn't matter who told, David. You didn't see Alicia's face today, how ashamed she was. She hates me."

"But Leo—" I begin.

He cuts me off.

"Look, it doesn't make any difference, none of that does now. What matters is that I've found my dad, which is where you come in."

"Me?"

"Yeah. Look, the thing is, I was wondering whether I could

maybe borrow some money? Just a loan, until I get settled in Tripton."

The thought of Leo leaving feels like a sharp slap across my face.

"David?" Leo prompts.

I realize I haven't answered him.

"Of course," I say, recovering myself. "How much do you need?"

"Well, the train fare down to Tripton is seventy-nine pounds. Plus I guess I'll need a bit extra, so I'm not just turning up empty-handed. Two hundred pounds maybe? Just to keep me going for a while until I sort myself out."

I take a deep breath. Although Leo is right beside me, I can feel him slipping through my fingers. His head is already in this Tripton place, filled with thoughts of the mysterious Jonathan Denton.

"I'll tell you what I can do," I say.

Leo nods eagerly.

"I'll lend you the money on one condition. That you let me come with you."

Leo's face crumples into a deep frown. "What?"

"Well, you can't go alone."

"And how'd you work that one out?"

"Because. You'll need moral support."

"I'll be fine," Leo says, folding his arms.

"I'm not saying you won't. But you can't be too careful. I mean, what if your dad turns out to be a crazy ax murderer or something?"

"He won't. He's my dad."

"But what if something else happens, if things don't quite go to plan," I say quietly. "You'll need a friend with you."

"I can handle it," he says firmly. "Whatever happens, I'm ready for it."

"That may be the case, but my offer is final," I reply. "If you're going, I'm coming too, the end."

He stares at me. "You're serious."

I nod solemnly. "I want to be there for you, Leo. Please let me."

I reach for his hand. Leo hesitates before letting me take it.

"Please?" I repeat.

There's a pause. He lets out a huge sigh.

"Okay, but while we're there we follow my rules."

"Fine."

"And you won't tell anyone."

"Not even Essie and Felix?"

"Especially not Essie and Felix. This is between us, okay?"

"Deal. So when do you want to go?"

"Is Friday too soon?"

DAVID

"You want us to do what?" Essie demands, her image slightly jerky on the computer screen.

It's Thursday. The screen in front of me settles to reveal Essie and Felix sitting on Felix's bed. Felix is sitting cross-legged with Essie behind him, her chin resting on his shoulder, her legs wrapped around his torso and her arms dangling down over his shoulders. It reminds me of a wildlife documentary I once watched about frogs mating.

I sigh and repeat my instructions once more.

"If my mum calls either of you for any reason this weekend, I need you to cover for me and say I'm with you but can't get to the phone right now. Then call me and I'll call her back. And if anyone at school asks about me tomorrow, I'm at home sick. Apart from Livvy. Whatever you do, do not speak to Livvy."

"But why?" Felix asks, his voice slightly out of sync with his lips. "Where on earth are you going?"

"I'm sworn to secrecy."

"By whom?"

"I can't tell you."

"But we tell each other everything, David," Essie wails. "You know stuff about me no human being should know about anyone."

"I know," I say reluctantly. "And I'm sorry. I just can't tell you this."

"You're not going to meet someone off the Internet, are you?" Essie asks.

"Look, if I tell you where I'm going, will you stop asking questions and just trust me?"

"Yes," Felix says, at the exact same time as Essie says, "No." Felix pokes her.

I take a deep breath.

"I'm going to a town called Tripton-on-Sea for the weekend. But that's all you're getting."

"Tripton-on-Sea? Isn't that some seaside place in Kent?" Felix says, pushing his glasses up on his nose. Trust Felix to have heard of it.

"Are you positive you're not meeting someone dodgy off the Internet?" Essie asks. "Because, I'm sorry, but this has dirty weekend written all over it."

"Look, I'll have my cell with me," I say. "I'll send you a text every now and again to reassure you I'm alive."

Essie continues to frown.

"And if you don't get a text, you have my permission to call me," I add.

"How very generous," she says huffily.

"Ess, please?"

"Okay, okay," she says. "But if you don't answer, we're coming to find you."

. . . . .

The next morning Mum drops Livvy and me off at school as usual. Livvy kisses Mum on the cheek before darting off to join her friends.

"Remember, I'm staying at Felix's until Sunday," I say, as I clamber out of the car.

I've told my parents that Felix, Essie, and I are working intensively on a science project all weekend.

"Are you sure Felix's parents don't mind having you for two whole nights?" Mum asks.

"I told you, no."

"Do you want your dad to pick you up on Sunday?"

"No!" I cry.

She looks up at me in faint alarm.

"No," I repeat, softly this time. "Felix's dad has already said he'll drop me back on Sunday afternoon."

"Okay, then. Well, have fun. And don't let Felix's mother force-feed you too much quinoa or goji berries or whatever superfood she's got her cupboards stuffed with these days."

"I won't. Bye, Mum."

I shut the door and watch her speed off.

I drop down to tie my shoelaces and then, instead of going

through the school gates, I take a sharp right, keeping close to the outside fence.

In the distance I can hear the bell ringing for homeroom. I take it as my cue to break into a light jog. Two minutes later I reach the relative safety of the bushes that mark one corner of the huge fence that encloses the school. I poke my head inside first, to check if the hiding place is empty. The bushes provide a hollow space in the center popular with couples, offering both privacy (to a degree) and shelter, as long as you don't mind sharing it with at least six other people at a time. It smells of cigarette smoke and cheap aftershave and the ground is littered with cigarette butts and candy wrappers. I set my backpack down and remove my blazer. I take a navy hoodie out and pull it on over my school shirt. I remove my school shoes and replace them with sneakers before stuffing them, along with my tie and rolled-up blazer, into my backpack. Next I take out my phone and, with suddenly shaking fingers, I dial the school. I select Option Two to report an absence and wait. There are a few bleeps before I'm put through to Ms. Clay, in the school office.

"Hello, this is Jo Piper and I'd like to report my son, David Piper, absent today," I say, just like I practiced last night. I wince, steeling myself for Ms. Clay's immediate suspicion but she simply thanks me for calling and hangs up.

I exit the bushes as discreetly as possible before legging it down the road, not daring to look back. I only begin to relax when I'm safely aboard the bus heading toward the train station.

When I arrive, Leo is waiting under the clock in the entrance hall. He looks nervous, glancing about the place like he's got a bomb strapped to his chest.

As I get closer, he notices me approaching and gives me a stiff nod.

"Morning, road-trip buddy," I say.

"Morning," he murmurs back, his eyes refusing to latch on to mine.

As we line up to buy our tickets, Leo doesn't say a word, just keeps his eyes fixed on the departure boards overhead, his eyes wide and unblinking.

Our assigned seats are at the front of the train.

"You do know we're only going for two nights, don't you?" Leo says as we walk along the platform, pointing at my bulging backpack. "What the hell have you got in there? A dead body?"

I look over my shoulder and lower my voice.

"It's girl stuff," I whisper.

"Girl stuff?" he repeats.

"You don't mind, do you? It's just that I thought this might be an ideal opportunity, seeing as there's pretty much zero chance of me bumping into anyone I know."

"Opportunity for what exactly?"

"Some real-life experience," I say.

I've been reading about real-life experience on the Internet. Sometimes the specialist doctors won't let you start taking medication until you can prove you're able to live in the world in your chosen gender. And so far I haven't even left the house as a girl. But now I have an entire weekend ahead of me in a

246

town where no one knows me. It's too perfect an opportunity to pass up.

"I thought you of all people would be supportive," I say.

Leo frowns. "I am, I just don't want us drawing too much attention to ourselves this weekend. It's supposed to be about my dad, remember."

"And it will be, I promise," I say. "I've just brought casual stuff with me. I'm not going to be strutting around Tripton dressed up like a drag queen if that's what you're worried about."

He continues to frown but doesn't say anything more and I persuade him to go ahead and find our seats. I board the train at the back and locate the nearest bathroom. I look both ways, relieved to find my fellow passengers busy reading newspapers or talking on cell phones. No one seems to be paying attention to the skinny boy hovering outside the bathroom.

As the train begins to chug out of the station, I press the button and the bathroom door slides open. I step inside and lock the door, checking it three times. I check the floor is clean before setting my bag on it, pull down my pants, and sit on the toilet seat. The metal is cold against my butt. I try to take a pee but it's as if my insides are seized up with nerves and nothing happens. I give up and take off my sneakers, pants, and socks. I take out a pair of tights from my bag, gathering them up in my hands before smoothing them over my legs and pulling them up high, over my belly button. I fish out a bra and fasten it around my rib cage, twisting it to the front and hooking the straps over my shoulders, adjusting it so the padding I've carefully stitched into each cup lies flat against my chest.

I take out a red shirtdress with a belt and buttons up the front, another reject from Essie (from her very brief preppy stage), and pull it over my head. It's a bit rumpled from where it's been rolled up in the bottom of my bag but it will have to do. I ease my feet into a pair of gray Ugg boots, the only feminine footwear I could find in my size.

I balance my makeup bag on the edge of the sink. The mirror is made from that misty sort of glass that might not be glass at all, the sort you find in scruffy public bathrooms and that makes your reflection look like a ghost. The cloudy glass softens everything so I'm just a series of blobby shapes—a dark blob for hair, a red blob for dress, a white blob for face. To apply my makeup I use the tiny mirror in my compact, holding it up as I put on foundation, concealer, blush, and mascara. Every so often the train sways violently from side to side. Reluctantly, I veto eyeliner.

Finally I kneel down to retrieve my wig from its netted bag. The train lurches suddenly and I have to put my hand out and hold on to the rail above my head to keep from pitching forward. I lower the wig onto my head. And it feels different somehow, putting it on here, rather than in the privacy of my bedroom. It's not just dress up anymore; this is real.

I bundle up my boy clothes and shove them into my bag. I inspect myself in my compact and realize I have no idea whether I look like a girl or not. I have stared at myself in the mirror so hard and for so many hours at a time, I no longer know for sure which features are masculine and which aren't. I wish I could see myself as a stranger might. I think of Leo, all the way in coach A, and wonder how I'll look to him.

There's a sharp rap on the door, making me jump.

"Nearly finished!" I call. My voice sounds like it doesn't belong to me.

I take one last look in the mirror, at the ghost girl looking back.

Another rap on the door, more urgent this time. I pick up my bag and open the door. It's a young woman with a toddler under one arm and a big pink changing bag hooked over the other. I don't meet her eyes as I squeeze past. On the way to my seat I keep waiting for people to notice my bigger-than-average feet, my jawline, the false shine of my wig, anything that might give me away. I accidentally knock a man's arm with my bag and he glances up, briefly annoyed, only for his face to relax into forgiveness when it latches on to mine.

"Sorry—sorry," I stammer.

"No problem, dear." He smiles, returning to his newspaper.

As I continue through the train, my palms are sweating and my heart is going crazy, pounding so hard I can't help but think of those old-fashioned cartoons, the ones where you can actually see the character's heart booming out of their chest. But all the nerves and fear are suddenly canceled out by blinding happiness.

Dear. That man, a complete stranger, called me dear.

I finally reach coach A. It's the designated quiet coach, the only seats they had left. I creep past businessmen and women tapping away at laptops or dozing. At the far end of the coach,

I spot Leo's sandy head, facing away from me. We have table seats. Opposite, an elderly couple is bent over the crossword.

As I slide into my seat beside him, Leo looks up and sort of does a double take. I feel my cheeks begin to burn all over again.

"Do I look okay?" I whisper.

"Sure," he whispers back, before shutting his eyes.

For the rest of the journey, Leo sleeps or at least pretends to. He looks peaceful and younger somehow. I try to read for a bit but keep reading the same paragraph over and over again.

Eventually we rumble into London. Once off the train, Leo leads the way, striding confidently through the station and toward the underground entrance.

"How do you know your way around?" I ask as we squeeze into a packed train.

"I come here for specialist appointments," he says in a low voice.

"Does your mum come with you?" I ask.

"She used to. Not so much now."

"But don't you get lonely? Coming all this way on your own?" I ask.

Leo meets my eyes. "Never."

Every few seconds I catch sight of the red material flapping around my thighs, or a strand of long hair, my hair, out of the corner of my eye, and it delights and terrifies me in equal amounts.

We get off the tube and board a second train, larger than the first but quieter. After about forty-five minutes, the tracks start running alongside water.

"Look," I say, pointing. "The sea."

Leo nods, his face blank.

I rest my forehead against the cold glass. The tide is way out, revealing wide flats of mud and silt the same color as the dingy gray sky.

Leo outlines the plan for the rest of the day. As he speaks his sight line hovers somewhere above my eyebrows, as if he can't quite bring himself to look straight at me. I guess I didn't give him much warning about coming dressed in girls' clothes, but I'm still a bit disappointed by his reaction. He proposes we go to the bed-and-breakfast first, to drop off our things, before grabbing something to eat and heading to Jimmy's house for what Leo refers to as recon. We'll return to the house tomorrow morning, which is when Leo will introduce himself. Once I'm satisfied he isn't about to get chopped up into tiny pieces and buried in the back garden, I will go, staying alone at the B&B before heading home on Sunday.

"What if he's in when we go by later?" I ask. "Won't you be tempted to knock on the door rather than wait until morning?"

"No," Leo says firmly. "I'm sticking to the plan."

For the rest of the journey I try to get Leo to play games but he refuses to bite, angling his body away from me and staring out the window. I can't help but feel annoyed. Ever since we made the decision to come here, I've been envisioning a cinematic adventure full of self-discovery, bonding, and life-defining moments, but so far Leo is failing to cooperate. Half an hour later a disembodied voice crackles over the intercom.

"Next stop—Tripton-on-Sea."

. . . . .

Tripton-on-Sea is a small station with only two platforms, and Leo and I are the only people to leave the train. Even though it's just a little after two o'clock, the light already seems like it's dimming into dusk.

As Leo digs a map out of his pocket, turning it around a few times to get his bearings, I text Essie to let her know I've arrived.

"I think the B&B is this way," he says, pointing down a steep cobblestone street. We follow it to the seafront, where we stand for a few moments, the beach spread out in front of us. It's gray and empty and gives me a hint of the thrill it used to when I was a kid and we went to Brighton. To our right stands a pier. It's not like Brighton's, with its amusement park and arcades and flashing lights. The Tripton-on-Sea pier is bleak in its emptiness and lack of decoration, stretching out into the water for what seems like miles.

"Sixth-longest pier in Britain," Leo says.

I look at him quizzically.

"Wikipedia."

"Get you, Mr. Trivia," I say.

In front of the beach there's a small amusement park, closed up for the winter. It's dominated by a modest roller coaster, its twisting metal form painted ice cream colors, exaggeratedly bright against the gray sky. The smaller rides are covered up with plastic tarps.

We take a left and walk along the front. Quite a few of the

places, the ice cream stalls and rock shops, have their grilles pulled down. They're interspersed with arcades, their bright lights flashing halfheartedly.

"I hate seeing places shut up like that," I say as we pass a gift shop, its windows dark. "I know they're only buildings, but it always makes me feel a bit sad. Do you know what I mean?"

Leo doesn't answer; he continues to study the map, looking up every so often to check the street signs. I shuffle along beside him, my Ugg boots dragging on the sidewalk.

"My sister's got some of those," Leo says after a moment, nodding at my feet. "Fake ones though."

"They're the only things I could get that fit," I admit.

"What size are you?" Leo asks.

"Nine," I say, sighing. "And growing. You?"

"Six," Leo replies in a low voice.

"Swap?"

He manages a brief smile.

We take a left and head up another steep road. Sea View is a tall, narrow house in the center of a terrace. We exchange nervous glances before going inside, ringing the bell on the reception desk. We're greeted by a middle-aged woman with silvery-gray hair, wearing a striped apron and the sort of expression adults seem to reserve exclusively for teenagers—a mixture of suspicion and impatience. She introduces herself as Mrs. Higgins.

"I have a reservation," Leo says in a grown-up voice I've never heard before. "A twin room under the name of Leo Denton?"

Mrs. Higgins's eyes drift to me.

"I'm Amber Denton, Leo's sister," I say quickly.

She holds my gaze for a few seconds before checking in her book. The wallpaper behind her is pink and chintzy and peeling slightly at the edges. I realize I'm holding my breath.

"Twin, you say?" Mrs. Higgins asks.

I nod eagerly.

"You didn't specify you wanted a twin when you booked."

"I'm pretty sure I did," Leo says.

Mrs. Higgins takes off her glasses.

"Let me assure you, if you specified a twin room, I would have given you a twin room," she replies snootily.

For a second I think Leo's going to lose it and start yelling at her. I can tell by the way his body stiffens, his fingers splaying out like a cat stretching its paws, preparing to pounce. But he keeps his cool and if Mrs. Higgins notices his simmering anger, she does a pretty good job of hiding it.

"Well, do you have any twin rooms available then?" he asks, his eyes still flashing.

"No. The family room is available, that has three beds, but that'll cost you an extra thirty-five pounds a night."

"You're joking," Leo says. "You're the one who messed up, why should we pay for it?"

Mrs. Higgins gives him a long look.

"I'm afraid that's the only alternative to a single bed, young man. Apart from that I'm fully booked tonight."

Leo swears under his breath.

"It's okay, bro," I whisper, tugging on his sleeve. "We've shared a room for enough years to figure something out."

Leo gives me a sharp look, clearly not appreciating my sisterly role-play. I widen my eyes. We can't risk being thrown out.

"Payment in advance," Mrs. Higgins says, holding out her hand.

As I take out my wallet and peel off the notes, I feel her eyes on me, possibly searching and failing to find the nonexistent family resemblance between Leo and me. When I hand over the money she makes a big show of counting it out.

"Room nine. Top of the stairs, turn left. No noise after 10 p.m., no food in the rooms. Breakfast is served 7 a.m. until 9 a.m. in the dining room."

She hands us a key on an oversize plastic key ring before disappearing into the back office.

"Well, have a nice stay!" I say in an American accent. I turn to Leo to share the joke but he's already halfway up the stairs.

Room nine is small and square and furnished with a tiny closet, a dresser, and a double bed covered in a flowery bedspread. It smells of potpourri and disinfectant. We stand there for a moment, both of us staring at the bed.

"Sorry," Leo says, dumping his bag on the floor, "I'm certain I booked a twin."

"And I bet you did," I say. "That silly cow downstairs clearly had it in for us the moment we walked in the door. Don't worry, we can put pillows down the middle or something."

I head over to the window and yank it open to lean out. The room looks onto the Dumpsters.

"Sea View, my foot!" I laugh. "Come see."

But Leo stays where he is.

"Let's get out of here," he says.

We have a late lunch of fish-and-chips. It's cheaper to take out so we sit on a bench overlooking the amusement park, flimsy Styrofoam containers balanced on our laps as we stab at our food with tiny wooden forks. The whole time Leo doesn't say a word, just stares out to sea.

LEO

Beside me David is swinging his legs and wolfing down his fish-and-chips, every so often commenting on the cold to fill in the silences.

I can't help but get a shock every time I look at him. Not that he looks bad, because he doesn't, but it's hard to get my head around him being here, dressed like, well, like that. But the weirdest thing is that it's not actually *that* weird, because the clothes he's wearing suit him, way better than anything else I've seen him wear. He seems less awkward in them, less self-conscious, and I find myself not thinking of him as "he" at all.

I shiver and pull my wool hat over my ears. I look down at the sidewalk beneath my feet and wonder if Dad has stepped on this exact same spot. Or even sat where I'm sitting now. The thought that he's close by makes my stomach flip-flop. I put aside my fish-and-chips. I've barely touched them.

"We should keep moving, check out Dad's before it gets dark," I say.

We dump our containers in a garbage can and continue along the front. Toward Dad's house.

When we turn onto Mariners Avenue, the last of the afternoon light is fading behind the houses. Dad lives at number eighteen. We count up from number two, my heart speeding up with every step. And for the first time I feel glad David is here. Not that I'm not grateful he lent me the money, because I am, but his presence has been clouding my vision and messing with my focus. But now, so close to Dad's house, I'm glad he's with me. Which, when you've spent most of your life longing to be alone, is a pretty alien feeling.

"Eighteen," David and I murmur in unison, coming to a slow stop on the sidewalk.

The house, big and painted white, stands in darkness and I can't help but feel relieved I'm not tempted to forget my plan of coming back tomorrow and march up to the door right now, waving my birth certificate above my head like a lunatic.

"C'mon," I say to David. "Let's go."

We head back down the street. After another ten minutes of walking we turn onto what must be the main street. It's littered with chain stores and fast food restaurants and the odd gift shop selling faded postcards and heart-shaped lollipops with *I love Tripton* on them.

"Oooooh, look, a bingo hall!" David cries, interrupting my thoughts. "I've always wanted to play bingo."

"Mam plays bingo," I say flatly.

"Have you ever gone with her?" David asks.

"No."

As if.

"Then it'll be a first for both of us!" he says, grabbing my arm and steering me toward the entrance.

I shake him off.

"David, I don't want to play bingo. Look, let's head back to the beach or something."

"But we've already seen the beach. C'mon, it'll be fun. My treat."

"No, you're paying for everything as it is."

Just then a drop of rain lands on my nose. I look up. The sky has turned a deep gray. There's a moment of quiet before the heavens open and the rain comes thrashing down in sheets. David pulls his coat up over his head to shield his hair and dashes into the entrance of the bingo hall. Reluctantly I jog after him.

"We're too young," I say. "It's over-eighteens only, look."

I point to the sign.

"So?" David says.

It strikes me then that the female version of David is much bolder than the boy version. It's like the wig, dress, and Ugg boots contain magical powers.

"I didn't have you down as such a goody-goody," he says. "Look, if they kick us out, they kick us out, so what? Got any better ideas?"

"Fine," I say, shoving my hands into the pockets of my hoodie as David heads to the counter. The guy behind the desk barely looks up from the newspaper he is reading, yawning openly as he takes David's money.

Beyond a pair of double doors, the bingo hall itself is

cavernous, the bored voice of the unseen bingo caller echoing off the walls. The place is mostly empty. Just a cluster of elderly women sitting near the front and a handful of solo players dotted about, their heads bent over their bingo cards.

David and I slide into a booth, David clapping his hands together like a kid at a birthday party as he gazes around the place.

A bored-looking girl in her early twenties with a name tag that reveals her name is Kayleigh comes over to take our drinks order.

"A Coke, please," David says.

My eyes dart down the sticky drinks menu, quickly identifying the cheapest pint of beer.

"Pint of Foster's, please," I say, figuring now we're in here it's worth a chance.

Kayleigh scribbles it down without blinking.

David looks up in surprise.

"Actually, I've changed my mind, I'll have a Foster's too," he says.

Kayleigh returns a few minutes later with our drinks, liquid slopping over the edge of the glasses as she sets them down on the scuffed plastic tabletop.

"Want to set up a tab?" she asks.

"Ooooh, yes please," David says. Kayleigh hands us a plastic token with the number seventeen on it.

"This is *so* fun," David says as soon as Kayleigh is out of earshot, his eyes sparkling.

I shake my head and watch as he leans forward and sips the foam off his pint. Immediately he makes a face.

"Yuck, it's horrible!" he cries.

"What? You never had a beer before?"

"No," he says, wiping his mouth on a napkin.

"It's an acquired taste I suppose," I say, taking a long gulp. The last time I drank beer was at Becky's party. With Alicia.

I keep thinking about what David said, about Alicia not being the one who told everyone. It should make me feel better but somehow it doesn't. Becky just got in there first, that's all. Besides, Alicia's face said it all.

The bingo caller announces the next game is about to start. I pick up my pen. David is already poised, his pen hovering expectantly over his card, his "eyes down," as instructed by the bingo caller.

The first two games we don't even come close to marking off all the numbers on our cards. The third game we're going for the house, the big one, the jackpot. It seems to go on forever. My eyes begin to blur. Another one of the old ladies at the front calls "house" but it turns out to be a false alarm. We keep playing, the numbers coming faster and faster. I just need one more to win. More numbers, another false alarm.

Then, "Danny La Rue, fifty-two."

"Fifty-two," David says, leaning over to inspect my card. "They just called fifty-two, Leo! House!" he yells, waving his arms in the air. "House! Over here!"

My winnings amount to one hundred pounds. It's the most money I've ever had. I return from the counter, the notes crisp and beautiful in my hand, unable to quite believe they are legitimately mine.

The old ladies at the front throw us dirty looks, which makes

David start giggling so hard he can't stop. And I don't know if it's the beer or what, because suddenly I'm giggling too. It's not even that funny, not really, but somehow that makes us laugh even harder. They're the sort of giggles I haven't had since I was a little kid, the sort that make you clutch your stomach and gasp for breath. Eventually we're laughing so loudly we have to abandon our bingo cards and stumble out into the street where it's finally stopped raining.

We're at the end of the main street and turning onto the seafront when David clasps his hand to his mouth and lets out a gasp.

"What's up?" I ask.

"I didn't pay our tab!"

We lose it. We have to hold on to each other we're laughing so hard.

I know then I'm officially drunk.

Considering it's a Friday night, the streets of Tripton are pretty quiet. In the distance we hear music. We head toward it. At some point, David links his arm through mine and by the time I realize it, it feels too late to shake him off. As we get closer, it's obvious the music is coming from a pub called the Mermaid Inn.

David pulls me back.

"We're underage," he whispers.

"So? You didn't care about that at the bingo hall."

He hesitates.

"There's no bouncer at the door," I add. "C'mon, I'm dying for another beer."

"Okay," David says. And for the first time since arriving in

Tripton, I can sense David's nerves as he grips my arm, his fingernails pressing into my skin, even through my multiple layers.

I push open the doors. The music we heard originates from the corner of the pub where a large woman is standing on a tiny stage belting out "Beautiful" by Christina Aguilera. It must be karaoke night. As we make our way toward the bar, no one gives us a second glance, which makes me think underage drinkers are a common sight in Tripton.

"Are people looking?" he whispers, his eyes wide and fearful.

"Nah."

"Do I look okay?"

"You look fine."

I peel a twenty-pound note out of my wallet.

"No, my round," David says. "I insist."

I open my mouth to protest but then snap it shut again. I need this money, pure and simple. If I've come here to live with Dad, I can't just turn up empty-handed, I need to contribute, earn my keep.

"Thank you. I'll have a beer."

"Here," David says, pressing the note into my hand. "You go up."

"No, you," I say, passing it back. "You've got a better chance of getting served."

"How come?"

"Everyone knows it's easier to get served if you're a girl."

David beams.

"What? Why are you smiling like that?"

"You just called me a girl," he says.

And I suppose I had, in a way.

As David heads to the bar, my eyes wander around the pub. It's one of those old-fashioned places, with lots of dark wood paneling and brass everywhere. Even though it's only November, it's already decorated for Christmas with a wonky plastic tree on the bar and fake snow sprayed unevenly all over the windows. On the stage now an old guy, clearly wearing a toupee, is also getting into the festive spirit, ready to belt out "Fairytale of New York."

David returns with a beer in each hand and at least five bags of potato chips shoved under one arm, a huge grin plastered across his face.

"He didn't even ask me for ID!" he says. "And he called me darling!"

I laugh. "Told you so," I say.

The old guy on the stage reaches the chorus and as most of the pub join in, I find myself murmuring along with them. David looks at me in surprise.

"It's my favorite Christmas song," I say with a shrug, fiddling with a coaster.

"Really? You don't find it depressing?"

"Nah, I like it. Besides, life is depressing, isn't it? It's a well-known fact murder rates rise on Christmas Day."

"But that's horrible! Christmas is meant to be a time for magic," David says.

I shake my head. "You're pretty cheesy sometimes, you know that? You're gonna tell me you still believe in Santa next."

David sticks his tongue out at me and sips his beer. His mouth leaves behind a lipstick mark on the glass. He holds it up to the light and admires it for a second.

"What's your favorite Christmas song then?" I ask.

"Guess."

I think for a moment before snapping my fingers.

"Mariah Carey, 'All I Want for Christmas Is You,'" I say.

"Wrong. It's 'Have Yourself a Merry Little Christmas,' the Nat King Cole version."

"Who?"

"Exactly. Don't think you know everything about me, Leo," David says, wagging his finger at me. "So really, how do I look?"

"I told you before, fine."

"Can you be a bit more specific?"

"You look . . . good," I say.

"But good how? Do I, you know, pass?"

"Pass?" I ask.

"You know what I mean! As in, do I pass as female?"

"Well, that's a hard one."

David's face falls.

"What I mean is, it's hard because I know you as a boy. But I reckon if I was a stranger and saw you on the street, I would assume you were a girl."

David bites his lip, no doubt to stop a huge grin from spreading across his entire face.

"Because you look totally like a boy," he says. "And sound like one too."

I glance over my shoulder, relieved to find all the people around us wrapped up in their own conversations.

"It's just practice," I say. "Knowing what works."

"Have you met a lot of people like us?" David asks.

I shake my head.

"What? Not any?"

"Nope."

"But what about the special clinic you go to? In London?"

I shrug. "It's easy enough to avoid the other patients if you need to. My therapist always goes on at me to go to support groups and stuff but it's not my thing. I'm stuck in this body, for now anyway, so what's moaning about it to a roomful of people going to do to change that? Nothing."

"Don't you find this helps though? Being able to talk to me and not have to hide anything. Doesn't that feel like a relief?"

I hesitate, anxious to divert the conversation away from me.

"So what's your girl name then?" I ask. "You can't seriously expect people to keep calling you David when you look like this."

"I suppose not," David says, carefully smoothing out his dress.

"So what is it? You must have thought about it."

"Of course I have," David says. "I take this stuff seriously, you know, it's not just a game."

"Jesus, I know that," I say, taking a swig of beer.

"Promise you won't laugh?"

"Of course."

David takes a deep breath.

"Okay then. It's Kate."

"Kate," I repeat. "How come?"

David leans in, his elbows resting on the table.

"I once asked my mum and dad what they would have called me if I was a girl, and they said it was going to be a toss-up between Kate and Olivia. I couldn't pick Olivia, because that's my little sister's name, so I went with Kate."

"Kate Piper," I say.

"What? Don't you like it?" David asks.

"No, no, I do. I just thought you would have picked something a bit more out-there, crazy. Kate is nice though. It suits you."

"Honestly?"

"Yeah."

"Thank you." He beams. "What about you? How did you pick your name?"

I pause to fold up one of the empty potato chip bags, smaller and smaller until I can't go any further, making my fingers slick with salt and grease.

"Mam helped me pick it," I say finally, wiping my hands on my jeans. "Leo's my star sign, not that I'm into that stuff. But Mam suggested it and it just kind of worked."

"Wow," David says. "I cannot imagine having that conversation with my mum, not for one second. How did you get everyone to start calling you that?"

"I refused to answer to anything else. And eventually it just stuck. I was never much of a Megan anyway."

There's a long pause.

"How are you going explain it to your dad?" David asks quietly.

"I'm just going to tell him straight out," I say boldly. "This is who I am now."

267

"Do you have a speech planned?" David asks.

"I don't need a speech."

The truth is, I have so many things I want to say I can't even begin to put them into a proper order. Every time I imagine the conversation we're going to have tomorrow, I stall, because so much of what I'm going to say depends on Dad.

David doesn't push the issue. We continue to chat about other stuff—music, movies, TV—our conversation sound-tracked by Tripton-on-Sea's residents belting out song after song, some more tunefully than others, and for a bit I can block out the un- certainty of tomorrow and just live in the moment. And it's a good moment, it's fun, and I feel almost free in a way that seems brand-new. The conversation moves on to school and David is talking about Zachary, the blond kid he likes, and how he won some all-county athletics thing last week.

"You really like him, don't you?" I say.

David goes red instantly.

"Yeah," he says, running his finger around the top of his glass. "It's hopeless though."

"Definitely?"

"Of course. Do you really think someone as popular and cool as Zachary would like someone like me? That's what's so frustrating sometimes. Being like this. It shuts down all these possibilities."

"It might not . . ." I say, but my lack of conviction shows in my voice as it trails off. After all, it was being like this that killed stuff with Alicia.

"Yes, it does," David says. "It has already. God, I long to be normal sometimes, and to be able to do normal teenage stuff."

"Like what?"

"Oh, nothing major. Just, I don't know, dance with a boy at the Christmas ball or something."

The ball. I was supposed to be taking Alicia.

"But normal is such a stupid word," I say, anger suddenly rising in my belly. "What does it even mean?"

"It means fitting in," David replies simply.

"And that's what you really want? To fit in?"

"Not all the time perhaps. But a lot of the time, yes, I think it would be a lot easier to just blend into the crowd. Isn't that why you don't tell people?"

"That's different."

"Is it though?"

I don't answer.

David leaves to go to the bathroom and I'm glad. Our conversation has got me thinking about Alicia again. I check my phone on the off chance there might be a message or missed call from her, but there's nothing, and even though I'm not surprised, I feel the sharp sting of disappointment.

David returns, his lipstick freshly applied, more drinks in his hands, and a mischievous look on his face. I sniff the liquid in the glass closest to me, almost poking myself in the eye with its little umbrella in the process.

"What is this?"

"I asked the bartender for a surprise," David says, slamming down on his chair hard and almost tumbling backward. I take a long sip. Whatever it is, it's sweet and strong and goes straight to my head. Opposite me, David's face looms larger, then smaller, then larger again, as if I'm looking at him in a wall of mirrors at the amusement park. Soon we're both laughing, over what I'm not too sure, but it's contagious and we can't stop and soon the people at the tables around us are laughing as well. David asks someone to take a photo of the two of us on his phone.

"No," I protest. "I look like crap in photos."

But it's too late. David is putting his arm around my shoulder and yelling, "Cheese," as the flash goes off, superbright, white dots dancing in front of my eyes. Then he makes me take some of him alone, his poses getting sillier and sillier. I'm snapping away when I hear my name over the microphone.

"Leo? Can we have Leo up onstage, please?" the MC, a small round man wearing a spangly waistcoat, calls hopefully.

"Over here!" David yelps.

"No! No way, David," I slur, trying to back away against the wall.

"Please!" David begs, putting his hands together as if praying. "Pretty please, Leonardo!"

"That's not my name," I say.

"Come on, lad, don't disappoint your girlfriend," a guy to my left says.

"She's not my girlfriend," I begin to say, but my voice is swallowed up as I'm pushed through the crowd. The pub is suddenly packed, as if the entire population of Tripton-on-Sea has turned out to witness my stage debut.

I don't know how I get up onstage, but somehow I find myself being passed the microphone as the introduction starts. I squint at the crowd. David has managed to make his way to the front and is sitting on a stool, clapping his hands in excitement.

"Go, Leo!" he yells, cupping his hands around his mouth.

I try to focus on the screen in front of me but the words are dancing about, refusing to stay still. I don't know the verse of the song so I just stand as still as I can and speak the words in rhythm with the white dot bouncing across the screen. But then the chorus kicks in and I realize I know the tune and it's like I'm having an out-of-body experience as I find myself singing louder and louder until, by the time I reach the second chorus, I'm belting out the words and strutting up and down the stage like a wannabe rock star.

"Right now, the time is ours! So let's fly higher!" I bellow. *"Light the stars on fire! Together we'll shine!"*

And I am drunk, so, so drunk. And all the time David is whooping his head off and it's so bizarre I start laughing and end up half-singing, half-laughing my way through the rest of the song. Then it's over and David is dragging me down from the stage and throwing his arms around me.

"You were like Justin Bieber up there!" he cries in my ear.

"I should kill you for that," I say.

"But you're not going to, are you?" David says, grinning wildly. And he's right. Because I'm grinning too.

"I'm going to get some air," I say, heading for the door.

"I'll come with you."

We step into the cold, past the smokers gathered outside, huddled together on picnic tables.

"I've had the best idea ever," David whispers in my ear, his breath warm with booze. "Let's go swimming!"

"Are you insane? It's November."

"So? Where is your sense of adventure? You're supposed to be the crazy one, remember? The junior-hacksaw killer!" he slurs, jabbing me in the chest.

"Shut up," I hiss. "People are looking."

I take David by the arm and lead him away from the pub. He shakes me off and grabs my arm instead, dragging me across the road toward the beach. I'm too floppy with drunkenness to do anything but let myself be dragged, stumbling, over the wet sand. The tide has come in and only a small stretch of beach remains. David collapses breathless on the sand, yanking off his Ugg boots before wriggling out of his tights. I turn my head away.

"C'mon, Leo!" he cries, pushing me down. And before I know it I'm taking off my sneakers and socks and rolling up my jeans to the knee and following David to the shore.

He takes my hand and looks at me, his eyes shining.

"After three?"

"This is nuts. You're nuts."

"Shush! After three?"

I find myself nodding.

"One, two, three!"

We run into the sea, the icy water hitting our ankles.

We scream in unison.

"It's freezing!" I yell.

"Oh my God! Oh my God!" David cries, holding on to both my hands and hopping from foot to foot.

"You're officially mental!" I yell.

"Good!" he yells back.

We splash about for five minutes, every few seconds screaming our heads off at the cold, until an unexpected wave hits us, soaking us from the waist down and sending us scrambling back to shore in wet defeat.

We run onto the sand, shivering as we hunt for socks, tights, and shoes in the darkness. David finds his phone and turns it on.

"Aw, look at your feet!" he says, shining the phone over them like a spotlight. "They're so tiny!"

I bat him away.

"Hey, I was still looking," he says. "They're so cute."

"Stop it, will you?" I say, pushing him. I catch him off guard and he goes toppling over on his side. He gurgles with laughter and rolls onto his back.

"Look, I'm a sand angel!" he crows, opening and closing his arms and legs.

I stand up.

"C'mon, Kate," I say, folding my arms across my chest. "I'm going to get hypothermia."

David stops flapping his arms and gazes up at me.

"What?" I ask. "Why are you looking at me like that?"

He closes his eyes, a blissed-out expression on his face.

"You called me Kate."

LEO

I'm dying. I've got to be. There's no other explanation. My head is throbbing and my throat feels like it's lined with razor blades. I groan and roll over. It takes me a few seconds to realize where I am, that I'm not in my bunk bed at number seven, Sycamore Gardens, but on a lumpy mattress in a bed-and-breakfast in Tripton-on-Sea. I open my eyes. The flimsy curtains hanging at the windows do nothing to stop the room from flooding with light. I wince and bury my head in the pillow before daring to open my eyes again, more slowly this time. On the radiator our things—my jeans and socks, and David's tights and dress—are draped haphazardly. I turn over. David is curled up with his back to me, snoring softly. Last night, just after he informed me he'd had the best night of his life, he threw up in the toilet. He then staggered around the room getting undressed, crashing into the closet before finally collapsing into bed.

I fumble on the floor for my cell. Last night I set the alarm for seven so that we could have breakfast and be camped out at

Dad's house by eight. I rub my eyes and squint at the display. It's blank. I frown and stab at the buttons. Nothing. The battery is dead.

"David," I say, poking him in the back. "David, wake up."

David groans and pulls the duvet more tightly around him.

"Not finished," he mumbles, yanking a pillow over his head.

Panic rising in my chest, I scramble over his dozing body, snatching his phone from the dresser on his side of the bed. I press the button. The display blinks into life: 11:46 a.m. I drop the phone on the floor and leap out of bed, grabbing my clothes.

We've missed breakfast by nearly three hours, not that it matters. Mrs. Higgins tuts loudly as I tear down the stairs, past the reception desk.

I run to the seafront, dodging pedestrians, my lungs and calves on fire, my head still banging from the worst hangover of my life. I only slow my pace when I turn into Dad's street, jogging along the sidewalk until I reach number eighteen. There is no car in front of the house. I press my face up to the window, looking for signs of life.

"Shit," I cry.

"Who are you after?" a voice calls.

I jump away from the window.

An elderly man is standing in the front garden of the house next door.

"Er, Jimmy, I mean, Jonathan, Jonathan Denton," I say. It feels odd saying Dad's name out loud to a stranger.

"You just missed him. Back later, I imagine."

"Right, thanks."

The man smiles and nods before going into his house.

I curse and sink down on the curb outside Dad's house, my head in my hands. Ten minutes later David, panting heavily, taps me on the knee.

"Get lost, David," I say. "I don't want you here."

"What's going on?" he asks, ignoring me.

"I was too late. He's gone out already."

"But he'll be back, right?"

"I don't know. He could be out all day and night for all I know."

"But probably not," David says.

I glare at him. "I should never have drunk so much last night. What was I even thinking? The night before something as important as this, how stupid can you get?"

"You were having fun, Leo. It was a really good night. Actually, scratch that, it was a great night."

"But it shouldn't have been!" I yell. "Don't you get it?"

David backs away, and for a second I think he's going to cry.

"So what are we going to do?" he asks.

"I'm going to wait. You can do what you want."

I sit down on the wall of the house directly opposite Dad's. I will David to go away but he perches beside me.

"I told you, go away," I say.

But he pretends he can't hear me.

It's cold, colder even than yesterday, and in the mad rush of leaving the B&B, I didn't bring my gloves or hat. To pass the time, David tries to encourage me to play games with him—I spy, and animal, vegetable, or mineral—but I refuse to join in. I'm not in the mood. Plus I'm too angry with him. If I'd come alone, I'd never have got myself in that state. I'd have been here at eight o'clock on the dot, fresh and prepared and focused. I block out David's voice and stare at Dad's house, scared if I take my eyes off it, it might crumble away to nothing. Finally David stops trying to talk to me and plays Candy Crush Saga on his cell instead.

After an hour my stomach begins to rumble. After two hours, the sound is almost deafening.

"We need to eat, Leo," David says quietly.

"I'm fine."

"I know you like to think you're superhuman, but you're not. Besides which, if I don't eat soon I might faint. There's a café at the end of the road. Let's go get warm for a few minutes and have something to eat. Then we'll come back."

My stomach lets out another angry rumble. I sigh and stand up.

The café is warm and steamy with red-and-white-checked cloths on the tables and ketchup and mustard in oversize plastic bottles. We order a mountain of grilled cheese sandwiches and mugs of hot chocolate. Although I'm starving, I have to force the food into my mouth, barely tasting it. While I'm picking at the last few pieces, David goes to the bathroom to fix his hastily applied makeup. He overdoes the blush but I don't have the energy to tell him.

· · · · ·

When we return to our spot, a shiny blue Volvo is parked outside Dad's house.

He's back.

I stare at the house.

"You ready?" David asks.

I stand up and cross the road, David close behind. Even though I've been imagining versions of this moment for years and years, I still have no idea what I'm going to find behind the front door of number eighteen. I've got my fantasy version of what happens—Dad recognizes me straightaway, flinging his arms around me in joy. He accepts his baby girl is now a teenage boy and invites me to live with him, and I get to start my life all over again. That's what would happen if my life was a feel-good family film, one with a plinky-plonky piano sound track and good-looking actors playing all the parts. But my life's never been a feel-good family film. Not even close. So perhaps this is my time. Maybe it's finally *my* turn for something good to happen.

I open the front gate and it's like I'm a puppet and some puppet master in the sky is controlling my movements and steering me up the short path. Somehow I make it to the door. I raise my hand to knock but before my knuckles have connected with the glass, it opens.

I know it's him within seconds. It's like he's stepped right out of the photograph in my wallet. He's piggybacking a little boy who is about four years old and wearing a Spider-Man costume beneath a navy duffel coat with fat red toggles. Whenever I've thought of Dad over the years, I've never ever thought of him with a family, not once. I've spent my whole life imagining him as a wanderer, going from place to place, a free spirit. I feel stupid.

"Can I help you?" he asks. His voice is deep and he's far more well-spoken than I was expecting. I search for some recognition in his eyes but find none.

I open my mouth to speak but no sound comes out. David, who I'd forgotten was beside me, jumps in.

"Are you Jonathan Denton?" he asks, although we all know the answer.

"Yes. Who wants to know?" Dad asks, a slight frown on his face.

This must be what it's like to see someone famous out and about. You convince yourself you know them because you've seen them on TV and in magazines, but it doesn't prepare you for seeing them up close. And you think you know exactly how you'll act when you do, but when the actual time comes you sort of fall apart.

I finally find my voice but it sounds like it doesn't quite belong to me.

"You used to know Samantha Binley?" I say.

Dad's face changes then, sort of darkens. He lets Spider-Man slide down his body. Spider-Man looks up at me. He has babyish versions of Dad's eyes. Green with amber flecks. My eyes. My half brother.

"Babe, have you got the keys?" a female voice says. Dad moves to the side and a woman appears beside him. She's pretty with tanned skin and dark brown curly hair. The next thing I notice is that she's pregnant. When she spots us on the doorstep she rests her hands protectively on her bump. A ring sparkles on her left hand.

"What's all this then?" she asks, not unkindly.

"Collecting for charity, aren't you?" Dad says smoothly.

"Ooh, what charity?" the woman asks.

"Animals," David says. "Endangered species."

"You get Archie in the car," Dad says to the woman. "I'll sort this out."

"Okay, babe," she says. "Come on, Archie, sweetheart."

Archie gives me one last curious look before scampering after his mum into the shiny blue Volvo. The Ford Fiesta from the photograph is clearly long gone.

As soon as the woman's back is turned, Dad's mask falls.

"C'mon then," he says grimly, leading us into the foyer. I can see through into the kitchen. It's bright and modern. The fridge is plastered with pictures Archie must have painted. They feature brightly colored stick people, the same set of three over and over again—Mum, Dad, and Archie. A picture-perfect family.

"You said you were here about Sammy?" he says, his voice brisk and businesslike. He looks through me, still obviously totally unaware who I am.

"I'm her kid," I blurt.

Dad's eyes narrow.

"You're one of Sammy's kids?" he says slowly.

I nod. "I'm Leo. Leo Denton."

Me saying Denton makes him flinch the tiniest bit.

"I'm one of the twins," I add, my voice almost a whisper. "Megan and Amber. I'm Megan. Only I'm not Megan anymore, I'm Leo."

I recite my date of birth. Dad's expression stays neutral,

unnaturally so, like he's trying his very hardest not to react to a word I say.

"I'm sorry, but I have no idea what you're talking about," he says, folding his arms across his chest, smiling this smile that doesn't go anywhere near his eyes, his voice artificially calm and cold.

"But you must. I'm telling you the truth, I swear. I can show you my birth certificate if you want." I start to fish in the pocket of my hoodie, my hands shaking, but I can't find it. I must have put it in another pocket. I start to turn them out, panicking that I've lost it.

"No need for any of that," Dad says briskly, resting his hand on my arm. "Now I don't know why you're here, kid, if it's money you're after or what, but I'm really not interested."

Fresh panic starts to rise in my belly.

"Look, this has nothing to do with money, or my mum, I swear. She has no idea I'm even here. I'm yours, I promise you I am. I'm transgender. It means I was born in the wrong body. I'm Leo now but I was born Megan, one of the twins, your twins."

Dad rubs his forehead and swears under his breath. "Look, I think it's time for the two of you to leave," he says, making a move toward the door.

"But you can see he's yours!" David chimes in desperately. "Any idiot can see he is. Look at his eyes, they're exactly like yours. They're identical."

For a second Dad does look at me and I can see that he sees it too. That he knows. But then he's rearranging his features and pushing us toward the door, his hand on the small of my back.

I shake him off. Red-hot rage is building up inside me, only this is different from the usual sort. It's loaded with something extra—desperation piled on top of the anger.

"But I've come all this way!" I cry. "You've got to let me talk to you. I'll come back tomorrow if you like. Or we could meet in town or something. I don't want money or to cause trouble or anything like that, I just want to know you, and for you to know me."

Because right now I'll take anything I can get.

Dad grabs me by the shoulders and for a hopeful split second I think he's going to have a change of heart.

"Please?" I say.

Dad's entire face is dark and mean, his mouth set in a firm line.

"Look, you've got the wrong man," he says. "So I'm going to tell you what's going to happen next. You two little freaks are going to walk out this door and never come back. Got me?"

Freaks. He practically spits the word.

"Babe, is everything all right?" the woman calls from outside.

"Yep, just coming," he calls back over his shoulder, from ice cold to sunny in the blink of an eye.

He opens the door and breaks into this big showman smile. And the penny drops then that this woman, his wife, has no idea about me and Amber, or Mam, or Cloverdale. Of course she doesn't. It's like that bit of Dad's life has been erased from his history.

The kid, Archie, is sitting in a booster seat in the back of the car, bouncing up and down. And in that moment I hate him.

I hate this innocent kid who hasn't done a thing wrong. And I hate the baby in the woman's belly too. I hate them so much I could burst.

Dad is behind us, forcing us out the door, onto the path. He locks the door behind him and overtakes us, striding down the path and climbing into the car. He starts the engine and drives off, his eyes looking resolutely ahead the whole time, leaving David and me standing in his front garden, frozen to the spot. The only person who pays us any attention is Archie. He twists around in his seat and stares right at me—his babyish eyes locked on my grown-up version—until the car snakes around the corner and out of sight.

DAVID

"Leo?" I whisper.

But Leo doesn't look at me. He just stands there, perfectly still apart from his fists, which clench and unclench, slowly at first, then faster and faster. There's a moment of absolute quiet before he lets out this terrible howl and takes off around the garden, tearing it up like a wild animal. He turns the garbage can upside down, scattering trash all over the neat paving stones. He takes the terra-cotta plant pots that sit in a neat row under the window-sill and smashes them in turn against the wall, before stamping on the rose bushes so they bend and snap. He kicks the front door repeatedly and for a moment I'm worried he might kick it right in. Then he's thumping it, his fists hammering against the glass. The entire time he continues to howl and I'm pleading with him to stop, screaming, begging him. A neighbor from across the road opens her window and yells at us, saying she's going to call the police. Leo raises his head and swears at her. She gasps and shuts her window.

"Leo, please!" I cry. He takes one final kick at the front door before pushing me out of the way and charging down the path, flinging open the gate so hard I think it's going to come off its hinges. He begins to stride down the road, toward the sea.

"Leo, wait!" I yell. "Wait!"

But he keeps walking, faster and faster, taking advantage of my handicapped speed due to my stupid Ugg boots as I half-run, half-shuffle after him.

I finally reach his side in front of a boarded-up gift shop on the seafront, my chest heaving with exhaustion.

"Leo!" I cry breathlessly. "Talk to me, please!"

He doesn't answer me. He doesn't even look at me.

"Leo," I say, grabbing hold of his hands. He shakes me off but stops walking and raises his eyes to meet mine. I can't help but shrink back in fear. They're gleaming with fury—black and murderous. He holds my gaze for a few seconds before breaking away and continuing along the front. As I run after him, I almost wish he would cry instead. I would know better what to do then, I could hold him, comfort him, contain him somehow. But he doesn't do anything but walk, his hands shoved deep in his pockets, his eyes trained on the wet ground in front of him.

"Leo, where are you going?" I plead again. But he ignores me and all I can do is try to keep him in sight as he increases the pace. We pass the strip of arcades. They're called things like Flamingo and Magic Land, their neon signs flashing wearily, some of the bulbs faded or missing altogether. Then Leo crosses the road diagonally without looking. A car has to brake suddenly, its driver winding down his window and swearing. But Leo barely blinks. I raise my hand in apology on Leo's behalf and dash after him.

As I reach the other side of the road, I realize Leo is heading for the pier. It stretches out toward the horizon. There are big signs saying you have to pay to use the walkway but there's no one patrolling the gate so we go straight through.

"Leo, it's going to get dark soon, they'll be shutting the walkway," I say. "We don't want to get locked in."

He doesn't answer. The murky green sea is visible through the gaps in the wooden slats beneath our feet. The farther we walk, the quieter it gets, the lights and sounds of Tripton fading behind us, until it feels like Leo and I are the only two people in the universe. More than once I almost slip and have to grab Leo to steady myself. He stiffens at my touch but lets me regain my balance before continuing on.

"Leo, where are we going?" I ask for about the tenth time.

At this stage it's a pretty stupid question because there is nowhere *to* go apart from the end of the pier, or else turn around and head back. But either Leo can't hear me or he chooses to ignore me, because he just keeps walking, his rhythm never faltering. The whole time he doesn't utter a single word.

The end of the pier opens up into a rectangular space dotted with metal benches and old-fashioned viewfinders. Leo walks to the edge, rests his hands on the rail and stares out to sea. I hover behind him, unsure what to do next. Out here the sea is choppier but it's still eerily quiet. The only sound comes from the lapping waves below us. I can't help thinking the weather ought to be wilder—stormy and dramatic—not this strange version of silence. One of the benches has several bunches of drooping flowers fastened to it. I wonder what terrible thing might have happened in this very spot and pull my coat tighter around my body as a shiver dances up my spine.

We stand like that for several minutes, Leo staring out to sea while I stand behind him.

"When I was little," he begins, his voice hoarse, "I wanted this toy garage really badly."

I dare to move in beside him.

"It had, like, five stories," he continues, indicating the height by motioning in the air. "And an elevator and I thought it was just amazing. I cut a picture of it out of a catalog and taped it to my headboard and I'd lie in bed for hours and just stare at it. I think I even dreamed about it, I wanted it that much. And because I wanted it so badly I sort of convinced myself that if I got it, everything would be okay. It was like all the other crap would disappear just because I had this garage. Anyway, I woke up on Christmas morning and went downstairs and there it was under the tree with a massive red bow on it. And I was so excited and for, like, two days I thought it had worked, that everything was going to be okay just because this load of plastic I'd wished for was actually mine. But then Mam's boyfriend at the time, Tony, tripped over it and broke the ramp and didn't even say he was sorry. And Tia kept putting her sticky hands all over it and losing the cars, and broke the elevator by being too rough with it, and by the new year it was ruined and I realized it hadn't made things better, not even close. And most of all I hated myself for being so stupid, for believing it would really make things better.

But that's the story of my life. Everything I want turns to crap, I should have learned that by now."

"You can't talk that way," I say urgently. "You've got so much going for you, Leo."

"I don't want to hear it. Just leave me alone, David."

I'm David today. Kate is clearly forgotten.

"I'm not leaving you," I tell him. "Not while you're like this."

"I'm not about to throw myself over the railing if that's what you're worried about," he says darkly.

"I know you're not," I bluff. "I'm still not leaving though. Friends don't do that."

He spins around to face me.

"How many times do I have to say this? I don't want to be friends with you or with anyone else. I just want to be left alone."

I open my mouth to argue but he gets in first.

"I mean it, David, go."

I remain where I am.

"Go!" he yells, tears building in his eyes. "Leave me alone, David. Just please get lost!"

I take a step toward him.

"Go away!" he yells one final time, before turning back to the railing, gripping it hard. I follow him, put my hands on his shoulders, and try to turn him to face me. At first he resists, thrashing angrily against me. Undeterred I try again, and this time I feel his exhausted body slowly giving in, going limp in my arms, his head collapsing on my shoulder.

I hold him tight and let him cry.

We walk back to Sea View in silence. Along the way, I steal a few glances at Leo's face, pale and stern. He stares straight ahead the entire time. We stop for pizza and smuggle it upstairs where we eat it in bed and watch bad TV—*The X Factor*, then half of some stupid action film from the eighties with really bad special effects. The whole time Leo barely speaks.

"Is it all right if we get ready for bed now?" he asks, as the credits of the film begin to roll. It's the most he's spoken since we were on the pier.

"Of course," I say. "Whatever you want."

We take turns using the bathroom. As we negotiate our way around the tiny bedroom, collecting toiletry bags and night clothes, it feels like we're doing an awkward dance.

When we're done, I turn out the light and climb into bed beside Leo. It shifts as he rolls over to face away from me. I roll over too so I'm facing the same way, my face inches from his curved back. I long to reach out and touch it, to let him know I am here for him, but I feel scared to, unsure of what might be pushing it too far.

"Leo?" I whisper.

"Yeah?"

"Are you okay?"

He makes a sound that I can't decipher.

"Leo, can I tell you something?"

The covers rustle. I choose to take it as an *okay*.

"I think you're the bravest person I've ever met, you know," I say.

Leo lets out a sharp laugh.

"You haven't met all that many people then."

"I'm serious," I say. "And your dad is crazy for not wanting to know you. 'Cause you're amazing."

I pause, worrying I've made a serious error by mentioning Jimmy.

"You sure you're not drunk again?" Leo says after a beat.

I take his joke as a good sign and poke him gently in the ribs.

"I mean it."

Silence.

My fingers search tentatively for Leo's in the darkness. I find them, daring to curl mine around his. I hear Leo take a deep breath before allowing his hand to relax into mine. His hand feels small and soft in my big palm, like a child's almost.

We lie in silence for a bit, our breathing falling into rhythm.

"Leo?"

"Yeah?"

"I think I'm going to tell them."

"Who? Your parents?"

"Yeah. I think I'm going to tell them tomorrow, when I get home. Before I do anything else."

"You're doing the right thing. Your mum seemed really cool and nice when she drove me home that time."

"I hope so. I'm still terrified though."

"Of course."

There's a pause.

"What's your dad like?" Leo asks quietly.

"I look like him apparently—not ideal as he's pretty much a giant."

"No, I meant what's he like as a person."

"He's just kind of a typical dad, I guess."

As soon as the words leave my mouth I regret them.

"Shit, sorry," I say quickly, "I didn't mean it like that. God, that was so stupid of me."

"It's okay," Leo says. "Go on."

I visualize my dad—big and goofy and embarrassing.

"Well, he likes soccer and golf and beer and cars and things like that," I say carefully. "When I was a kid he used to try and get me to kick a ball with him in the garden and stuff, but as soon as I made it clear I wasn't into all that, he never put pressure on me or made me feel like it was a big problem. And when I was asking for dolls for Christmas and wanting to paint my bedroom girlie colors, he never batted an eyelid, or at least if he did, he didn't let me see. He's always just let me be me, I guess."

"He sounds pretty great," Leo says.

"Yeah," I murmur, realizing that he sort of does.

"Why are you so scared of telling them if they're so cool?" Leo asks, practically reading my mind.

"Because I'm pretty sure they have no idea this is coming. It's going to knock them sideways and I don't know how they're going to react. I mean, they're hardly going to be setting off firecrackers and unfurling banners, are they?"

"They'll be okay, I know it. Even if they're shocked at first, they'll come around eventually, I bet."

My grip on Leo's hand tightens.

"Thanks, Leo, that means a lot."

We lie there in silence for a few moments.

"Are you going to tell your family about what happened today? Amber or your mum or anyone?" I ask.

"I don't know. I don't think so. What good would it do? It's funny, Amber had him figured out from the beginning, but I could never see it. I was just blinded by this idea of him. Jimmy the hero . . ."

He coughs. "Look, I'm really tired, I'm going to go to sleep now."

"Okay."

"Night, David."

"Night, Leo."

I lie there for a long time before I drop off. And although he doesn't say another word, I can tell Leo is awake too. The whole time he doesn't let go of my hand.

LEO

David and I wake up at dawn and creep out of Sea View before breakfast.

David travels back in his boy clothes.

"You still going to tell them today?" I ask.

After two days as Kate, he looks strange in a baggy hoodie and skinny jeans, with his boy haircut.

"Yes," David replies firmly.

He looks petrified though.

We don't talk much for the rest of the journey. I think we've said enough the past few days to last us a lifetime.

We say goodbye at the train station, outside by the taxi line.

"Will I see you at school tomorrow?" David asks.

"I don't know yet," I admit.

"You'll be old news by now, I bet," he says brightly.

"Sure," I say, rolling my eyes, not believing it for one second.

"All we need is for someone to release a sex tape to take the heat off and you're home free," he adds with a grin.

I fake a smile.

David looks at his feet for a moment. The laces of his sneakers are too long and drag on the sidewalk.

"Stupid jokes aside, I really hope you do come back."

"Yeah, well, we'll see."

I turn to go and David grabs hold of my hand and pulls me into a hug. I find myself returning it. We break apart and nod at each other before going our separate ways. And it's funny, because as I head across the street and toward the bus stop, I sort of miss him.

As I cross the estate, the whole place seems changed somehow in a way I can't quite put my finger on. I've been away just over forty-eight hours but it seems longer. I feel different too, raw, like I've had a layer of skin ripped off and the layer underneath is red and delicate and painful to the touch.

It's past noon but I expect everyone will be in bed. Apart from Tia maybe, who still rises at dawn like a newborn, and will have been glued to the TV for hours by now.

I'm digging about in the bottom of my backpack for my keys when the door flies open and Tia flings her tiny body at me.

"He's back!" she screams. "Leo's back!"

"Steady on, Tia," I say. "Let me get in the house at least."

I'm kicking off my sneakers when I notice a figure in the doorway to the living room. At first I think it's Mam. It takes me a moment to realize it's Auntie Kerry, puffing furiously on a cigarette and glaring at me.

"What are you doing here?" I ask, disentangling myself from

Tia, who still has her skinny arms around my waist. There's a wet patch on my hoodie from her soggy tears.

"Tia, go upstairs," Auntie Kerry says.

"But I want to watch cartoons with Leo," Tia protests, lacing her fingers through mine.

"I said upstairs!" Auntie Kerry shouts, setting Tia's lower lip wobbling.

"Go on, T," I say.

Tia nods and heads up the stairs, her head bowed.

"Give your mam and Spike a call," Auntie Kerry calls after her. "And your big sister. Tell them they can come home now."

She turns and walks into the living room. It's clear she expects me to follow. She waits until we're in the center of the room before spinning around and slapping me across the cheek. It shocks more than it hurts.

"Where the hell have you been?" she barks.

"What the hell was that for?" I cry, holding on to my cheek.

"Answer the damn question, Leo, before I really do lose my patience."

"Away," I mutter.

"Away? What d'you mean, away? Away where?"

"Why the drama?" I ask. "I left a note."

"What note? No one's seen a note."

"I left it on top of the TV," I say, crossing over to the television set. But the spot where I left my note is bare. I hunt around, eventually finding it behind the set, tucked under the radiator. I fish it out and hand it to Auntie Kerry. She doesn't bother to read it, flinging it onto the coffee table instead.

"That's it? You go gallivanting off for two whole days and all we get is a note?"

"I thought someone would see it," I say.

"Do you know where your mam and Spike are right now?" she asks, jabbing a finger in my chest. "Where they've been for the past two nights?"

I shake my head.

"Driving around looking for you, that's where. Tia's been in tears since yesterday morning, Amber and Carl have been all over the estate searching for you. The police, well, they've been no help."

"The police? What did you call them for?"

"What did you expect us to do? We had no idea where you were. Your phone was off."

"I forgot my charger," I say, looking at my feet.

Auntie Kerry just glares at me.

"I didn't think Mam would care," I say. "I didn't even think she'd notice."

Auntie Kerry's face turns a fresh shade of red.

"Your mam may not be winning any prizes for the world's best mother anytime soon, but I would think very carefully before accusing her of not noticing her own kid is missing."

"She seems to do a pretty good job of not noticing me when I am around, so what am I supposed to think?" I retort.

"Raising three kids alone isn't a walk in the park, you know."

"It's not our fault she can't hold on to a boyfriend."

Auntie Kerry slaps me again. Hard. This time it hurts.

"You have no idea, Leo," she says, pointing a shaking finger right up in my face. "Until you've walked in your mam's shoes, you will have no idea what her life has been like, bringing up the three of you alone, so don't you even pretend you do."

I slump down on the sofa, my arms folded. In front of me Auntie Kerry fumbles in her purse for a pack of cigarettes. She takes one out and swipes a plastic pink lighter from the coffee table, lighting up with still-trembling hands. She does the whole thing without taking her eyes off me for a second.

"Leo, remember that weekend when your mam came home with a black eye?"

I frown.

"It was just after all that bother at school," she prompts.

All that bother. Whenever anyone talks about what happened back in February, they always seem to speak in some special code.

"Yeah," I say. "What about it?"

"What was his name again? The ringleader?" Auntie Kerry asks.

"Alex Bonner," I murmur, my voice flat. Just saying his name out loud makes me feel sick.

"That's him, nasty piece of work. Your mam went to have it out with Alex but he wasn't in. His mam was though, giving a load of lip."

"What?"

I know Alex's mother, everyone does. She's one of those people you just can't miss. Annette, her name is. She looks just like Alex, with the same jet-black hair, hard face, and Terminator build.

"Hang on, Annette Bonner gave Mam that black eye?"

"You should have seen Annette. She was in a state once your mam had finished with her. People had to drag your mam off her in the end."

I stare at Auntie Kerry. I can't believe what I'm hearing. Mam went up against Annette Bonner for me?

"Why didn't she tell me?" I ask.

"God knows. God knows why your mam does a lot of the stuff she does."

Silence. I can sense Auntie Kerry watching me as she smokes.

"Come on then, where were you?" she says, folding her arms. Like Mam, she's tiny, built like a sparrow. Which makes it all the more incredible Mam beat up big old Annette Bonner. Jesus.

"Don't keep me in suspense," Auntie Kerry says, taking a long drag on her cigarette, the smoke misting the air between us. "Where have you been?"

"You really want to know?" I ask.

"Yes, I do."

I take a deep breath.

"I was in Kent."

Auntie Kerry's forehead creases in confusion.

"Kent? But that's miles away. What the hell's in Kent?"

I get my wallet and slide out the photograph of Dad. She takes it between her fingers, her eyes bulging. She looks down at me.

"Where'd you get this, Leo?"

"Does it matter?"

"Where did you get this, Leo?" she repeats.

"Mam's bedroom. I've had it for years."

"We turned the house upside down looking for this," she says softly. "Your mam thought she must have thrown it out by accident."

I look up. I always assumed Mam didn't miss it. She certainly never said anything about it.

"That was his first car," Auntie Kerry says, her fingers tracing its outline.

"Drives a brand-new Volvo these days. Midnight blue. Very nice," I say.

Auntie Kerry's head snaps up.

"You saw him?"

"Oh yeah. We had a great chat, me and old Jimmy," I say with a bitter laugh.

She just stares at me, her mouth hanging open slightly.

"Didn't like me turning up on his doorstep very much," I say. "Didn't like it at all in fact. You probably knew as much though, didn't you?"

Auntie Kerry sinks onto the sofa beside me, the photograph fluttering to the floor.

"How did he look?" she asks.

"Like this, I suppose, but older," I say, leaning forward to pick up the photograph. "Amber and I got his eyes," I add.

"I know you did," Auntie Kerry says.

"He's got a wife and kid of his own now," I say. "Fancy house and all that."

"Has he now?" she murmurs, her face white. It's not a real question though.

"He wasn't interested, of course. Called me a freak."

"Oh, Leo."

I crumple up the photograph in my hand and let it drop. I don't cry. I'm not planning on wasting any more tears on Jonathan Denton.

"What happened, Auntie Kerry? Why did he leave?"

"You mean, what did your mam do to make him leave?" she snaps. "I know that's what you're thinking, Leo."

I look down at my feet. Because she's right, that's exactly what I was thinking.

"Your mam and I are well aware that you've always had her down as the bad guy and your dad as the hero," Auntie Kerry continues. "We may not have done well at school and passed many exams, but we know that much."

She picks up her cigarette again. It's burned down to nothing. She tuts to herself and lights another.

"Then tell me the truth," I say.

She raises her eyebrows.

"The truth, eh? You want the truth?"

I nod.

"You sure?"

"For God's sake, Auntie Kerry."

She takes a deep drag on her cigarette and lets her eyes fall shut as she exhales. Her eyelids are waxy and shiny. She opens them again.

"Your mam met Jimmy Denton when she was twenty-one. He was twenty-three and drop-dead gorgeous. All the girls in

Cloverdale wanted him but he chose your mam. Anyway, they'd been going out for six months when she found out she was pregnant with twins. And at first Jimmy was so excited, telling everyone he met. He even proposed, brought her home this flashy ring. Everyone on the estate was green with envy, including me."

"So then what happened?"

"He started getting distant, staying out late. Your mam just put it down to him being a bit stressed about money being tight. Anyway, one day, about six weeks before she was going to pop, your mam got home from doing the grocery shopping and found a note on the coffee table."

I glance at my note, nestled among the ashtrays and mugs.

"We thought it was a joke at first," Auntie Kerry continues. "But then we went upstairs and his clothes were gone from the closet and he wasn't answering his phone. I assumed he'd got cold feet and would come back, but he never did. Your mam never heard from him again."

"But that can't be right. I remember him. I remember him changing my diaper," I say.

Auntie Kerry shakes her head.

"You can't, Leo. He was gone before you were born."

I squeeze my eyes shut and try to conjure up the image of Dad singing as he bent over me.

"It must be my ex, Chris, that you remember. He helped out quite a bit when you and Amber were small. Or your granddad maybe, before he died."

I shake my head firmly.

"No, I'm certain it was him, Auntie Kerry, I can picture his face."

But already it's fading, his features growing hazier by the second.

Auntie Kerry puts down her cigarette and takes my hand, looking right into my eyes. Her fingers are rough and freezing cold.

"It wasn't him, Leo. Trust me, it wasn't."

I stare hard at the carpet, so hard my vision blurs.

"Why didn't she just tell us?"

"What, tell a couple of little kids their dad skipped town before they were even born? Easier said than done, Leo."

"Better that than not telling us anything at all."

"Your gran told your mam to tell you and Amber he was dead, but she couldn't bring herself to do it. And anyway, as soon as you could talk you were obsessed with the idea of him. It was easier to let you dream, easier for your mam to be the villain who drove him away."

"Did she love him?" I ask.

She sighs and shakes her head.

"She really did, the fool that she is."

I stare at the carpet.

"I always assumed she'd driven him away, like she did all the rest."

"No, Leo."

"That's why she does it though," I murmur.

"Does what?"

I look up. Because it all makes weird, messed-up sense now.

"Pushes them away. So they won't leave her like Jimmy did."

Not Dad. Not anymore. Jimmy.

Auntie Kerry lets out a heavy sigh.

"You and your mam have let that man haunt you for too long now. It's time to move on, Leo, for both of you."

DAVID

I turn my key carefully in the lock and ease the front door open. The hallway is empty. I creep forward and press my ear up against the kitchen door.

I can hear my family on the other side: the rustle of newspapers, muffled voices, the occasional clink of glasses and cutlery, the radio playing in the background. A perfect family scene. And I'm about to turn it upside down.

I back away and head upstairs to my bedroom where I dump my backpack on the floor and remove my coat. I hunt around in my desk for the unsent letter to my parents, the one I almost posted under their bedroom door. I take it out of its envelope and read it through before smoothing it out and carefully gluing it onto the next available page of my scrapbook.

Mum and Dad look up in surprise as I enter the kitchen.

"You're back early," Dad says. "We didn't expect you until dinnertime."

"You look like shit," Livvy observes.

"Livvy!" Mum scolds. "Language."

"But he does!" Livvy protests, pointing at me with her yogurt spoon.

"That's no excuse."

Livvy drops the spoon onto her plate with a clatter and stands up to leave the table.

"Excuse me, madam, we clear up after ourselves in this household," Dad says.

Livvy rolls her eyes but heads over to the dishwasher with her dirty brunch dishes, loading them noisily before going into the backyard with Phil. The whole time I just stand there, clutching my scrapbook.

Mum peers up at me.

"You do look on the tired side, David," she admits. "Up chatting all night, I expect. Now, do you want some scrambled eggs maybe? I think there might even be a bit of smoked salmon left if you're lucky."

I don't say anything.

I simply walk over, put my scrapbook down on the table, and walk out again, shutting the kitchen door behind me.

I go upstairs, curl up on my bed, and wait.

. . . . .

It's only an hour before I hear the knock at the door, but it feels like days. And even though I've been expecting to hear it, it still makes me jump.

"Come in," I say, sitting up.

The door opens and in step Mum and Dad, the scrapbook tucked under Dad's arm, their faces serious.

I stare up at them and realize my whole body is quaking. I wonder whether there'll ever be a time when my body does what I want it to.

Dad clears his throat.

"David," he says. "Before we say anything more, we want you to know one important thing. And that's that your mum and I love you very much. We always have and we always will. But we also need a bit of time to digest this, okay?"

I nod.

"Does this have anything to do with Leo?" Mum asks.

"Yes, but not in the way you might think. He made me realize I needed to tell you guys, nothing more."

"And you're certain this is what you want, David?" she says, edging forward. "You're not just confused?"

"No, I'm sure, Mum. I've been sure for years now."

"I see," she says quietly, lowering her eyes.

As I watch her move across the room, it's almost like I can see all the plans she had for my future slowly crumbling inside her head.

"Why didn't you tell us earlier?" she asks, her eyes glistening with tears as she sits down on the bed beside me. Dad reaches across and squeezes her hand.

"I don't know," I say. "I was scared, I think. I was worried you would disown me or something."

Mum starts crying then. Of course that sets me off, and then

Dad too, which is miraculous in itself because I haven't seen Dad cry over anything non-soccer-related since his parents died. Noisy crying must be genetic because we're so loud Livvy comes barging in assuming Granny must have just died. Mum whisks her out of the room, reassuring her Granny is very much alive. She ends up dropping her off at Cressy's for the afternoon, leaving the three of us to talk without interruption.

When Mum gets home, we go through my scrapbook, page by page. Then I show them the videos I've been watching on YouTube, the forums I've visited, the Web sites I've pored over. I tell them about the specialist clinic in London, the one where Leo goes. I monitor their faces out of the corner of my eye as they stare at the computer screen, their eyes wide, and I can almost see the cogs in their heads whirring as they try to process everything they're seeing and hearing. Some of the more explicit stuff makes them frown and wince and I can tell Mum is fighting back more tears. But they keep watching, reading, listening. All the time I have to keep reminding myself I've had pretty much my whole life to get used to the idea, while they've only had a few hours.

Dad goes off to make tea. He comes back with a tray of cookies (the fancy ones we usually only get out when we have guests), cheese-and-pickle sandwiches, and mugs of tea. We sit on my floor and have a sort of picnic, sitting in a triangle, our knees touching.

"I'm sorry," I say, as we slurp tea, my throat exhausted, my tear ducts sore.

Mum frowns. "What do you mean, David?"

"For not being normal. I know it would be easier for everyone if I was."

She and Dad exchange looks.

"I'm not going to lie to you," she says. "Of course I'd prefer it if things were more straightforward. I love you and I don't want to see you have a hard time unnecessarily. And the road ahead, if this is what you really want to do . . ."

"It is," I say firmly.

"Well, then, the road ahead is going to be tough. It's going to be long and painful and frustrating and you're going to encounter people who don't understand it. I'm not even sure I understand it right now."

"I know. But I'm ready, I promise I am."

"What I'm trying to say, David," she says, "is that we're going to support you, no matter what."

"Besides," Dad says, "who wants to be normal anyway? Imagine that on your gravestone. 'Here lies so-and-so. They were entirely normal.'"

I smile. But I can tell he's putting on a brave face with all the fake jolliness.

The phone rings. Mum and Dad both claim it must be for them, leaving me alone among the remnants of our picnic.

When Livvy gets home from Cressy's, we eat dinner and Mum and Dad act like nothing has changed, when really, three out of four of us know that everything has.

. . . . .

I go to bed early. Mum tucks me in, something she hasn't done in years. She's been crying some more, I can tell because her face is covered in fresh blotches.

"Can I show you something?" I ask as she turns to leave.

"Of course," she says, although she looks slightly fearful.

I pick up my phone and scroll through the photos until I find one of the shots Leo took of me in Tripton. I'm beaming away, rosy cheeked, high on alcohol and life. I pass the phone over to Mum and hold my breath. She stares at the screen for ages.

"When was this taken?" she asks, not taking her eyes off it.

"Not long ago," I reply, biting my lip.

I try to read her expression but I can't quite work it out.

"You look really happy," she says finally.

"Thank you," I whisper.

She peers closer at the photograph and her expression changes ever so slightly. She turns her head to look at me, a different kind of frown on her face from the one she's been wearing for the majority of the day.

"Was this taken in a pub?" she asks.

"Of course not," I lie. "You know I don't drink."

LEO

The next day I go back to school.

David is waiting for me at the bus stop. The moment I step through the school gates, kids are staring at me, their mouths hanging open like goldfish.

At lunchtime Essie screeches, "Get a life" at any kid who looks our way, which I don't think really helps. I appreciate the effort though.

On Tuesday I have English. As I stare at the back of Alicia's head, my insides twist. At the end of the class she packs up her stuff quickly and leaves without looking back. I hear through the grapevine she reached the finals of the singing competition. I want to tell her congratulations but I know I can't.

On Wednesday I eat lunch with David, Essie, and Felix in the cafeteria. Harry comes over to our table and calls us "the mutant, the geek, and the two superfreaks" and asks us whether we've thought about opening our own traveling carnival. Essie tells him to curl up and die. I start to stand up. David grabs my wrist and pulls me back down. Harry saunters off, smirking.

On Thursday Becky keeps calling me Megan during homeroom. I don't bite and keep staring straight ahead until the bell rings and I can escape.

Later that morning, I'm walking down the hallway alone when some year-twelve kid stops me and asks if I'd be interested in joining the Math Challenge team. At first I assume it's a trick and he's about to follow up with some nasty insult, but he doesn't, giving me a flyer instead.

"We need some new blood," he says. "And Mr. Steele gave me your name. Think about it?"

I find myself promising I will.

On Friday before school I have an appointment with Jenny. It's the first time I've seen her in three weeks, having canceled my previous two sessions. She looks pleased to find me waiting in the reception area.

"I had a long conversation with Mr. Toolan at the beginning of the week," she says as I sit down in her office.

"Oh yeah," I say. "Did he tell you I did a runner from the school trip?"

"He did," Jenny admits. "But he also told me you came back on Monday with your head held high."

My face colors. Jenny lowers my file onto her lap and smiles.

"I'm really proud of you, Leo."

"You are?"

"Big-time. I know how hard it must have been for you to go

to school this week, but you did it, and you'll keep doing it, I know you will."

"Thanks," I mumble.

"Mr. Toolan also told me you've made some friends," she says tentatively. "Is that right?"

I'm about to tell Jenny she's got it wrong when I realize I don't want or need to. Instead I tell her about David.

That day I make it down the hallway without anyone saying anything nasty. It's only a small triumph but it's one I'm prepared to accept.

The bottom line is, I survived the week. And if I can survive one week, I can survive the next one, and the one after that.

When I get home from school Mam summons me and Amber to the living room. At first she doesn't say anything, chain-smoking as she fiddles with her hoop earrings and not looking us in the eye. Eventually though she sets her cigarettes and lighter down, takes a deep breath, and starts to talk.

And finally we get to hear everything, right from the very beginning with no gaps—Mam's story in her own words.

DAVID

It's the last Friday before the Christmas holidays and Essie and Felix have been acting odd all week: lots of urgent whispering when they think I'm not looking, and fixed smiles when they think I am. At first I put it down to boyfriend-girlfriend stuff but something tells me it's more than that.

Today is definitely the pinnacle of their weirdness. In History Essie is totally manic, babbling nonstop. Even Felix seems on edge.

"What's going on, guys?" I ask, for at least the one-hundredth time this week.

"Nothing," they reply in unison.

"We're still on for tonight, aren't we?" I ask.

"Of course we are," Essie replies. "Why wouldn't we be?"

"Just checking," I murmur.

For the first time ever we've decided to boycott the Christmas Ball. We're going to hang out at my place, gorge on pizza (Essie and I anyway; Felix will be bringing his own cauliflower-crust alternative), and watch Christmas movies. And although I know we'll have fun and everything, and even though the Christmas Ball has proved the most disappointing night of the year every year for the past three, I can't help but feel a small ache of regret that tonight it's going ahead without me.

The final class before lunch is Math. Mr. Steele gives us a quiz. I'm pretty sure *quiz* is just a slightly friendlier word for test, but I surprise myself by actually doing okay. After class I head to the cafeteria. I'm unloading my tray when I sense someone by my side. I look up. It's Leo.

Upon his return to school following our weekend in Tripton, the teachers quickly figured out what was going on and a series of special assemblies were arranged, explaining what being transgender means, and making it clear that anyone found guilty of bullying would face a harsh punishment. Although the name-calling and cruel whispers haven't stopped altogether, they've certainly died down.

Leo and I have been hanging out more. He's still tutoring me, plus we've been to the movies a couple of times, and sometimes to McDonald's or Nando's afterward. He's been over to my house a few times too, and charmed the pants off my mum and, to my surprise, Livvy. A couple of times a week he eats lunch with Essie, Felix, and me. He never says a lot, just listens and occasionally chimes in with a sarcastic comment. Earlier in the week, the four of us went to see the drama club's production of *Oh! What a Lovely War*. Alicia was in it. She looked very beautiful and sang two solos.

Leo talked to his therapist, Jenny, about me, and she gave him the details of some support groups that might be helpful while I'm waiting for my referral to the specialist clinic in London to be accepted. Leo promises he'll come with me in the new year, although I'm not sure he actually will. He avoids the subject of his gender whenever possible, even with me.

"Hey," I say, opening my can of Coke.

I notice Leo's lack of food.

"Don't tell me you weren't tempted by the driest turkey in the land," I say, presenting my plate as if it's the top prize in a game show.

"I can't stay," he replies. "I just came by to give you this."

He hands me a note.

I frown and open it, immediately recognizing Essie's spidery handwriting.

If anyone asks, you don't know where we are. See you at yours tonight? xoxo Us.

I look up at Leo.

"You know what's going on?" I ask.

"No idea. They just asked me to make sure you got this. What does it say?"

"That they're cutting school this afternoon," I say.

Leo shrugs. "I don't know why. Like I said, they didn't say anything else."

He stands up and turns to go.

"Hey," I call after him. "Are you going to the ball tonight?"

"What do you think?"

"Essie, Felix, and I are hanging out at my house if you want to come?"

"Thanks for the offer, but I reckon I'm just going to stay in."

I try not to show my disappointment.

"Look, I've got to go. See you around?"

I nod and watch him leave.

That afternoon, usual classes are canceled and replaced with DVDs or games, which makes Essie and Felix's disappearing act even more puzzling.

. . . . .

On the way home Mum plays Christmas songs in the car.

In the backseat Livvy bounces up and down.

"Excited about your first ball, Liv?" I ask over my shoulder.

"Duh?" she replies. "Of course I am. It's going to be epic. Mum, did I tell you there's going to be an actual snow machine?"

"You did, darling," Mum says, winking at me.

"Ten of us are going to Cressy's to get ready. Cressy's mum has hired a limo and everything, a white one."

"Sounds great," I murmur.

"Not just great, epic," Livvy says dreamily.

After an initial freak-out, Livvy has taken the news of what my parents are referring to as my "gender issues" far better than expected, the blow possibly softened by my parents' promise to coincide my first clinic appointment in London with a trip to see *Wicked* afterward. I often sense Livvy looking at me though, through narrowed eyes, as if she's trying to figure me out by telepathy or some other cosmic means, rather than just asking me.

"Did you get ice cream for tonight?" I ask Mum.

"Of course."

"What flavors?"

"Oh, you know, a variety," she says vaguely.

"And did you get the nondairy stuff for Felix?"

"I think so . . ."

We pull into the driveway. As I'm climbing out of the car I'm certain I see the curtain twitch, which is odd as Dad doesn't normally get home from work until at least five-thirty.

Mum opens the door, nudging me through first, to reveal Essie and Felix in a tableau on the stairs, Essie with her arms outstretched, Felix crouching beside her.

"Surprise!" they yell.

Essie is wearing a pair of fairy wings and has glitter smeared on her cheeks, and Felix is sporting plastic mouse ears and what looks suspiciously like a silver unitard.

"Don't ask," he says.

"What are you guys doing here?" I ask. "You're not supposed to be coming over until seven."

"We were lying!" Essie singsongs with delight.

I turn to Mum.

"Did you know about this?"

She just shrugs innocently and ushers Livvy into the kitchen.

Essie scampers down the stairs, followed by Felix, his hands hovering awkwardly over his crotch.

"What's going on?" I ask.

"She's got a thing planned," Felix whispers.

"Oh. Okay."

Essie produces a wand from behind her back and starts swinging it about above her head.

"Do not fear, sweet thing, for tonight, Cinderella, you shall go to the ball!" she cries.

She points her wand at Felix, almost poking him in the eye. He dashes up the stairs, returning a few seconds later with a shiny black box in his hands. I peer at it, realizing it's a brand-new makeup kit.

Essie waves her wand again and Felix hurtles back up the stairs. He returns with a wig on a polystyrene head.

"Is that *my* wig?" I ask. It's been styled into soft waves and has a small tiara nestled on top.

"Yep," Essie says proudly. "Kudos to your mum for her pretty incredible hairdressing skills."

I peer down the hallway but Mum has shut the kitchen door.

"And now for the pièce de résistance!" Essie cries.

She waves her wand a final time. Felix goes dashing up the stairs once more, emerging a few seconds later carrying a dress bag.

"Open it," Essie whispers, her eyes glittering.

Slowly I unzip the dress bag to reveal just about the most beautiful dress I've ever seen. It's light blue with delicate shoulder straps, a full skirt, and a gauzy sash around the waist.

"It's like the movie star dresses in my scrapbook," I breathe, running my fingers over the silky fabric.

"I know," Essie says excitedly.

"It's incredible, it really is. But I can't wear it," I say, doing up the zipper.

Essie's face drops.

"What do you mean, you can't wear it?" she demands.

"Are you serious? Wear this to the ball? With a wig and makeup and stuff? Can you imagine what Harry would do? I'd be a laughingstock until the end of time. Look, I'm really touched you've done this for me, I'm bowled over, but I can't go to the ball wearing this, I'm sorry." I shove the dress back into Felix's arms, tears in my eyes.

"When Ess said 'you shall go to the ball,' she didn't specify which ball," Felix says gently.

"What do you mean?"

"We're not going to the Eden Park Christmas Ball," he says.

"Then where are we going? We're not crashing some other school's ball, are we?"

"Not exactly."

"Then where are we going?"

"You'll have to just trust us," Essie says.

I hesitate.

"Look, just start getting ready," she continues. "All will become clear, I promise. Oh, wait, one last thing."

She runs up to my bedroom, returning a minute later with a shoe box. I take off the lid to discover a pair of silver-sequined Converse.

"Tennis shoes?" I say.

She smiles mysteriously.

"I told you, all will become clear."

. . . . .

Having my mum do my makeup is probably one of the most surreal episodes in my life so far (and probably hers). It's almost as surreal as having Felix sitting on my bed dressed as a mouse watching. Dad arrives home from work and orders us pizzas (salad for Felix) before dropping Livvy off at Cressy's house. Things get even more surreal as I sit at the kitchen table in my bathrobe wearing full makeup, chomping on a slice of Hawaiian pizza with my parents and friends as if it's the most normal thing in the world.

. . . . .

At 6:30 p.m. I am standing alone in my bedroom staring at myself in the mirror, not entirely sure what to make of the person staring back at me.

There's a knock at the door.

"C'mon out!" Essie calls. "We wanna see."

"Hang on," I yell back.

Because I want this moment to last a few seconds longer. Just me and the mirror. And me finally liking what I see in the reflection, even if it also makes me feel like I might faint or vomit or both at any second.

More knocking.

"All right, all right, I'm coming," I say, taking one final look. "But first, close your eyes."

"They're closed!" Essie and Felix call back in unison.

I take a deep breath and cautiously step out onto the landing. Essie and Felix are poised, holding hands, their eyes screwed shut, Felix has ditched the mouse costume for a slightly too-large tuxedo, Essie in a very short purple dress and artfully ripped fishnet tights.

"Okay, you can open them now," I instruct.

Essie opens hers first, gasps, and hugs me.

Felix pulls me into a hug.

"You look awesome," he whispers.

I laugh and hug him even harder than I already was.

The doorbell rings.

"That'll be Leo," Felix says. "I'll get it."

"Leo?" I say.

"Well, you can't go to the ball without a date," Essie says.

"Wait—" I begin to protest. But Felix is already bounding down the stairs. Dad beats him to the door. Essie and I hang over the banister and watch as Leo steps into the hallway, looking self-conscious in a gray suit and a blue tie.

Essie wolf-whistles. "Nice threads, Denton!" she calls.

He rolls his eyes in response.

"Aw, check out Leo's tie," Essie whispers, as Dad takes Leo's jacket and offers him a slice of leftover pizza. "It matches your dress!"

"Don't even go there," I warn her.

"Why not? You're single, he's single . . ."

"We're just friends, Ess."

"But you guys would be so cute together!"

"Ess, I mean it," I say firmly.

"You're no fun at all," she says. She's smiling though.

I kept my promise to Leo. I haven't told Essie or Felix I was with him the weekend I went to Tripton. They suspect though, and have probably been driving themselves insane trying to figure out what we were up to down there. And maybe one day, with Leo's permission, I'll tell them, but for now that weekend is our secret—just Leo's and mine.

Essie takes my hand and we head downstairs. I trip on my dress on the bottom step and Leo has to jump up to steady me, but apart from that it's a perfectly graceful descent.

"You totally lied to me this afternoon," I say lightly.

"I've had a lot of practice," Leo replies, one eyebrow raised.

We smile at each other.

"You look nice," he says.

"Honestly? I can't decide whether I feel amazing or ridiculous."

"Go for the former."

"Thanks. You look nice too. It *suits* you. Get it?"

"Ha-ha."

"I do try. Hey, do you know where we're going tonight?"

"I might."

"But you're not going to tell me, are you?"

"Nope."

Mum and Dad swoop in then, armed with a camera each, and make us pose for a series of photographs in the foyer. As they snap away, calling out instructions, I wonder what they're think-ing, whether they're silently freaking out at sending their only son off to a phantom ball dressed up as a girl. Whatever their feelings are, they're keeping them well hidden, covered up with wild enthusiasm. Since I told them, their behavior has been slightly hysterical, torn between acceptance and horror, trying to make up for the horror bit with overt support. Only the other night I heard Mum crying again and Dad soothing her, so I get the feeling we still have a long way to go. But I love them for trying so hard, so much it makes my heart ache sometimes.

As we pose for my parents I notice that instead of wearing dress shoes or high heels, all four of us are wearing tennis shoes. I'm about to ask why when there's a loud honk from outside. Essie runs into the living room and sticks her head under the curtains.

"The limo's here!" she calls.

Leo frowns.

"A limo, Essie, are you serious?" he says. "You do remember where we're going, don't you?"

"Oh relax, I couldn't resist," Essie says, shooing him away. "C'mon, everyone, time to go!"

I'm the last to leave.

"Be safe, kiddo," Dad says, hugging me.

"I will."

Mum takes me in her arms then, hugging me close.

"You look wonderful," she whispers in my ear.

"Thank you, Mum."

We pull apart. Her eyes are wet.

"Now look after each other and have fun," she says, wiping her cheek with her sleeve. "That's an order, by the way!"

. . . . .

The limo is pink with leopard-print upholstery and flashing lights. It is the ugliest vehicle I have ever seen.

"It's so tacky! I adore it!" Essie proclaims, sprawling over the seats. "I asked the company for the most disgusting limo they had and they have not let me down!"

"I feel like I'm in an incredibly low-rent music video," Felix murmurs, gingerly sliding in beside her.

Leo is still frowning. "We're not supposed to be drawing attention to ourselves, remember?" he hisses.

"You're no fun," Essie says, pouting.

"I hate to say it, but I think Leo's right," Felix says. "We're going to stick out like a sore thumb in this thing."

"Can someone *please* tell me where we're going?" I ask.

Everyone ignores me.

Essie sighs. "How about we get out around the corner from the venue and do the last bit on foot?"

"I guess we'll have to," Leo says grimly.

As the limo creeps through the evening traffic, I try to narrow down our likely destination. We head out of Eden Park, on our way passing several limousines heading in the opposite direction, toward school.

"Suckers!" Essie yells out of the sunroof.

After that we head south through the city center, then over the bridge. It's only then it dawns on me where we're going.

We're heading for Cloverdale.

．　．　．　．　．

Leo guides the limo driver around the back of the estate, avoiding the main streets and dropping us off on the corner of Renton Road, home of the old Cloverdale swimming pool. As Leo helps me climb out of the limo, I notice the line of people snaking down the side of the fence. I begin to feel nervous, holding on tight to Leo's hand. He squeezes back.

"Oh my God!" Essie cries, grabbing Felix's arm and jumping up and down. "People have come! They've actually come."

As we get closer, I realize I recognize most of the people in the line. There are a couple of girls from my textiles class, some emo kids from year eleven, a lesbian couple from year nine holding hands, a large group of goths. As we walk past them I can feel their eyes on me, their nudges and whispers tumbling down the line like dominoes. My legs feel like they're made of paper.

"I've got you," Leo whispers as he steers me toward the front of the line, where we find find Amber holding a clipboard, her hair scraped back in a tight don't-mess-with-me ponytail, accompanied by a burly boy wearing black who is introduced as her boyfriend, Carl.

"A.k.a. the muscle," Essie says, her eyes lingering on Carl's arms.

"What's going on?" I ask, as Essie turns to speak to Amber. "You keep saying 'all will become clear,' but so far absolutely nothing is."

"Just trust us," Felix says.

I glance at Leo.

"What he said," he adds.

Essie gives Carl a nod. He pulls aside the loose fence panel. Essie bangs the fence three times with a stick. The crowd quiets down.

"I now declare the very first Alternative Eden Park Christmas Ball open!" she yells to polite applause.

I don't have a chance to ask any questions because I'm being pushed down on my hands and knees. One by one we crawl through the hole which has been carefully lined with a tarp. Once through the hole and standing upright again, I can see the route to the pool has been lit with hundreds of tea lights in jam jars. We follow it into the foyer where there are more lights, guiding us toward the pool itself. The four of us lead the way, the excited murmurs of our schoolmates humming behind us.

"How did you get all these people here?" I ask, glancing behind me.

"We just conducted a rather militant underground advertising campaign," Felix says casually.

"Consisting of what?"

"Oh, it was very easy," Essie says. "The second Leo described this place we knew we had a venue. We then simply gave people an alternative."

As we get closer I realize I can hear music.

"Is that a DJ?" I ask.

"It might be," Felix says, his face twitching.

As we turn the corner to the poolside, I let out a gasp. It looks insane. There are more lights, as well as white balloons and silver streamers everywhere. Plus, suspended from the top diving board, there's a slowly turning disco ball, casting millions of chinks of light around the space.

"This is what you were doing," I say. "This afternoon."

"And last night. And the night before that," Essie says. "Getting a generator in here was no picnic, you know."

At the other end of the pool, near the shallow end, music is blasting out of a set of massive speakers. The DJ himself looks suspiciously like one of Felix's older brothers.

"Felix, is that Nick?" I ask, squinting.

"It is."

"He doesn't mind DJ'ing a high school ball?"

Felix turns to me, his face grave.

"I won't lie to you, I've promised to be his slave for Christmas Day in return."

I look at the three of them, their faces aglow from the flickering candles dotted everywhere.

"I can't believe you've gone to all this trouble," I say. "Just for me."

I feel myself welling up for about the fifth time this evening.

"Oh no you don't!" Essie cries. "You are not crying tonight. It's not allowed, for one thing it will totally ruin your makeup. And for another, your emotion is misplaced. It's not just for you. Take a look around."

I do as I'm told. Gradually the pool, for tonight rechristened the dance floor, is filling up with awestruck kids: the oddballs of Eden Park High. But then I realize it's not just the goths and the emos and the nerds out there. There are other kids too, kids I never dreamed would choose a ball in an abandoned swimming pool in Cloverdale over Harry Beaumont's snow-machine extravaganza.

Nick begins to play a Bruno Mars song.

"Come on," Essie says. "Let's dance."

"I don't know," I say, planting my feet firmly on the ground.

I can't forget the fact I'm here as a girl, as Kate. And down on the dance floor are a ton of kids whose reaction to my appearance I am yet to experience.

"Go," Leo whispers in my ear. I hesitate before letting Essie guide me toward the ladder. We clamber down onto the dance floor, the surface of which slopes gently toward the deep end.

"I get the Converse now," I say, nodding at my feet.

"See, I told you all would become clear," she says, grinning, pulling me into the center. I glance over my shoulder. Leo and Felix are getting drinks. Leo catches my eye and gives me a thumbs-up.

As the chorus kicks in I can feel people looking at me. Essie immediately begins to dance, flinging her arms in the air and singing along. But I'm rooted to the spot, too afraid to make any sudden movements. Even though Leo has paved the way at school in some respects, I'm still a boy in a dress to most people: David Piper in drag.

Essie grabs my hands.

"What's wrong?" she asks.

"I don't think I can do this, Ess, everyone's looking."

She yells something I don't catch over the music.

"What?" I yell back.

"Dance like no one is watching!" she shouts in my ear. "Pretend it's just you and me!"

I shut my eyes for a second and try to imagine it's just Essie and me dancing around her bedroom. I begin to move, just my arms at first, slowly introducing the rest of my body. After twenty seconds I dare to open my eyes and although half of the kids on the dance floor are still staring at me, I manage to more or less block them out for the rest of the song, just concentrating on my best friend's grinning face as she bounces up and down in front of me.

We've danced to a couple of songs and I'm almost in the swing of things when I hear it.

"Freak Show."

I look over my shoulder but the dance floor is crowded and I can't work out where it came from. I stop dancing.

"You okay?" Essie asks, tugging at my arm.

I nod. But I'm not okay. This is too much, too soon. I try to keep moving but my limbs feel heavy and clumsy.

The next time I hear it clearly. I spin around. A group of kids from the year below are standing in a semicircle, staring at me, their lips curled in disgust.

"Tranny," one of them says.

The others dissolve into giggles.

"Yeah, are you, like, a drag queen?" another asks.

Leo appears as if from nowhere and cuts them off.

"Get lost, why don't you. If you can't be cool, then you may as well go to the school ball."

"Yeah," Essie chimes in. "If you've got a problem with anything you see, then you're not wanted here."

"Well?" Leo growls. "Got anything more to say?"

The year-nine kids look at one another before wandering off, throwing us dirty glances over their shoulders.

"Idiots," Essie mutters. "You okay?"

"Fine," I say, although I'm shaking.

"Thanks," I murmur to Leo, as the next song kicks in.

He shrugs.

"Is it always going to be like this?" I ask.

"For a while, yeah. But it'll get better, I promise. It already has for me. And this comes from someone with a bit of experience."

I nod gratefully.

As Felix joins us we start to dance again and Leo surprises me by not being that bad a dancer, although he does bow out of some of Essie's more outrageous dance-move suggestions. We dance to song after song and slowly I look around to find fewer kids are looking in my direction; they're too busy dancing themselves. Our dance circle slowly expands until I'm dancing alongside kids I've never even spoken to before.

At one point I'm conscious of Simon Allen shuffling about beside me in a rented tuxedo, still smelling distinctly of plasticine.

"Hey, Simon," I say.

"Hey," he replies. "Look, I, er, just wanted to say, I think you've got real balls."

The second the words leave his mouth, he goes bright red, like, tomato red.

"Oh my God—sorry—bad choice of words," he stammers. "What I mean is, I think you're really, really brave."

I'm a little taken aback. In all our years of sitting next to each other in homeroom, Simon and I have barely spoken. We've always had this nonverbal agreement that associating with each other may draw unwanted attention to our individual oddness.

"Thank you, Simon," I say. "I really appreciate you saying that."

"You're welcome," he says, looking at his feet before turning to shuffle off again.

"Wait," I say.

He turns, his face still pink.

"Dance with us?"

He hesitates before nodding, and ends up staying for another two songs.

Nick has been instructed to play as many requests as possible so the music lurches from rock to pop to punk to folk.

"Want a drink?" Leo asks when a particularly obscure goth-rock song starts to play.

"Good idea."

We sit on the edge of the pool with our Cokes, watching our classmates dance below us.

"Is it freaky?" I ask after a few seconds. "Having your special place invaded like this?"

I can hardly believe this is the same space Leo and I spent that freezing cold evening, sitting on what is now a dance floor teeming with kids.

"A bit," Leo admits. "Not that it's going to be mine for much longer. They're bulldozing it in the new year."

"No way?"

"Yup. They're going to flatten it to the ground." He takes a long sip of Coke. "It's good it's going out in style."

"I wonder how things are at the real ball," I muse.

"Did you know I was supposed to take Alicia once upon a time?" Leo says, fiddling with the tab on his can.

"Really?"

He nods and looks really sad for a second.

"For what it's worth, she tweeted that she was boycotting it this year," I say.

"Doesn't make much difference though really, does it?"

"I suppose not."

I pause. Leo is looking deep into his Coke can.

"You still like her, don't you?"

"It makes no difference whether I do or not. We each go around school acting like the other one doesn't exist."

He looks up and puts on a bright smile.

"Enough about Alicia. Tonight's about looking forward, not back."

Just then the music stops abruptly, resulting in a collective groan from the goth kids on the dance floor. It takes me just a few seconds to recognize the introduction to the next song. "Have Yourself a Merry Little Christmas"—the Nat King Cole version. It's the first slow number of the night and quickly kids start partnering off.

"Your favorite Christmas song, right?" Leo says.

I nod.

He jumps down onto the surface of the pool.

"Want to dance then?" he asks, holding out his hand.

"Seriously?" I ask, glancing around me.

"No one's looking," he lies. "C'mon."

I let him help me down to the dance floor. Even though we've shared a bed, and hugged and held hands, and told each other some pretty personal stuff, somehow negotiating where our hands should go while we are dancing is suddenly the most awkward thing in the world. Eventually we get into position and begin to sway back and forth with the music. I keep my eyes on Leo in an effort to drown out the whispers and nudges coming at us from every angle. Not that I blame them in some ways, it's kind of a scoop, the two of us slow dancing together.

"I'm sorry I'm not Zachary," Leo says as we reach the second verse.

"What do you mean?"

"You know, your fantasy? Dancing with a boy at the Christmas Ball? I'm kind of guessing this wasn't quite what you had in mind."

I look up at Leo and smile.

"You're right, it's not. But this is better. One hundred times better."

And I swear Leo, king of the poker face, is blushing.

It's when we're dancing to the final chorus that I notice her standing on the side of the pool, combing the packed dance floor, her face all tearstained.

Livvy.

"Excuse me," I say to Leo.

He frowns but lets me go.

"Livvy!" I call. When her eyes finally latch onto me, there's a moment of confusion before her face melts into recognition.

"What are you doing here?" I ask as I climb up the ladder at the side of the pool.

"I got a taxi," she replies.

"But why? Why aren't you at school?"

She looks at her feet.

"Cressy and I had a fight."

"What about?"

"She started it," she says. "She danced with Daniel Addison. She doesn't even like him! And she knows how much I do, I've told her so, like, a million times."

Her eyes start to well up with tears.

"Come here," I say.

She lets me hold her.

"I'm sorry, Liv," I say, stroking her hair. "That was a sucky thing for Cressy to do."

She nods fiercely, a bubble of snot protruding out of her right nostril.

"Here," I say, passing her a napkin from the refreshment table.

She blows her nose hard.

"How was the ball apart from that?" I ask.

She shrugs. "Not like I imagined it."

"Yeah, they're kind of like that," I say.

"The snow machine didn't work," she says. "It snowed for about three seconds, then got clogged up. When I left, Harry Beaumont was outside screaming about it to someone on his cell."

I grin. "I'm glad you're here, Liv."

She nods and looks out at the dance floor.

"I like your dress," she says.

"Thanks, Liv. I like yours too."

She bites her lip to stop herself from smiling.

"Why don't you come dance?" I say.

"I don't know. I might just sit and watch," she says, motioning to the fold-down seats behind her.

"Don't be stupid. Come on, dancing will make you feel better, I promise. Only you better take off your heels first."

And this is how I end up spending most of the ball dancing with my little sister.

. . . . .

It's almost the end of the night when I hear the opening chords of a familiar song. And for a moment I'm back at the Mermaid Inn, Tripton-on-Sea, high on life, as Leo nervously shuffles about the tiny stage in front of me, clinging to the microphone and looking as if he would like to kill me.

"I'll be back, Liv," I say.

She waves me away, happily dancing with a group of year-eight kids. I wade across the dance floor, scouring the bobbing heads for his. As the chorus kicks in, I swear under my breath. I turn around in a slow circle. He's got to be here somewhere. Then I see him, fighting his way across the dance floor toward me. I break into a grin and push my way through the crowd. We collide in the middle of the dance floor.

"It's your song!" I yell.

"No it isn't," Leo yells back. "It's ours."

Essie and Felix join us then. We put our arms around one another and jump in a circle, bellowing the lyrics.

Right now, the time is ours!
So let's fly higher!
Light the stars on fire!
Together we'll shine!

And even though I know there's a ton of stuff ahead I'm terrified about, tonight I can't help but feel like no matter how hard it gets, everything might just be okay in the end.

LEO

It's Boxing Day. Amber is at Carl's house. Mam and Spike, in matching pajamas, are passed out on the sofa, crumpled paper hats perched on their heads. In front of them on the coffee table are the remains of lunch: turkey sandwiches, Pringles, pickled onions, and chocolate cake. Tia is sitting cross-legged on the floor watching *Brave* on DVD, a pair of glittery fairy wings on her back.

Christmas Day was all right in the end. It turns out Spike is half-decent in the kitchen, so he took care of Christmas lunch while Amber and Tia made a huge raspberry trifle for dessert. The Jell-O layer hadn't set properly so it was a bit runny but it still tasted good. Mam was in a great mood and even agreed to a game of Tia's Monopoly Junior (we let Tia win). In the evening Auntie Kerry and her boyfriend and a few friends of Spike's came over. One of them brought his ukulele with him and played loads of Christmas songs, Spike accompanying him by drumming on the coffee table. We all joined in the choruses and Mam sang so loudly she lost her voice. When we did "Fairytale of New York" I thought of being in the Mermaid Inn in Tripton with David. It feels like years ago. Whenever I think of Tripton now, it's this stuff—winning at bingo, splashing around in the freezing-cold sea, holding back David's hair as he threw up—that pops into my head. The other bits, the bad stuff with my dad, I keep buried. Jenny reckons I need to work through it. And I will. But for now, I just want to forget him and move on.

When Mam, Spike, and Amber got home from searching for me all those weeks ago, I thought they'd be angry. I expected shouting and swearing and slamming doors. Instead Mam held me really, really tight while Spike put the kettle on and Amber collapsed on the sofa, the three of them pale with exhaustion. I kept telling them I was sorry, over and over, but Mam just told me to "shut up." We've been getting on better since. The entire house has felt quieter, calmer. It's almost like we've hit an invisible reset button.

Someone knocks on the door. I glance at Mam and Spike but they're comatose. I sigh and heave myself out of the armchair.

It's Kate, bundled up under loads of layers. She's wearing makeup and I can see her wig peeking out from beneath her green wool hat.

"Hey, someone cut the grass," she says, gesturing at the lawn behind her.

"Oh yeah," I say. "Spike and a couple of his friends did it the other week."

"Looks good."

"Yeah. We've got an actual front path again."

"I almost forgot, Merry Christmas," she says.

"Merry Christmas," I reply. "You, er, want to come in or something?"

"Best not, I said I'd only be five minutes," she says. Over her shoulder I can see her mum and dad and Livvy in the car. They wave. I raise my hand in greeting.

"So how's your Christmas been?" I ask.

"Weird but good. We told my gran yesterday."

"Wow. And? How'd she react?"

"Um, okay, I think. Shocked. I'm pretty sure she almost choked on her Christmas pudding. She clearly thinks it's a phase but, hey, she hasn't disowned me yet so that's something, right?"

I nod and laugh.

"Oh, and guess what else?"

"What?"

"My referral to the clinic in London was accepted. The letter came on Christmas Eve, would you believe."

"That's great news," I say. And I mean it.

"I know," Kate says, beaming. "It still might be another three months before I get an appointment but it's a step in the right direction. I feel like things are finally happening, you know?"

"Definitely."

"And we've got an appointment to see Mr. Toolan in the new year, to maybe talk about me coming to school in role, maybe once I start seeing someone at the clinic."

"Wow."

"I know, right? So far, so terrifying."

She's grinning ear to ear though.

"Anyway, the real reason I'm here is to give you this," she says, reaching inside her coat and pulling out a slim package in silver wrapping paper. She thrusts it into my hands.

"What is it?" I ask.

"Duh. What do you think it is? It's a Christmas present."

"But I don't have anything for you."

"That's okay. It's small. Aren't you going to open it?"

"You want me to open it now?"

She nods.

I rip off the paper to reveal a paperback book. I turn it over and study the front cover.

"*Alan Turing: The Enigma*," I read aloud.

"He was a really brilliant mathematician apparently," Kate says. "He cracked codes during the Second World War. They made a film about him."

"I think I've heard of him," I say, thumbing through the pages.

"It got tons of good reviews on Amazon," she adds.

"It's great, thank you," I say, closing it.

"You're not just saying that? I was worried it might be a bit boring."

"Nah, it looks really cool."

She smiles.

"What about you? How's your Christmas been?" she asks.

I glance behind me, at the scene of relative peace in the living room.

"It's been . . . okay actually."

There's a sudden gust of cold wind. I zip up my hoodie all the way to my chin.

Her dad beeps the car horn.

"I'd better go. You must be freezing. We're going to see *The Nutcracker* at the theater tonight. Family Boxing Day tradition."

"Nice. Enjoy it."

"Cute guys in tights! What's not to enjoy?" Kate quips.

"Thanks again for the present," I say, clearing my throat and holding the book up. "I might read some tonight."

"You're very welcome," she replies. "So see you next year?"

"God, yeah, see you next year."

"Harry's going to have it in for us big-time, I bet."

"Maybe, maybe not. What's he going to do though? Realistically?"

We stand there for a moment, smiling, not really needing to say anything.

"You better run," I say.

"Yeah, you're right."

She hugs me hard before dashing down the path.

I stand on the doorstep in my socks and watch her go.

．．．．．

About an hour later, just as it's getting dark, it begins to snow. Mam and Spike have headed out to the pub for the night, and Amber is still at Carl's, so it's just me and Tia at home.

As soon as she sees the snow she goes mental, tearing around the living room and begging me to come out into the backyard and make a snowman with her.

"There's not enough snow for that," I tell her.

"Snowballs then!" she says.

In the end I watch from the doorway. Not enough snow has fallen yet to scrape up a decent snowball, so after a few failed tries Tia just stands there instead, her arms outstretched and her head lifted up to the sky, trying to catch snowflakes in her open mouth.

"Get your coat at least," I call to her. But she doesn't listen. It's like the snow has put a spell on her.

I get cold just standing there watching, so I close the door and go back inside. But Tia's outside for another ten minutes, just in her crocs, jeans, T-shirt, and fairy wings. When she eventually comes in, her face is bright red and her teeth are chattering. When I touch her hands, they're like ice cubes, but she doesn't even seem to notice. Sometimes I do wonder if Tia is wired up right. I make her some cocoa and leave her curled up on the sofa watching *Beauty and the Beast*, an old picnic blanket draped over her tiny body.

I head upstairs and sit on Amber's bunk where I watch the snow fall out the window, the flakes getting increasingly fat, settling fast. As I'm watching them fall, faster and faster still, I get this funny feeling, sort of like déjà vu, of being in the snow with Jimmy, when I was really, really tiny. Of course I now know this is impossible; it's just my mind playing tricks on me. In the past I would have tried to cling to this "memory," but tonight I let it dissolve into nothingness, just like the snowflakes on Tia's tongue.

As I look out the window, I imagine that I'm not in Cloverdale at all—but somewhere far, far away instead. It's funny how snow changes that, takes everything ugly and gray—the garbage cans and piles of trash and rusty cars—and hides them under a sparkling white blanket. It won't last. By tomorrow night the snow will have turned slushy and stained. But for tonight, with not a soul in sight, it's perfect. I push open the window a crack and listen to the absolute stillness. I shimmy down the bed so I'm lying on my back, and all I can see is the sky, the falling snow-flakes lit up in orange by the street lamp outside the window.

I don't know how long I've been lying there like that, when I hear someone knocking at the door. It'll be Mam and Spike I expect, having forgotten their keys. Or belated carolers.

I sit up and listen as Tia calls, "What do you want?"

A few seconds later she yells my name up the stairs. I climb down the ladder.

"It's for you," Tia says, blinking up at me from the hallway, her fairy wings all crooked from where she's been lying on the sofa.

"I gathered that," I say. "Who is it?"

She just shrugs and wanders back into the living room.

I pad down the stairs. Behind the glass of the front door, there's a shadowy figure. I open it.

It's Alicia. She's wearing a purple coat and fluffy white ear-muffs. There's snow on her shoulders and in her hair. I stare at her. I'm pretty sure my mouth is hanging open.

She takes a deep breath.

"I want you to know it wasn't me," she blurts. "I didn't tell a soul about what you told me, I wouldn't have. But then Becky went digging on the Internet and blabbed. She's not my favorite

343

person these days, if that's any consolation. Look, what I'm try-ing to say is, I'm sorry. For everything, but mostly for taking so long to say so."

She says this quickly, her eyes wide and startled, as if she's sur-prised she wound up on my doorstep in the first place.

"No, I'm sorry," I say. "I should have told you from the start. I shouldn't have let things go that far."

She puts her finger to my lips to silence me and looks into my eyes.

"Leo, can I ask you something?"

I nod.

"Can we please forget about all that and, I don't know, start again?"

"Start again?"

"As friends."

"Friends," I repeat.

She holds out her hand and takes another deep breath.

"Hi. I'm Alicia Baker. Nice to meet you."

I hesitate before taking her hand in mine and shaking it.

"And I'm Leo, Leo Denton."

She breaks into a smile. That smile.

"Merry Christmas, Leo Denton."

ACKNOWLEDGMENTS

A huge thank-you to everyone and anyone who supported me during the writing of this book, but especially:

My hands-down amazing agent, Catherine Clarke, for making me feel I'm in safe hands every step of the way.

Catherine Drayton at Inkwell Management for her help and guidance.

The entire team at FSG, especially my wonderful editor, Margaret Ferguson, whose care and attention to detail has made the editing process a joy from start to finish. I'm thrilled *The Art of Being Normal* has found such a happy home across the pond!

Everyone at David Fickling Books, including but not limited to Phil Earle, David Fickling, Rose Fickling, Anthony Hinton, Simon Mason, Philippa Perry, Linda Sargent, and last (but never least), my UK editor, Bella Pearson, who believed in me from the very start.

To the staff of the Gender Identity Development Service, London, and its many service users: a million thanks.